: savior stones chronicles :

Lost Stones

: savior stones chronicles :

Lost Stones

Michelle Janene

STRONG TOWER
PRESS

Strong Tower Press, Sacramento, CA
strongtowerpress.com

Scriptures are taken from Holy Bible, New Living Translation, copyright © 1996, 2004, 2015 by Tyndale House Foundation. Used by permission of Tyndale House, Inc., Carol Stream, Illinois 60188. All rights reserved.

Definitions from "Dictionary.com." *Dictionary.com*, Dictionary.com, 2020, www.dictionary.com/

Cover Art by: Whetstone Designs
Images: jakkaje879, shutterstock.com / Sergey Nivens, 123RF.com
Tribal Tattoos: 123RF.com, image 22960286, alisher
Fonts: Cardinal Alternate and under world, 1001Fonts.com

ISBN-978-1-942320-30-2

To Nat: *God designed you with a mind quick to grasp
information,
Intelligence to use your knowledge wisely,
And a strength found in Him that makes you unstoppable.*

To Jer: *God's heart lies within you to care for those you meet,
Your care mends the broken-hearted as you share His love,
And your upstanding character mirrors the One your creator.*

To Cay: *God has gifted you with strength,
A steel will that won't let you give up,
And determination to work out the most challenging situations.*

To Gannon and Jacob:
Thanks for the assist,
The laughter,
And the kindness you shared.

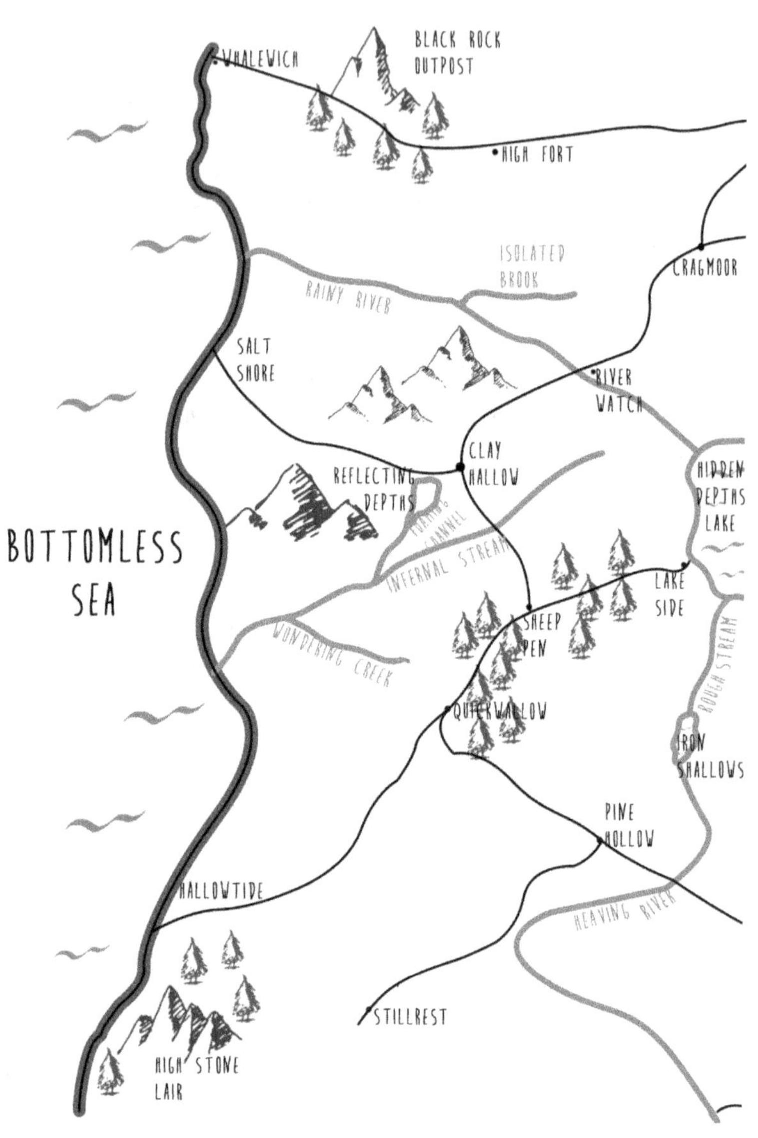

WHALEWICH
BLACK ROCK OUTPOST
HIGH FORT
ISOLATED BROOK
CRAGMOOR
RAINY RIVER
SALT SHORE
RIVER WATCH
CLAY HALLOW
REFLECTING DEPTHS
HIDDEN DEPTHS LAKE
TURNIP CHANNEL
INFERNAL STREAM
BOTTOMLESS SEA
LAKE SIDE
WONDERING CREEK
SHEEP PEN
ROUGH STREAM
QUICKWALLOW
IRON SHALLOWS
PINE HOLLOW
HALLOWTIDE
HEAVING RIVER
STILLREST
HIGH STONE LAIR

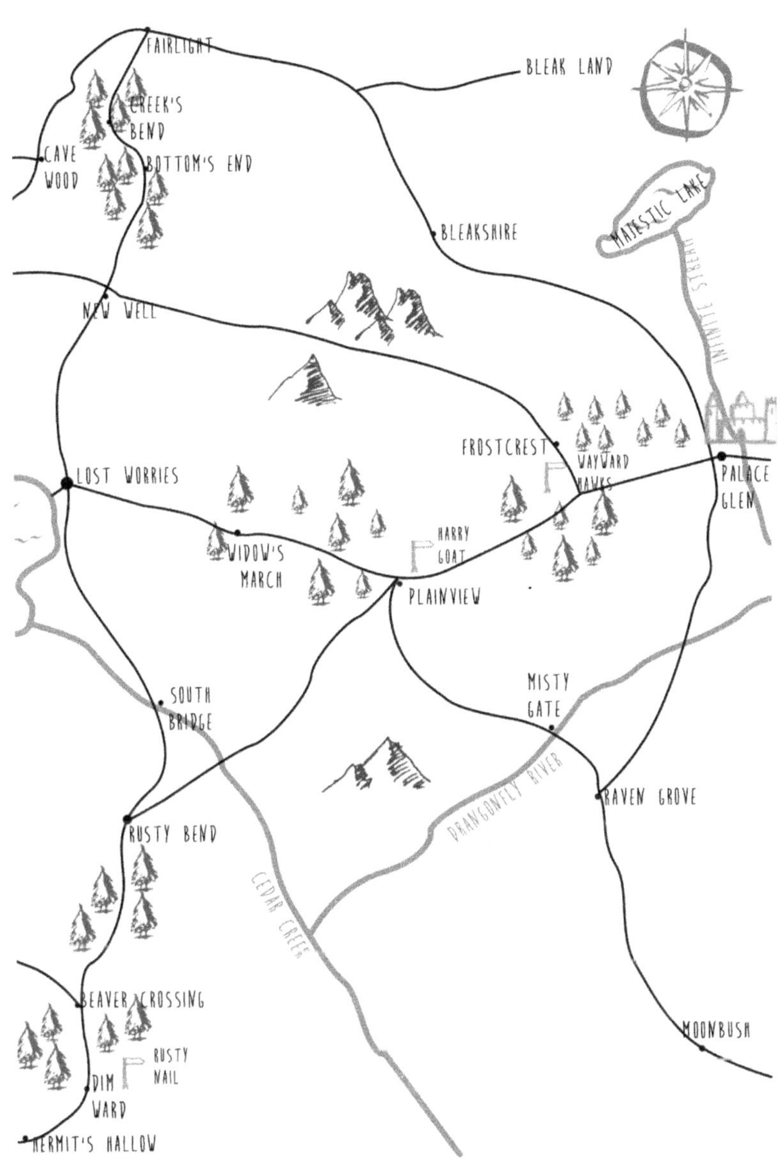

FAIRLIGHT
CREEK'S BEND
CAVE WOOD
BOTTOM'S END
BLEAK LAND
BLEAKSHIRE
MAJESTIC LAKE
NEW WELL
WHITE STREAM
FROSTCREST
WAYWARD HAWKS
PALACE GLEN
LOST WORRIES
HARRY GOAT
WIDOW'S MARCH
PLAINVIEW
MISTY GATE
SOUTH BRIDGE
DRAGONFLY RIVER
RAVEN GROVE
RUSTY BEND
CEDAR CREEK
BEAVER CROSSING
RUSTY NAIL
MOONBUSH
DIM WARD
HERMIT'S HALLOW

Make the chestpiece of a single piece of cloth folded to form a pouch nine
inches square.
Mount four rows of gemstones on it.
The first row will contain
a red carnelian, a pale-green peridot, and an emerald.
The second row will contain
a turquoise, a blue lapis lazuli, and a white moonstone.
The third row will contain
an orange jacinth, an agate, and a purple amethyst.
The fourth row will contain
a blue-green beryl, an onyx, and a green jasper.
All these stones will be set in gold filigree.
Each stone will represent one of the twelve sons of Israel,
and the name of that tribe will be engraved on it like a seal.

Exodus 28:16-21

For ever since the world was created, people have seen the earth and sky.
Through everything God made, they can clearly see His invisible qualities—
His eternal power and divine nature.
So they have no excuse for not knowing God.

Romans 1:20

Chapter 1

Venomous laughter snaked up the stairs. Nat left the scrub brush on the floor and sat back on her heels. She snatched the two ends of her braids, tied them together at the base of her skull, and made sure to tuck in the ends. She wouldn't give them anything to grab hold of this time.

Nat picked up the brush again. Mud-covered boots stomped up beside her on the rough wood-plank landing. She didn't need to look up to know the three girls towering over her were the daughters of the housemistress. Their entire reason for living seemed to be to make her life as miserable as possible.

"Look, it's the unwanted old maid," Rachel mocked.

Nat could hardly be considered an old maid, but at thirteen, she was the oldest girl in the home.

"Why does Mother keep her here? Surely, she could sell her to a workhouse," Gretchen, the oldest, responded.

"Even they don't want the wretch." Violet's smug tone, only slightly less annoying than her squeaky voice, sounded like it came through her nose.

Nat sat still and waited. Years of their torment had proven she could do nothing against it without being punished by their mother. Even if she tried to get back at them, she'd still have to redo the stairs and floors because of all the mud they tracked in. Best to wait them out and then return to her cleaning. She made a quick calculation. The added work at this hour of the day when she'd been almost finished would mean she'd miss supper. It couldn't be helped now, though.

Gretchen stepped back as if to judge the effect of her taunts. Maybe there was a way to pay back the wicked girl. A year younger than Nat, Gretchen didn't stand nearly as tall. It could work. Nat scratched at the back of her right hand. The water bucket moved to the right. Nat could move things just by looking at them. Not big things, and not far, but she could pull a book from a high shelf or call a brush to her hand from a foot away.

The effort of moving the heavy water bucket proved more challenging. It inched another finger width toward her target. She scratched at her hand again since it bothered her more than normal. Could she have used too much lye in the cleaning water today?

"Look, she's too dumb to even know she's been insulted," Gretchen laughed.

"She's become ever so boring, sisters." Rachel crossed her arms. "I remember the days when she'd cry and run for Mother."

A little closer and the bucket would end up right where Nat wanted it.

Gretchen sighed. "But Mother punished *her* because of all the fuss she made. Mother never believes we would do her any harm."

"And Mother wouldn't care if we did," Violet added.

Almost in position.

"When the sissy learned she'd get no aid from any of the other girls, she just became dull." Rachel stomped her foot, leaving more of the mud from her boots for Nat to clean.

With a hard breath, the bucket finally arrived behind Gretchen's legs. Nat rose up on her knees as though to turn and resume her work. It had the desired effect and all three girls startled away from her with a small yelp.

Gretchen's backward momentum caused her legs to bump into the bucket. She lost her balance and her fat behind fell into the soapy water, splashing out much of the contents over her and the floor.

The other two jumped away from their sister as Gretchen screamed.

Nat returned to her heels and bit her lip to keep from laughing.

Now, Nataline, we are not to revel in the downfall of our enemies. Have I not taught you to love them?

The voice in her head was a familiar one. It had come to her since her first days at the Stepping Stones Home for Wayward Girls. What a ridiculous name for a place where there were no steps to a better life from here, and they were not lost and wandering girls, but orphans.

"You horrid creature!" Gretchen screamed as she struggled to get out of the bucket, but she seemed to be stuck.

The more Gretchen wiggled, the harder Nat clutched her hands together and closed her eyes. The laughter clawing at her insides grew painful to hold in.

Nataline, we are not to repay evil for evil. You are better than that, my sweet girl.

As always, the voice came with a near-crushing wave of peace and love. Why is this the only affection she'd ever received?

Now, you know that is not true.

The voice knew her every thought.

You are deeply loved. Beautifully made for the delight of the Almighty Himself. You have always been loved with an unrelenting power.

That voice, which only she could hear, with those words, was the only thing keeping her from dissolving into tears most days.

Rachel and Violet finally helped their sister out of her mess, though they snickered at her mishap.

"You wicked cow!" Gretchen screamed as her skirt soaked her hose.

"I sat here and watched you track mud all over the floor I scrubbed. What could I have done from here?" Nat spoke in quiet words drawing on the strength and calm of the voice, though she bit her cheek to stop the giggle still tickling inside her.

"You put that bucket there."

She tipped her head and look at the furious girl. Her pretty yellow dress with its many ruffles now hung soaked and limp. "Of course, I brought the bucket. How else am I supposed to clean?" she asked sweetly.

"You moved it so I'd fall into it."

"From over here? How?"

"You're a sorcerer," Gretchen screeched.

"If I was, I'd be a sorcer*ess*. Are you foolish enough to believe such things even exist, Mistress Gretchen?"

"*OOF!*" Gretchen stomped her foot and clenched her fists at her sides. Her face, which often unnaturally flushed, was now bright red. "I'm telling Mother. She'll cane you for sure."

As usual, Nat had no control over what these girls did or the response of their mother. Mistress Swanson was a cruel woman and her rage-filled outbursts were unpredictable. Though in truth, Nat had suffered fewer beatings than many, and she had been here the longest. There were times she thought the voice somehow saved her—but that didn't make sense because it was only a voice in her head.

"You'll pay," Gretchen vowed as she stomped down the hall. She left a trail of water and mud in her wake. The other two eyed Nat with a mixture of hatred and bewilderment and hurried after their sister.

Nat waited until a door slammed shut before she threw back her head and laughed until her sides hurt.

You must always be careful, Nataline.

The voice was the only one to use her full name. She wasn't even sure Mistress Swanson knew it.

"By the great tower, what has happened to you?" Mistress Swanson's yell oozed from under the door.

"It wasn't me, Mother. Nat did it," Gretchen cried.

Nat leapt up and collected the bucket.

They are already beginning to suspect things are different with you, my girl. Do not give them cause to scrutinize you more closely. You must never reveal what you can do.

"I know," Nat whispered as she hurried down the stairs. She wove a pattern between the mud splotches so as not to track it anywhere else in the house. "Keep it a secret—always."

It is for your own safety I urge this of you, Nataline. You must stay hidden.

"But for how long?"

The Almighty alone knows, dear.

"Nat!"

Nat fled Mistress Swanson's screech and slipped through the kitchen and out the back of the girls' home to the pump over the well. Best find a way to linger here. If she was at all lucky, Mistress Swanson would become busy with other matters in preparation for the meal and Nat could continue her work without a whipping.

"Please," she begged quietly.

Chapter 2

Nat stood at one of the many windows of the dorm room she shared with several younger girls. She looked out at the dark city. As she'd predicted, cleaning the mud had made her too late to make it in time for dinner. Nat could almost hear Mistress Swanson say the first words of one of her many rules. After about the third word, all the girls would finish the well-known rule as a sing-song chorus. Nat muttered it under her breath now. "If you wish to eat, you arrived on time or you will eat nothing at all." Not that Nat missed the flavorless mush, but something in her belly was better than nothing.

She had been lucky enough not to have been seen by the mistress while cleaning the muddy stairs while working her way back up to the second-floor landing where she'd had the incident with her daughters.

Nat turned her attention from her bleak mood to the even gloomier view outside. Like the name of the orphanage she stood in, the city itself was badly named. Fairlight was neither pleasant to live in nor was it light. Most of the buildings were four- or five-story stone structures. All of them were coated in the same thick black gunk that hung in the air and blocked out much of the sun. And all of them were crammed so close together that a horse-drawn cart could hardly maneuver in the streets and allow people to pass at the same time. And there were buildings as far as she could see in every direction. It was a bleak place to live. Bleak or not, Nat had not been outside further than the street in front of the home since her arrival seven years ago.

Nat shivered and drew the holey threadbare blanket from her bed. She wrapped it around herself and moved to the small round stove which stood against the wall at the end of the aisle between the many beds. She added a chunk of coal. Mistress Swanson rationed the black fuel to the dormitory on the third floor in order to keep her chambers on the second floor more than comfortable. When she was younger, Nat had rested against her door on nights when the coal ran out upstairs.

Though she turned to another window, the dark, gloomy view didn't alter. She rubbed her arms to drive away the chill. Icicles grew around the leaky window frames and sheets of frost climbed up the inside of the glass in winter. Spring was supposed to be on the way, but under the thick perpetual coal smoke, it was hard to tell if the seasons ever changed. Nat had read in a book once that trees in some places had leaves that turned yellow, orange, and red. She could only see one tree from her window perch. Its leaves were always brown.

With a deep breath, she leaned against the thin strip of wall between two windows and closed her eyes. It hadn't always been this way. Deep in her memory, she knew she'd once lived in a grand house surrounded by a garden with trees and flowers and bushes. The walls inside were so bright she squinted against them even in her memory. White, yellow, and gold covered every surface. Chairs had bumpy carved edges and soft fabric seats, and there were long cushioned sofas too. And fat beds piled high with covers and pillows. Nat remembered that all the many rooms shone like the sun never did in Fairlight.

There had been more. Laughter. A pretty woman with streaks of gold in her hair. A man with dark hair and a short beard. And she thought there had been a little boy—or maybe two. It was just before her sixth birthday the last she'd seen them. The recollection of those times grew fainter each year.

Crying, Nat pushed off the wall and shoved the memories away. They only brought pain. She'd lived in the SSHWG—Sh-Wig as the girls called it when Mistress Swanson wasn't around to hear—ever since. In the beginning, there were hopes that she would return home again, that someone who knew her family would come and rescue her. As more years went by, even the hope of being adopted or leaving to work as a maid in some rich person's home faded. She had long since resigned herself to living here, toiling under Mistress Swanson's cruel hand until *the Almighty deemed her ready to leave.* Whatever that meant.

Quiet footsteps drew Nat's attention to the door. The other girls returned from dinner. Eighteen girls currently called Sh-Wig home. They ranged in age from six to ten. She was the one exception at thirteen. And all of them wore the same coarse, tattered style of garment that barely covered their arms to their elbows and their legs below their knees. Their only other possession was a pair of slippers with holes, handed down from one girl to the next until they were useless.

The girls' shoulders slouched forward, and their arms hung. Though it was only about seven in the evening, each one shuffled to her cot, wrapped in her one blanket, and curled into a ball. Some cried, but none dared to do so loudly. They were trained to be silent and stay out of Mistress Swanson's way.

Nat moved between the beds. She assured where she could, rubbed the back of another, and smiled at one other. It was her self-imposed job to make sure the girls were as well as they might be in this situation, and she cared for them as a big sister would. Again, she wondered if those boys from the life in the big bright house might have been her siblings.

Once everyone was fast asleep, Nat crept out of the room. She'd lived in Sh-Wig long enough to know every creak in every board and how to avoid them. She had a set pattern on the stairs she could walk down in her sleep without making a sound.

On the bottom floor, she turned away from the kitchen and dining room. Anything left over had been given to Wolf and Bane, Mistress Swanson's two beastly black dogs. To take from them meant losing a hand. Nat shuddered and went around the stairs toward the front of the home.

Prospective parents and workhouse managers came to view the girls in this area. Therefore, it was kept neat and in good order. Visitors were never allowed upstairs, or even to the stairs for that matter. The first room was a sitting area. It was a room with light green wallpaper for meeting with individual girls. The second larger room had desks on one side and shelves of books on the other. It gave the appearance that Mistress Swanson educated her girls in order to provide them that "step up" the title of her institution promised. In truth, no one ever sat at those desks unless the city manager came for an inspection.

Nat had been fortunate in that she'd just begun to learn her letters and to read some simple words before she'd arrived here. A couple of older girls at the time had helped her learn more. That was before they were sent off to work in a dress shop or a laundry and Mistress Swanson deemed Nat the one girl no one else could befriend.

Nat pushed the old hurts away and slid between two bookcases. Over the years she had gone row by row, shelf by shelf, from the back to the front, reading every single book. She learned history, mathematics, science, medicine, and poetry. But her favorite were the stories.

She curled in her blanket. This was the one spot in the entire house she was convinced didn't have a draft. With slow movement, she pulled the book she'd hidden on the bottom shelf into her lap and let her mind escape the heartbreaking memories of the past and the torment of the present. In the worlds of myth and legend, she learned of heroes and bravery. She found strength and a tiny measure of joy.

"Nat!" A harsh whisper cut down the stairs. "Oh, you worthless girl. Where are you? Nat, come here this moment."

Chapter 3

The pounding of his racing feet was echoed by another's beside him. Heavier footfalls followed them. "Stop! Thieves. Someone, stop them!"

A whistle blew several times. "Halt!" More whistles.

Jer cut tight at a corner, and Burt fell a step behind. The city of Dimward had many places to hide if one could get to them without being seen. Jer jumped over trash as he raced down an alley and burst out onto the cobblestone street beyond. Two hapless steps brought him directly in front of a fancy black carriage. The shiny paint on the vehicle gleamed in the harsh afternoon sun.

The horses reared at his sudden appearance. He whirled and ducked to keep from suffering a hoof to his face. Atop his perch, the driver shook his fist at him and roared. "Dumb kid! Get out of the road."

Burt dashed behind the carriage as it lurched forward. He joined Jer, to charge through a curtained market area in a wider alley. They wove between the stands and milling shoppers and turned into a tavern halfway down the lane. Through a back room and out into a different lane, they crossed another market area and stepped into a shop with many hats. They tried on several and watched closely as the constables ran past, still blowing their whistles.

Before the shop owner could raise an alarm, they dropped the hats and headed out in the opposite direction from the officers. As the shouts and whistles faded behind them, they slowed and continued on their way to the edge of town. Burt laughed and held up a leather pouch of coins he'd nicked. He glanced at Jer and shook them. "Worth every heart-pounding moment."

Jer wiped sweat from his brow and shrugged. He didn't want to steal. The voice in his head forbade it and, though he couldn't prove it, Jer believed she prevented his involvement in any crimes—other than as a distraction to their target.

As they approached the workhouse area, tall apartments gave way to single-story, wide structures. Many had tall smoke stacks. Few of these buildings had windows. Between a red brick warehouse used to make fabric and a gray stone one where shoes were made, they approached a narrow tunnel used to access the sewer system. A gang of kids had found a spot away from the smells to create a makeshift home down in the darkness.

A figure stepped from the shadow of the opening as they neared. "Boys. So, have you earned your keep today?" The boy who claimed to be their leader, Litton Shark, was the oldest of the kids in the tunnel. At fifteen, he stood only a few inches taller than Jer who was eleven. Shark wore gentleman's knickers that stopped below his knee with an oversized nobleman's dress shirt. A fat man's vest with a pocket watch on its gold chain hung under a long jacket. Shark had pushed the jacket open. One hand rested on a folded knife at his waist. Though his tall socks had holes, Shark was the only one to have decent shoes.

Of course, everything Shark had, he'd stolen or had one of the other kids nick for him. The clump of black hair on the top of his head stood on end, making him look taller than he was. His dark eyes and a ragged red scar down his right cheek added to his formidable appearance.

Burt brushed his long brown hair out of his eyes and held up the pouch. Everyone knew better than to hide any of their stolen goods from Shark. His bite was quick and deadly.

Shark patted Burt on the shoulder, took the pouch, and put it in his coat pocket. What a ridiculous display to wear any jacket on a day like today. Here in Dimward far to the south, spring had already taken hold this year, and even if Jer hadn't run through half the town, he would still be hot. But Shark only cared about appearances. "There's grub inside. I'll see you get your split." Which meant Burt might see a coin for all his efforts, but he would get a meal and a place to sleep for tonight.

"And you?" Shark raised his chin toward Jer as Burt disappeared without a backward glance.

"Nothing again," Jer shrugged as he dug the toe of his shoe into the dirt gathered around the tunnel entrance.

"Nothing?" Shark mimicked him. His right hand came down with a loud thump on Jer's shoulder. "You know the rule. No booty, no entry."

Jer nodded. Where else could he go? Last year he outgrew the boy's home, and no one would hire or trust a street kid.

Shark put his left hand on Jer's other shoulder. His thumb stroked Jer's throat and increased in pressure. "I've tried to do right by ya, kid. Took ya in when the growns wers done with ya. Spent my valuable time trainin' ya. But ya have yet to bring back anythin'. Not a roll, or an apple, or a watch."

"I know." Jer tried to swallow around the force on his neck.

"If ya aren't going to be a team player and do yar part ..." The words faded as the pressure on his throat increased to the point Jer couldn't breathe. He needed help. The back of his right hand tingled like bees buzzed in it.

Not the rats again, Jeremicum, the voice in his head warned. *You'll get a reputation. Everyone will start thinking that the vile little creatures follow you around.*

But I need help, Jer thought.

There are other creatures about, her soothing voice said. *Calm yourself, Jeremicum, and you will find them.*

A moment later, a deep string of barks made Shark yelp, release Jer, and wobble back a step. A huge dog whose shoulder came even with Jer's waist approached, head down, ears back, teeth bared. The beast growled. She seemed to ignore Jer and focus solely on Shark.

"I don't want—" Shark's voice cracked as he staggered back another step. "Get out of here."

A little unclear as to whether Shark had spoken to the dog or to him, Jer turned and walked back the way he'd come. The dog's tail wagged as she ambled along beside him.

Jer coughed a few times and rubbed his neck with one hand as he buried his fingers in the dog's thick fur with the other. "Well, that was interesting." His voice came out hoarse and raspy.

Indeed. Seems the Shark is scared of dogs.

"If we ever cross paths again, kid, ya'll regret it." Shark waved his knife in the air but scurried away when the dog turned and growled at him again.

"Now what do I do?"

Jer continued to pet the dog that had come to his rescue. He had a way with animals. He couldn't talk to them in the strictest sense, but some level of communication happened. Like with this dog, they would come to his aid when he needed them, and they seemed to know what he wanted them to do. Jer had also never met any creature that was afraid of him.

Head toward Hermit's Hallow, Jeremicum.

The gentle voice never failed to help him get what he needed, but he was tired of being alone.

You are never alone, my dear boy.

He knew better than to think such things. The voice could hear his thoughts as though it lived in his head. "Well, it sure feels like it," he whispered. His throat was still sore from Shark trying to strangle him. He couldn't go back to the tunnels.

The Almighty will provide, she assured. But Jer couldn't see how.

A cluster of tiny homes with thatch roofs made up the area of town known as Hermit's Hollow. Many of the people who lived here worked in the warehouses he passed on the way to the tunnel hideout.

Turn right at this lane and go to the back door of the third house on the left.

Though it seemed impossible that the voice in his head could know anything about where he was or the house he approached, she had never failed him before, so he followed her instruction.

Knock three times.

A blond girl about his age opened the door and stared at him. A white apron covered a short black dress. Jer didn't say anything, but the servant girl nodded, held up one finger, and glanced over her shoulder. She brought the same finger to her lips to make sure he stayed quiet when she left the door open and stepped away. He waited. After a moment, she returned with an apple, the end of a loaf of bread, and a couple slices of meat.

"Thank you," he said with silent lips.

She smiled and closed the door without a sound.

The big dog licked her lips and her tail picked up speed. Jer continued down the lane. He knew a place by the river where he could eat and not be bothered by anyone.

Tucked in a hidden spot between a bunch of big rocks, Jer listened to the water lap against the stones. He kept the meat for himself, eating it slowly, then split the bread with the dog. She ate and rested her head, which was probably bigger than his own, on his leg. The apple he dropped down his shirt to save for later. Though he had no idea where his next meal might come from, he only knew it would not be from the little blond servant girl.

While he watched the sky turn orange, then pink, and finally dark purple, he reclined against one of the rocks. Perhaps he should find somewhere warm for the night. At that thought, the dog snuggled in closer. Soon her body heat drove the chill away.

He petted her and let his mind wander. There had to be more than this. The voice said things would be different in the future too. She promised that the Almighty had great plans for him. Jer wasn't sure he could believe that any more.

His eyes slid closed. In the moment between awake and asleep, he thought he saw a man with a dark beard smile at him.

Jer woke from the best sleep he'd had since he'd left the boys' home.

The dog kept him warm and, because he knew she'd warn him of danger, he was able to rest well. He liked this spot tucked in the hidden place among the rocks. As long as no one saw him coming or going, this would be a great place for him and his dog. He rubbed her head. "You need a name." She looked up at him. "There was a nice boy in the home once named Kevin. I could give you his name."

The dog sneezed and tossed her head.

"Not keen on that name?"

Again, she sneezed.

"Spot? You have tan spots on your white fur."

Once more the dog shook her head as if in disapproval.

"Soo?"

Her ears perked up.

"One of the boys in the home named a cockroach that once. He said the name meant "long life". What do you think about Soo?"

The dog wagged her tail and gave a quick bark.

"Soo it is, and I hope, if we can stick together, both of us will have very long lives."

Soo barked again.

Jer crept out of his new home, making sure that no one saw him. Soo stretched out her long legs in front of her and raised her rump up in the air. She yawned, and, after a moment, she shook. Dust and myriad hairs escaped into the air and floated in the first rays of sunlight. There wasn't a cloud in the sky. It was going to be another warm day.

The apple he'd hidden away wouldn't quiet his hunger for long. He needed to stay away from Shark and his gang, but since they roamed nearly every street in search of victims, that seemed impossible.

Chapter 5

Jer turned away from the river and headed toward the center of town. At this time of day, Shark and his gang wouldn't be up prowling the streets for targets, so Jer took the opportunity to see if he could find something less illegal to occupy his time.

Soo trotted beside him. Her tail swayed gently. Her fur was light with tan splotches, and her coat was short, but it was so thick it seemed like a fuzzy blanket. Jer couldn't keep his fingers out of it as they ambled down a quiet lane.

Anyone they came across shied away from the dirty boy and his huge dog. Jer stood a little taller. Soo made him brave.

He started to turn left at one corner and head to the market to see if anyone needed help setting up for the day's business, but the hairs on his neck and arms stood on end, and a low growl came from Soo. Jer couldn't see anyone or anything ahead of him that might be dangerous. The voice didn't warn him not to go that way, which it usually did if there was trouble.

When the growling didn't stop, Jer turned the opposite direction. Soo quieted, and her tail wagged again. The unease vanished as well. "Weird," Jer whispered, and Soo looked up at him as if he were a dunce.

Around the next corner into an alley they came face to face with a charging horse. He reared and snorted a loud neigh. Soo barked. The horse dropped back down to his hooves, shook his head with another snort, and pawed at the brick path.

Jer opened and closed his right fist as it buzzed and tickled.

The horse looked at him with eyes so wide and wild Jer could see his own reflection in them. The large animal pranced and reared again. But this time when he came back down, the breath he expelled came quieter. He dipped his head to Jer a couple of times, eased forward, and pressed against Jer.

"Hey, kid," a man behind the horse whispered so quietly Jer almost didn't hear him. "How'd you do that?"

Jer shrugged. The voice in his head continually warned him—until he was sick of hearing it—that he could never *ever* tell anyone about talking to animals. "I guess he figured he didn't have anywhere else to go. He can't really turn around in this narrow alley."

"Do you think you can bring him back to the stables?"

Jer stroked the front of the horse's face and stared into eyes that watched him with great attention. The horse seemed agreeable, so Jer judged the distance to either end of the lane they were stuck in. "I'll lead him this way and turn him around at that end," Jer pointed behind him, "and come back."

The man nodded.

When Jer turned them around, he saw three men standing at the other end of the alley. Two were pudgy and wore thick pants and stained shirts with heavy leather aprons. The third was tall and skinny. He wore a shirt and dark pants that seemed cleaner than the others. From his travels around town, Jer recognized the two with aprons as farriers.

Jer glanced down at the odd *clop, clop, thunk, clop* of the horse's hooves on the stones. "Looks like you ran off before you were fitted with all your shoes." He patted the horse on the neck as the large animal blew out a long breath. "What spooked you?" The horse didn't respond.

Jer tried to act as though he didn't notice all the other animals in the stable quiet. An almost unnatural calm blanketed the structure when he entered. As he led the horse to a stall where he could be secured, Jer saw the looks exchanged between the men.

"You trouble?" the tall man asked Jer as he turned to leave.

"I'm trying very hard not to be, sir. There aren't many options in Dimward for an orphan once they outgrow the boy's home."

"You sayin' you *want* to work?" The man crossed his arms and his gaze narrowed.

"I'd be willing to do any honest work for a few coins."

The man nodded. "We'll see. You can muck the stalls. And as long as your beast doesn't disturb the livestock, it can stay as well."

Soo plopped down in a bit of shade right inside the door. She watched but didn't make any other move. "Thank you, sir. I confess, I've never mucked anything. I'm happy to do it if you don't mind giving me some directions."

"Call me Olrog." He extended his hand.

Jer stared at it.

"It's the proper way to greet a body."

Jer put his hand out too. Olrog took it so their thumbs hooked and their fingers tightened around the other's hand. "Make the grip firm so men respect you, but not so hard as to challenge them." Olrog raised and lowered their hands twice. "Good, now follow me." Olrog led him to the shovel and cart and told Jer what he was supposed to do with the dung and foul straw he removed from each stall.

Jer worked hard all day but didn't quite finish the large stable.

Olrog inspected his work, then looked him up and down with a raised brow. "How old are you, boy?"

"Eleven—I think, sir."

Olrog's hand slammed down on his shoulder; it almost knocked Jer off his feet. "Well, you near did the day's work of a man twice your age. You'll always have work here if you keep that up." He dropped three coppers into Jer's hand.

"Thank you, sir. Thank you."

"You got a place to lay your head?"

"Yes, sir. As long as the weather holds."

"Well, you can bunk in the loft if you need." Olrog pointed to an area above them that held many bales of hay.

"I'll remember that." He hid his coins where they wouldn't easily be nicked by Shark or his gang and hurried off to the market. It was late, but he might be able to buy some fruit or something else to eat before the last of the vendors packed up for the night.

He'd reached the market just in time. Now with a meat pie in hand and two apples for tomorrow tucked in his shirt, Jer walked back to the river and the hideaway between the rocks. Soo ambled beside him and bumped into him many times as she tried to get a bite of the rich-smelling pie. Jer smiled and scratched her head, then pulled a bone the butcher gave him from his pocket. Tucked out of sight of robbers and away from the wind, they ate happily.

His legs, back, and arms ached from the long day's work, but it felt good to not be a thief today.

"Where'd he go?" a voice asked over the soft waves.

"Don't know. Thought I saw him head this way."

Jer pulled Soo close and told her not to make a sound.

Chapter 6

Mura drew her wayward spirit back within the confines of her skin and sat up before the key turned in the lock. The heavy steel door whined with a nerve-grating cry as the two guards stepped into the stone chamber that held her iron cage. King Thedo Brax revealed his growing fear when he placed her in the bowels of the dungeon, inside a cage, inside a stone chamber. The Savior Stone, once gifted to her, caused Mura to be an empath. She could read others' thoughts, impose her own will into the mind's of others, and influence them to a desired action. But her gifts could do nothing against steel and stone.

Mura lumbered to her feet and hobbled to the door. She took great care to maintain the expected appearance of one who had lain on a stone slab all day for the last three years. Her skin itched as she not been allowed to bathe or to clean in any way in the last year. Her once red gown was black below her knees. The dangling sleeves looked the same. She pushed them up and slid both her pale arms through the space between two bars.

One of the guards secured the manacles around her wrists before he opened the cell. She held still while shackles were added to her ankles. Then one guard led her out and the other followed as they climbed the winding stone stairs.

She had never resisted or fought them or made any attempt at escape. There was no point. Her charges were well hidden and still too young to fight against Brax's ongoing struggle for ultimate power. Therefore, she had no urge to leave. She could learn far more by remaining his prisoner.

They reached the main floor and inched down the hall. Mura couldn't move fast in the chains. They were only long enough to allow her to climb one step to the next from the dungeon. The hallway was dark with few of its torches lit. Father had never permitted darkness to invade any corner of their home. But then, Father no longer ruled the kingdom of Purlan. Thedo Brax had swooped in before they could crown a new ruler after Father died.

Brax was of the Everblood line, a group of outcasts in their society that believed they were better than everyone else, known for their cruelty. Brax had seemed sweet when he'c first arrived, though, acting the part of a grieving citizen. Before anyone knew what he was up to, he wore the crown and hunted those with the holy stones.

Mura and her two guards entered the throne room and, as always, her heart broke. Blood stained the once-gleaming walls and marble floor. The windows that once welcomed the bright sun remained covered with heavy fabric. The beautiful throne carved with emblems of their faith had been replaced with one made of the bones of Brax's victims. And the former kind and generous king was forgotten because the cruel spawn from the fiery depths who stole his crown was all anyone dared think about.

Thedo Brax's bones poked through his ghostly skin. He looked like one of the walking undead from children's nightmares. His hair was white as new snow and stood straight up as though afraid to touch him.

He sneered at her. It hadn't always been this way between them. After Mura's sister fled the palace with her family, Brax had tried to enchant Mura. Now she understood that he'd hoped to win her to his side before his true intentions were revealed. To win one from the line of the Truefaith and make her his queen would have cemented his rule and squashed any rebellion before it could begin.

Mura's empathic gift and the protection of the Almighty had saved her. Though she could not read Brax's thoughts as she could with most she met, she was always uncomfortable around him. The secret blackness within him made his thoughts impossible to read. Only after he killed the man she had intended to marry could Mura understand the depths of evil which filled his heart.

When she refused Brax's hand in marriage, he stripped her of her title as Crown Princess of Purlan and moved Mura to the servants' quarters. She was convinced it had only been her gift to influence those who counseled him that saved her life. She gave them the thought that killing her for her Savior Stone would taint it in a way that would make it unusable for him.

Later, when Brax came to believe she actively worked against him, he locked Mura in the dungeon behind three doors. Now she only came before him when he wanted something. At this moment, she stood tall, shoulders back, chin high. She glared at him as she waited for his order. This was her home, and she would see it restored to glory one day. She had faith in the Almighty to do great things.

Brax rose, drew his sword, and slowly stomped down each step.

Chapter 7

Mura stood near the entry inside the throne room and waited as she looked on the thief of the Purlan crown. Two men in military overcoats knelt below the raised platform where Brax had been sitting on his disgusting bone chair moments ago.

As he descended the stairs, sword in hand, Brax pointed a gloved finger at her and then at the men. "Come here and tell me which of these men lies." His voice was rough, like he had injured it at some point.

Mura hobbled forward, and her chains clattered against the floor. "You know I can do nothing that will lead to another's death." She didn't curtsy or call him "Majesty" or "Lord". He deserved no such honor for what he had stolen.

"They both will die if you do not. At least one may be spared if you do as you are told."

Mura came to a stop beside the soldiers. She refused to lower her gaze as was expected of a servant before the king. This man had robbed her of her family, her station, and all comfort. If ever her compassionate heart could hate anyone, it would be Thedo Brax. But even she could afford him a sliver of understanding. The Everblood line had lost the crown centuries ago. That alone would have been hard enough for them to take, but the first king of the Truefaith line had stripped them of all land and titles when they continued to offer sacrifices to other gods. But it was the Everbloods' killing of their own children that had made them unworthy to be part of the kingdom again.

Brax stalked down another two steps and pointed his sword at her. "Do as you are told, slave."

"You may call me anything you like, but all know I am an heir to the throne you have taken."

He stomped down another step and extended his sword-bearing arm toward her. "It is time I kill you."

But Mura didn't flinch. He said the same thing whenever they met. She could only assume it was the Almighty alone who kept him from doing the deed. As long as her charges needed her protection, she figured Brax's threats would never come to pass.

They stared at one another. Finally, Brax turned his sword tip toward the soldiers and descended the final step.

"A brush."

He stopped cold; his sword lowered as his brows pinched together. "What?"

"In payment for my services, I require a hairbrush."

He closed the distance between him and the men. "I'll just kill them both and be done with it."

Mura suspected they wouldn't leave this chamber alive regardless of what they had to say or anything she might reveal. She stood her ground. He had given in last time and provided her a blanket, but that could have been in an attempt to keep her alive for when he needed her next.

"I will decide after I have heard your report if your words warrant such a reward."

"You have not proven yourself to be a man of your word. I will hold the brush before I begin."

Brax's head snapped in her direction, and the hate that filled his eyes stole her breath. "I tire of you, slave."

She didn't respond.

After enough time passed to cook an egg, Brax nodded to a nearby page. The lad dashed off and returned with her own silver-handled brush from the personal chamber she had once used.

"Not that one, you fool. Slaves do not get priceless treasures."

The page ran away again, and this time he returned with a wooden-handled brush with half of its bristles missing.

Mura refused to accept it. They waited again for the boy to return with a better one. Mura took it and pushed it up her sleeve, then turned and knelt in front of one of the men. "Tell me what he wants to know." The man was muscled with a long beard but short hair. His blue eyes were wide, and she looked deep into his soul. Though not a holy man, she didn't find him to be truly evil like Thedo Brax., but what his thoughts showed her, made her shudder.

Chapter 8

Mura sat on her knees in front of the soldiers Brax wished for her to interrogate. It was up to her to determine if they lied and to report to him all she saw within their hearts.

The man, Boyd, also knelt with his hands shackled, but unlike Mura's, his were chained behind him. His voice trembled as he spoke. "I tell you true, my lady. I found the one King Brax sought, and I ended his life. I do not lie."

Mura's heart stuttered. She saw his victim in Boyd's memories; a man Boyd had hunted for no other reason than he was a believer in the Almighty. For that alone a brother in the faith had died.

She slid on her knees to come before the other man, Alt. He was shorter with long black hair pulled back and bound. His dark eyes challenged her.

Unease stole her breath—and it had nothing to do with the man before her. She closed her eyes against the nausea rolling in her empty belly. *Not that way. Don't go there.* She couldn't go to her young charge now. Mura breathed again. The lad remained safe. His furry companion had warned him.

Calmer now, she opened her eyes and focused once more on the soldier.

"I do not lie either. I hunted three of these misguided men who would dare turn against their king. I know, even now, where they can be found, and as soon as I am allowed to complete my duty, they, too, will be as dead as Boyd's man." Alt tipped his head toward Boyd beside him.

Mura nodded to the guards, who helped her stand. She turned to Brax. "They both speak the truth."

"You lie!" The tip of Brax's sword sliced her chin.

Mura never flinched. "The men your soldiers hunt are good, honest men. To get justice for them, I *should* lie and tell you Boyd didn't kill his target so you would kill him in return. Boyd would receive the punishment deserved for his crime and no more of the holy brothers and sisters would be lost at his hand. And I *should* tell you that Alt lied and allowed those he chased to escape. But I tell you the truth—as I always have—that three more of the brethren will fall at his hands if you release him."

"Return her to the pit," Brax waved her away with a swish of his gloved hand, "and retrieve her reward."

The guards took her by the elbows, turned her back toward the hall that led to her dungeon cage, and they searched for the brush. She did not have the power to convince them that she never had it, but she let the sound of wood clattering to the floor echo from her mind into the hall. Her ability created the illusion she had lost the brush and they could recover it after they secured her. It worked, and the three of them continued downward to her cell where the guards locked her away.

They left the dungeon, and she waited to hear the upstairs door clang secure. Then she stood on the stone slab, which was her bed, pulled the brush from her sleeve, and tucked it away in a hidden spot. Even if they came to search and looked in its direction, they would not see her reward without a long hunt. With a deep breath, she settled on her bed. She'd wait for a few days, before she worked the brush through her hair a few strokes each day.

But now she had other matters to attend. Another of her charges needed to be checked on, and she had a warning to deliver. She wrapped her right hand in the long tail of her sleeve, pressed the back of it to the stone beneath her, and covered it with the blanket.

Mura's hand warmed as she drew on the power of the Savior Stone within her. After allowing her spirit to ease from her body, she sent it hurtling to the east. It would cost her precious minutes with her youngest charge, but she could not let the men she had seen in Alt's memories die without at least trying to warn them. She allowed her spirit to become visible as she floated through the wall where two of the men waited.

"Your Highness." Both men took a knee.

"They know where you are. Take your families and leave. Warn anyone who has worked with you. Do not delay. Run. They are nearly upon you."

"Yes, my lady."

Her image dissolved and she sped to the west. Though she wanted to stay longer, her strength would not allow her to remain more than a few moments once she reached her destination.

Chapter 9

The large metal bucket clattered over the ground as Cay pulled it behind him toward the stream. He was the smallest and youngest on the farm. Why did Kint assign him the task of watering the new field? It was on the other side of the property a *million* steps from the water. Cay plopped the bucket down on the bank. He rubbed the back of his right hand against his pants as he looked around. He was usually alone, but he had to be sure.

A wave crept up from the water like the neck of an imaginary sea creature. It waved a moment and then bent over the bucket as if to see it was safe before it splashed inside. The bucket filled, and the ripple returned to the stream as it wound past the farm.

Cay rubbed his hand some more. It always tickled when he made the water and earth bend to his will. The dirt under the bucket rose in a long ribbon as if a giant mole dug a tunnel under it. It pushed the heavy bucket forward and then settled back into place behind him as if the earth had never been disturbed. All Cay had to do was walk beside the bucket and keep it from tipping over.

Calebus, you know better.

She'd caught him again. How did she always know when he did something he shouldn't? Cay looked around. He saw her on the other side of the stream. Well, as much as he ever saw her. Her vague shadow of light still showed the shape of a pretty woman in a long dress, but he could see the trees on the edge of the next field through her. He waved a greeting to her as the earth went flat beneath the bucket.

He tried to lift it but couldn't.

Calebus, you must be more careful. She stood beside him now.

He stomped his foot. "It's too heavy. I bet it weighs more than me. I can't water the whole field before dark. You know what'll happen if I don't finish, don't you? Kint will pull off his belt—the one he added metal chunks to the end of—and whip me." Cay rubbed the back of his thigh, remembering the last time that belt had bit into him. It still hurt to sit.

She crouched in front of him and looked in his eyes. *You are a smart lad, my sweet. You can come up with a better way.* Her slender finger reached up as if to tap his forehead, but he didn't feel her touch him. Instead, the spot grew warm, and his insides filled with the love that always came when she was near.

"If the river was closer…"

Yes? She smiled at him, and one brow rose.

He knew he was on the right track, and he also knew she would never tell him the answer. He'd have to think it out. She said thinking out his problems now was good for when he got older. But he was nine, and there were days he didn't feel like he'd ever get any older. "If there was a canal dug along there," he pointed to the edge of the field beside the path, "that went all the way to the new field …"

You've got it. She smiled at him as she stood and brushed her hand over his head. It didn't ruffle his hair, but a warm tickle made him giggle.

Cay rubbed his right hand against his pants again as dirt jumped out of the canal.

Calebus!

Cay stomped his foot again and put his hands on his hips. "But Mura, how else am I supposed to make it?"

The way any boy would. She faded even more, and he could no longer see her. *Be careful, my sweet.*

"There you are." Lor walked up with a sigh. She was a couple years older than Cay and had been at the farm as long as he had. Most kids didn't last long under Kint. They either ran off or were hurt too much to work. If they were caught running away from the master—Cay shuddered. Death would be better than what happened to runaways.

"Yeah, I'm here. Trying to water the new field."

"That's why he sent me. Said you probably couldn't lift the pails." She brushed her brown bangs from her face. All it did was smear the sweat and dust into streaks of mud, and her hair fell right back in her eyes. She dropped an empty pail at his feet and took hold of the full one with both hands. She strained to pick it up, then waddled away. "Fill that one. I'll be back."

Cay moved to the stream and, when she was out of sight, he made the earth form into steps that took him to the water's edge. There he dipped in the bucket, pulled it up onto the path, and waited for Lor to return.

Lor looked out for him, and Cay hoped that Kint really had sent her. It would be awful to watch her get punished for helping him. Cay scanned the fields for any sign of the angry farmer.

Chapter 10

Before Cay realized what was happening, Lor had gotten all the other children away from their chores. They formed a line to carry the water from the stream to the new field. Cay filled the bucket and passed it to Lor. She walked a little ways and passed it off to Wart. And on it went until Slade dumped it on the new field. They almost never all worked together—or did anything at the same time.

They were given their little bit of food when their chores were done. They would be handed a biscuit, some jerky, and maybe an orange or apple—when they were in season. Cay would eat it as fast as he could so none of the bigger kids could take the food away from him. The sky was always dark before he'd find a spot to lay down. It had to be a place he could escape from easily if anyone else wanted it. Then he'd try to sleep.

Many of the kids who came to the farm outside Quickwallow said it wasn't a bad place to work. They said the coal mines that went deep into the earth were the worst. There were others who came from the quarries where they chiseled out rock for the many monuments for the king. The kids who had been in the mines or quarries said the farm was the best place they had ever worked.

Cay always grew sad after hearing that. If this was the best place, the rest of the world must be terrible. Cay looked out to the edge of the property and the rolling hills beyond. It didn't look like a bad place, but then, he couldn't remember being anywhere else. But he had. Lor had told him he arrived about a week after she had. He was only two, and she had to watch him *and* still get all her chores done. At first Lor hated him, but over time they came to watch out for each other.

"What is the meaning of this?" Kint stomped up and scanned the line of children. Cay looked up so far it made his neck hurt. Kint was almost as tall as he was fat. And his head looked too small for his body. His hairy arms stuck out of his rolled-up sleeves, and his pants bunched at the tops of his black boots.

"We are watering the new field, master," Cay muttered, dropping his head to look at the ground.

"All of you?" Kint's deep voice made Cay's chest vibrate.

"The buckets are too heavy for us to move so far. We each take it a little ways and it goes much faster." Only Cay talked since it was his chore to do. The others stood, hands held behind them, heads down, ready to bolt back to their own tasks at the slightest nod of Kint's head.

The long thin strands of gray-brown hair that Kint combed from one side of his nearly bald head to the other waved in the breeze he created when he scanned back and forth along the line.

If not for Kint's silence and anger, Cay might have laughed, but as it was, he glanced sideways at the man, who raised his hand to unhook his belt. Cay's heart pounded.

"And what's that?" Kint pointed to the canal Cay had started to dig as the end of the belt fell free. The newly created whip came to rest in one hand at Kint's side.

"I thought if we dug a canal from the stream to the new field, the water could flow by itself, and we could have time to work on more important chores." Cay squeezed his eyes closed and waited for the snap of the belt and the sting against his flesh.

"And how would you keep it from flooding the field, you dumb kid?" He spit, the glob landing on Cay's foot. *Gross!*

Cay knelt at Kint's feet. Cay scraped the top of his foot over the ground to rub the spit off as he used his finger to draw in the mud next to the stream. "A gate could be made that could be raised to let water in and closed to stop it," he said as he sketched the idea.

"Finish this up—*quickly*. Then help Lor milk the cows." Kint stomped off, securing the belt around his waist as he went.

All six kids let out a long sigh once he was out of sight. After a dozen more buckets of water, each one returned to their normal chores.

Cay carried one of the empty buckets, letting it clatter over the ground on the way to the milking shed and the two dozen cows. "Thank you," he said to Lor, who walked beside him with the other bucket.

"We just have to look out for each other. No one else is gonna." When they entered the shed, she pulled over a three-legged stool to sit beside the first cow. She brushed her hands over her pants several times to warm them before she began to milk the animal.

"You want me to milk too?"

"No, they don't like how rough you are. Just pour the milk into the containers and give me an empty bucket when I move."

Cay wiped his forehead with his arm. It was still cold in the mornings and evenings with spring just starting. But in the milking shed, with all the cows, the stuffy air made Cay sticky. It strengthened the smell of his dirty body. He needed to take a dip in the stream soon.

"Pay attention, Cay. We survived not being whipped once today. We'll not be so lucky again." Lor passed him the first bucket of milk, and he exchanged it for an empty one as Lor moved her stool to the next cow.

Careful not to spill any, he poured the warm creamy liquid into a tall container. It took three pails before the milk can was full and he could seal it tight. Wart or one of the other bigger boys would put all the full milk cans in the back of the wagon, and Kint would drive it into Quickwallow before sunset each day. He'd come back after dark and lumber off to the house while the kids unhooked the animals, fed them, and put them in their stalls. Then the children could get a little sleep too.

Every day was the same as the one before. There were the same activities of planting and caring for the fields and animals. Harvest was the hardest time with even longer hours, harder work, and less sleep. In winter, they had to keep the animals comfortable in the cold and try not to freeze themselves. This time of year, they had to be careful of frost with the new crops just planted, as well as make sure the plants received enough water and were free of bugs.

Cay sighed as he looked out the door and across the land again. Mura, the ghostly woman who often visited him, said it hadn't always been this way and that one day it would be better. They just had to trust the Almighty and wait. Nine years—his whole life—was a long time to wait.

"Cay! Where is your head, kid?"

He turned, picked up the milk, and added it to the can.

"Saddle my horse," Kint yelled. But he hadn't said who should do the job. Cay stepped forward to do it, but he knew he was too small. Maybe one of the others would. But if everyone thought that someone else went to see to the farmer's demands, Kint would whip the first kid he saw.

Cay stood between the milk can he'd been filling and the door, not sure whether he should stay or go. His stomach knotted and the old sores on the backs of his legs stung.

Chapter 11

Nat trudged up the steps again. She'd climbed these stairs behind Mistress Swanson last night. The laughter of the headmistress had cut deep. As Nat often did, she'd sneaked down to the library to read after the other girls were asleep. But this time she'd been caught.

"Nat!" A harsh whisper had cut down the stairs. "Oh, you worthless girl. Where are you? Nat, come here this moment."

She had jerked up and shoved her book onto the shelf. It stuck out so that anyone who looked would see, but she didn't have time to fix it. Nat scurried to the meeting area and sat on the chair across the table of two empty chairs as though she was being interviewed for adoption by imaginary parents. She'd just settled when Mistress Swanson passed the doorway. The light from her lamp cast light on Nat.

"What are you doing in here?" The headmistress' face lay hidden in shadow behind the harsh light thrust in her direction. The mistress' words spewed more harsh than normal.

"I was imagining what it would feel like to sit here and have someone want me." It wasn't a complete lie. She had dreamed of it— many times—but she'd never had the courage to come sit in this chair. Someone had to be truly brave to endure that kind of hopeless pain.

Mistress Swanson stood silent for a moment. Then she started to laugh. A snort flew from her mouth, then grew into a deep belly laugh. "Want you?" Her cruel enjoyment grew causing the lamp in her hand to jostle and make light dance across the walls. "No one has ever wanted you, you stupid girl."

In her heart, Nat knew that wasn't true. She remembered the home, her family. And the voice loved her, wanted her. But the headmistress' words still bit like a rat.

"Come on, no more time for ridiculous fantasies, girl. Edith is crying. It is your job to keep them quiet through the night, Nat. If you can't even do that simple task, how can you hope to dream of someone thinking you're worth having around?"

They parted at the second-floor landing. Mistress Swanson's continued laughter chased Nat up to the third floor. Except for a small whimper, the room seemed quiet, but Nat went to Edith, the newest and youngest of the girls, sat beside her bed, and talked softly. "Shh, Edith. It's all right. You don't have to be afraid. I'll sit here with you." Nat rubbed Edith's back until she fell asleep.

Now in the light of the new day, the laughter and cruel words of last night still stung, and Nat struggled to ignore the humiliation as she set the half-full ash bucket down with care and knelt next to the stove. She pushed the few lumps of coal aside and scooped out the heaps of collected ash.

The room was quiet as most of the other girls were off working in different areas of the girls' home. Today Margy remained behind. She had lived in the home for a couple years. At seven years old, her long blond braided hair often swayed across her back when she walked.

Though Margy was supposed to help Nat, she plopped on her bed, shoulders slumped and arms limp in her lap. "Why didn't they want me?" The girl had almost been adopted last week, but at the last minute, the couple changed their minds.

"Mistress Swanson will never say. A friend once told me, 'The Almighty does what's best.'" Though the *friend* was only a voice in her head, it was the only friend Nat had.

She glanced out the window at the bleak sky. There was no joy to be found in Fairlight. Every life seemed darkened and soiled by the sooty air they were all forced to breathe.

"Look, it's the ash maid," Gretchen snickered.

Nat sighed and sat back on her heels. When had these three crept into the room? And what were they planning now?

"No wonder she's always so filthy. Always covered in soot and blackened by the fire. She can't even do the simplest of things right. You're such a waste of space." Rachel scooped up a handful of ash and tossed it at Nat.

The fine dust covered Nat's hair and shoulders and pricked her eyes. It stung and brought tears to wash it away.

Violet laughed. "Look, we made the baby cry."

"Girls? Where are you? Come here. Mr. Jamerson will be here any moment," Mistress Swanson called.

Each of the three girls took a handful of ash and threw it on Nat before running from the room in fits of giggles.

Nat brushed off as much as she could back into the bucket as Margy brought her the pitcher of water they used to clean. "Put the basin in your lap," Margy said. "Turn your head, and I'll pour water over your face to try to wash the ash out of your eyes."

The stream of water flowed across her face. It soothed her eyes, and tickled her cheeks, before it dripped into the basin. Once she could blink without tears, Margy helped her clean up the remainder of the spilled ash, and they carried the bucket down the stairs together.

Almost an hour had passed before they cleaned up the mess. As Nat and Marty passed the second-floor landing, Mistress Swanson's voice hammered through the door of her private chambers. "What is the matter with you three? We had an opportunity to get out of this place. We could have had a real home and family. What have you done? You greeted Mr. Jamerson covered in filth and even dared to shake his hand with your grimy fingers. You horrible little urchins. You've ruined everything!"

Nat and Margy glanced at each other and hurried downstairs before the mistress' girls could blame their woes on someone else.

A horrid-smelling cold liquid splashed over Nat and jerked her from sleep. Her eyes stung, and she spit whatever it was out of her mouth.

Giggles met her next. The girls sleeping closest to Nat woke and muttered at the nasty odor which now covered Nat. She was soaked, as was her bed and blanket. With nothing dry to wipe her face, she grabbed hold of Rachel's nightgown and rubbed her face against it.

"Stop it!"

"That's so gross." Gretchen stepped out of reach.

The noise in the room grew louder until everyone was awake. The other girls pressed their blankets over their noses and mouths.

A light preceded Mistress Swanson as she entered with a lantern swinging from her raised hand. "What is the meaning of this racket?" The foul odor hit her and she gagged, then covered her mouth with her other arm. "Oh, what have you done now, Nat?"

"It wasn't her fault, Mis'ress S'anson," Edith dared speak up. "Rachel, Gre'chen, and Violet did it. Nat was just sleepin'."

All the girls gasped. No one ever dared challenge Mistress Swanson, and heaven forbid anyone blame her girls for anything.

Mistress Swanson turned and glared at Nat, who continued to shiver on her soaked bed. She tried again to spit whatever she'd been doused with out of her mouth. She was going to get sick. Nat knew it. She shivered. And Mistress Swanson would make her go around in her disgusting dress—or possibly even naked—until laundry day. Nat shuddered again. Oh, how she hated this place.

Mistress Swanson stomped two steps toward Nat but stopped

abruptly. "You wretched child! Oh, that I could get rid of you for good. You will …" She trembled as her words faded. Then she muttered. "Yes, Mr. Hideman is due for an inspection. Right. Can't leave the room like this. The smell will invade the entire house."

Her eyes scanned the dormitory. Her voice sounded almost like a machine as she gave a list of instructions. "Margy, grab a bucket of water. Gretchen, get your old nightgown and give it to Nat. Nat, go to the well and clean up as best you can. All you girls divide up the work and clean everything. Violet and Rachel, remove the soiled mattress."

"Mother!" her daughters all shouted at once.

Again, Mistress Swanson babbled as though she talked to someone not there.

It reminded Nat of when the voice first talked to her.

Mistress Swanson nodded. "True. They caused this. Their fault, and we are all losing sleep before the inspection."

"We don't even know that Mr. Hideman is coming tomorrow," Rachel whined.

"We are due for a visit, and with my luck, he will be here early in the morning. We can't have the dormitory in such a state. It would mean a fine for sure. If that happens," she waved her finger in the face of each of her daughters, "the money will come out of your candy and toy fund."

"Mother!" they yelled as one.

"I'll hear no more about it. I will be back in one hour and this room will be spotless, and you three," she singled out her daughters, "*will* help."

Chapter 12

Jer arched his back and stretched his aching muscles. Shadows reached far across the stable floor. He came to the city stables early every morning. Out in the corral, he cleaned up the manure around the cattle, then moved inside. It was cooler inside with less of a chance he would be seen by Shark and his gang of thugs.

Jer caught a whiff of himself and almost gagged. It had been a while since his last bath, and shoveling the droppings of large animals was leaving its mark on him. But it was also the smell of honest work. He'd take that over living in sewer tunnels with thieves any day.

"There you are, lad." Olrog came in smiling. "Don't know how this place ran before you came. The animals all seem more at peace, and it is a good deal cleaner." He reached out his hand toward Jer and dropped three coppers in Jer's upturned palm. "Worth every cent, you are."

Jer stood still as Olrog patted him on the shoulder. While it was a kind gesture, it felt more like a mighty hammer driving a post into hard soil. "Thank you, sir."

"Never seen anyone thank another for a hard day's work."

"Better this than being a thief on the streets. I like my hands." Jer shuddered at the thought of the constables cutting off his hand if he were caught stealing. Shark and his group liked the challenge and the rush of the danger. It made Jer sick.

"How you spending all that coin, anyway?"

"I'm eating good again. And I save some." He inhaled deeply again. "Might be time to get another set of clothes and launder these, but you never know what tomorrow will bring."

"You got a safe place to keep them?" Olrog nodded toward Jer's hand with the coins.

"Yes, sir." It wasn't super safe. Some sat in a hole inside one of his shoes. He'd also found a scrap of cloth that he'd formed into a pouch. It was tied to a string around his waist and dangled inside his pant leg. With his savings split up, he hoped if Shark or his gang ever robbed him, they wouldn't find all of it.

He tucked two coppers away and held the third tight in his hand as he headed toward the market. Soo walked beside him as she never wandered far away.

He'd almost reached the place where he bought meat pies when Burt stepped from the shadows into his path. Few vendors or shoppers remained in the market square. As they met next to an empty bakery and tailor's shop, no one stood near them. But someone or something else was there on the edge of Jer's senses. It reminded him of when the voice talked to him.

Burt now had a black eye, and Jer wondered if that was from one of his victims or if Shark had punched him. "Well, look who it is."

Jer took a step back and Soo moved closer, head down and ears back. The sense of being watched made the hairs on Jer's neck stand on end. It wasn't a threatening presence, but it lurked out of his eyesight.

"You too good to hang with us now? I'd say you aren't willing to get your hands dirty, but you scoop poop all day." Burt plugged his nose. "You smell like the back end of a cow. That's so much better than nicking goods with us." Burt pretended like he stole an imaginary wallet.

"Let me pass."

Burt took a wide stance. "Give me your money."

"No." Jer spoke with a calm that surprised him. Maybe it was Soo at his side or maybe the presences he couldn't identify but he wasn't afraid of this kid.

Burt leaned forward, his voice low and menacing. "Give it, you wimp."

Soo growled. It made the hairs on Jer's arms stand on end. Did he also hear a roar? Something was definitely nearby, though Burt didn't seem to notice it.

Burt flicked out his blade and pointed it at Soo. "I can slit his throat as easily as I can yours."

Jer sunk his fingers into Soo's fur and sent her a warning to be careful. Burt was dangerous. Soo lowered a little as though she wanted to lunge at their attacker.

"You all right, lad?" Olrog came down the lane behind him. The stable owner whistled loudly to attract the attention of any constable on duty.

Burt tucked away his blade. "You haven't seen the last of me. And Shark is looking for you too. You aren't hard to find." He melted into the shadows. The presence at the edge of Jer's senses evaporated as well.

"I think you need some new friends, lad." Olrog pounded his shoulder.

"They were never my friends. They only wanted me to be part of their group for what I could do for them."

"I'll see you to the market. Don't know that there's anything left to purchase for a meal at this late hour, though. Will you be safe the rest of the way to wherever you stay?"

"Soo will make sure no one hurts me."

Olrog patted Jer's shoulder again. "You have a way with the beasts, lad."

"They do seem to like me." Jer purchased the last meat pie Mr. Wills had and went a different direction the ususal to his rocky hideout. He watched for anyone who might have followed him, and he didn't slip inside until darkness fell.

He'd have to be on his guard all the time now. He didn't want to give up his job. He liked eating and didn't want to let Olrog down. The stable owner had been good to him. But he knew he'd have no chance against Shark, Burt, and the rest of the gang.

Chapter 13

Cay leaned against a tree and wiped his forehead. Each day seemed to get a little hotter. And as the plants grew, his work became harder. He hated helping the plants grow almost as much as he hated the harvest. There was always too much to do. Kint made them dig the trench from the river to the new field. A smithy in town had made the metal gate. Cay thought that would have made his life easier, but Kint gave him new work to replace carrying the water. "I hate working on this farm."

But the worst had to be pulling weeds in the blazing sun. Cay stepped into the shade of the tree for a moment. Wart looked up from his end of the row they were weeding. "And just what do you think you're doing?"

"Taking five breaths in the shade before my brain melts."

"You don't have a brain if you think you can stop working and leave it all to me."

"I haven't stopped—"

"Sure looks like it." Wart picked up a small rock from near his knee and chucked it. It hit Cay's chest with a stinging blow. "Get back to it before I break your neck." Wart was only a couple years older, but he was big compared to Cay.

"He wouldn't really break my neck," Cay muttered to himself, but he shoved off the tree. Best not take the chance and find out.

He staggered back between the rows of newly sprouted grain and knelt. The rough soil dug into his skin, but its dampness didn't cool him. It only made his pants dirtier and him stinkier.

"I hate this," Cay grumbled at the dirt. "Pulling weeds is stupid. The dumb weeds are almost the same color and size as the new grain." Cay had to be careful not to pull the wrong one. But even pulling out the weed made the dirt loose around the grain so it could fall out too. "Dumb, dumb weeds. Why can't they just grow someplace else?" He dragged the back of his hand over his forehead again. This heat was already unbearable, and it wasn't even summer yet.

"I'm done with my half. And I'm tired of listening to you whine. The rest is yours." Wart stood and brushed off his trousers.

"We still have ten more rows."

"You have ten rows. I'm going back to muck the stables."

Cay sat back on his heels and yelled at Wart's back as he disappeared into the distance. "That's not fair! You didn't do half. Come back and help." He knew it wouldn't make a difference, but it felt better to say it.

The only good thing was now he was alone. He sunk his fingers into the soil. He used his control of the earth to hold the stack of grain in place while he made the ground let go of the weed. The dumb weeds almost fell out of the dirt on their own. Cay made sure to keep an eye out for anyone who might see what he could do.

Cay finished the current row and moved to the next. Even with the help of his special skill, there was no point in hurrying. He only made more mistakes that way, which cost him even more time. The sun sat straight overhead. Cay stepped into the shade to get a drink. He filled the cup half full and poured it over his head. He closed his eyes and dreamed that the trails of water were the fingers of his mother—or even the ghost lady, Mira—rubbing his head. His stomach grumbled. "No point in making noise," he told it, "since Kint won't let us eat until the end of the day."

But as he said that, Cay's stomach growled louder, and he plopped down to weed again.

"Why aren't you helping with the milking?" Kint stomped to the edge of the field on his way from the stables to the silo.

Cay jerked, sat upright, and yanked his fingers from the soil. His mind had wandered, and he'd missed that someone walked up. "I haven't finished weeding this field."

"Where's that other kid?"

Cay shrugged. He knew better than to get one of the others in trouble, but he also wasn't about to suffer Kint's belt by lying to the big man. "Wart said he had to clean the stables."

"No-good, rotten kids. Can't be trained. Why don't any of you do as you're told?" Kint muttered as he continued on his way. He shouted back to Cay. "Get to the milking so I can get to town on time. Then come back and finish."

Cay stood with a groan. "Now I'm going to be weeding in the dark. It's hard enough pulling the right plant in the light." Cay took a quick drink and rushed off toward the milking shed.

"What are you doing here? You can't be done already." Wart stood in his path, crossed his arms, and tapped his foot.

"Kint sent me back to help with the milking so he can make deliveries. Then I go back."

Wart laughed. "Weeding through dinner. I get your grub."

"I'll get what's mine, then finish with the dumb weeds. Oh, and just so you know, Kint asked why you weren't helping me out there."

Wart jerked so straight and tight it looked like he'd break if he fell over. "What'd ya tell him?"

"The truth, that you said you went to clean the stables."

Wart raced toward Cay and punched him in the shoulder as he passed. "If I get a whippin,' you're so gonna pay."

Cay's arms and legs shuddered as he struggled to lift the last of the pails of milk up to pour into the larger jug. He sealed it, then leaned against it. He'd work hard—as always—today. His hunger dug a hole in his belly. "I hate living like this."

Three of the older boys came in and worked to move the tall cans to the wagon.

Cay hurried to grab his food before someone else tried to take it. He needed to go back to the field and finish the weeding. Cay glanced up at the darkening sky. At least the moon would be up tonight. Not quite whole but enough to give him some hope of pulling only the weeds. He needed to get done before Kint came back since Cay would have to take care of the horses. But if he still hadn't finished the weeding, he'd have to go back out. Cay didn't want to be in the open fields when all the night critters came out. He shuddered. Working in the hot sun or being whipped wasn't the absolute worst, after all. No, getting eaten by a wild animal would be even worse.

Chapter 14

Mura gripped the rough rusted metal as she hung from the bars on the top of her cell. She drew her knees up to her chest, lowered her legs all the way until they dangled over the floor, and repeated. Then she raised her knees as if she sat in a chair, twisted her waist, brought her knees up first on her right side, then on her left. Even in the cool underground cell, sweat collected on her body as she worked to keep herself limber and strengthened in preparation for the time she would eventually leave this pit.

She dropped to the cell floor and ran in place until her heart pounded against her ribs. Next, she went through the forms of sword fighting she had studied for years and practiced her attack and defense, using her hairbrush as a practice weapon. As she went through the many movements, memories floated to her mind.

Father had learned she often sneaked out of her lessons in mathematics to watch the young squires train. She would hide in the shadows and mirror their movements with a waster, a heavy wooden practice sword. She pulled the wooden from the pile of others the squires used before they arrived. She'd trained in this way for months before Mura had been spotted by a young maid, who had run immediately to the king.

Father had called her to his study. He stood behind his desk, arms crossed, with a deep scowl that marred his kind face. "What are you up to, young lady? Is it true you lurk around the squires and thrash a waster about?"

"I want to learn how to use a sword, Father."

"No daughter of mine will wield a sword. I forbid it. You will return to your studies at once."

Mura had but one chance to change his mind. "May I make a bargain with you, Daddy? I want to know how to fight. If what the priest says is true and there is evil stirring, I want to be prepared and not wait for someone to protect me. What if my defender dies? Then what hope is there for me? I have been diligent in studying as all the squires do. Put me to the test. Have one of the second-years meet me in a match. See if I am ready."

"Mura, you cannot best one so much more experienced than you. He'll have a year's more training."

"Then he should win easily." Mura crossed her arms to mirror him. "I just want to show you I'm serious. After you see what I can do—or not—I will do as you ask and stop training if you wish."

Father frowned at her, something rare between them. As his first born, Daddy loved her—but no more or than her sister. He initially gave her a firm no, but after a few days of her pouting, he set up a challenge.

Mura entered the empty training area with Scout—a boy two years older than her and a head taller. Even at twelve, Mura had a well-developed stubborn nature. She'd pointed her waster at the boy. "So help me, you go easy on me because I'm a girl and the princess, I'll knock you on your backside."

Scout straightened, raised a brow, and looked to the king.

"Treat her as any other first year, lad, and don't hold back." Father leaned back against the corral's railing and crossed his ankles and arms.

Mura took up her starting form and waited only until Scout raised his waster before she came at him with a fierce attack. He almost lost his mock weapon as she hammered against it. Scout recovered quickly, and they went blow for blow for several minutes, neither giving ground.

As they spun around each other looking for an advantage, Mura saw Father straighten and stand with his feet apart.

As Mura pressed Scout with unrelenting blows, he whirled away from her and snatched up a shield from the pile nearby.

Mura grabbed another waster and charged him. As he raised his shield to block her overhand swing, she slipped one fake blade under it and poked him in the ribs. She spun away from him, crouched, and slammed the flat of both her wooden swords behind his knees. He dropped to his back. She kicked the shield away, stood on his sword arm, and pointed both of her mock weapons at his throat.

She looked up to see the king's back as he stomped away. Mura had thought he was angry with her, but by that afternoon, she was dressed in a combination of wide-legged trousers and a skirt that was open in the front. She train in a back corner of the castle grounds with one of Father's personal guards four days every week.

Now all these years later, she swiped at a tear for that brave knight who had been among the first to fall when Brax made his move. In remembrance of him, she spent any time she could practicing the forms and movement he taught her all those years ago. Even then, few knew that she had been trained in war craft—fewer now with so many dead. Father had allowed it, saw that the Almighty gifted her in it, but he still didn't approve of it being her first line of defense.

With Father on her mind, Mura moved back to the stone bed and rested the few moments until the guards arrived at her cell with her meal. She hobbled forward appearing the weak and defenseless captive they thought her to be. At least for now.

Chapter 15

Nat yawned; her borrowed dress pinched her arm as she tried to cover her mouth. It was too tight and too short, but at least Mistress Swanson had given her something to wear. Nat put the chamber pot back in the corner and gagged at the memory of its contents which had been dumped on her a few hours ago.

"Mistress Swanson, he's coming. Mr. Hideman is heading this way," Margy yelled up the stairs.

Cursing and door slamming followed. "Girls, take your places immediately."

Everyone ran. No on wanted to be sold for disobeying mistress.

As she raced down the stairs behind all the other girls, Nat stumbled to a stop when Mistress Swanson stepped into her path. She grabbed and pulled Nat by the ear until she perched on her toes. Mistress Swanson's lips pulled back to reveal yellow teeth, and she almost pressed her long, pointed nose to Nat's.

After one whiff, Mistress Swanson pulled back with a disgusted snarl. "You say one word against my girls or try to blame them for the mishap that occurred early this morning, and I don't care what the evil spirit of this dreadful house says, you won't see tomorrow."

Still holding to her ear, Mistress Swanson spun around and thrust Nat toward the lower stairs. She stumbled and grasped at the railing to keep from crashing down to the bottom. After finding her balance, Nat resumed her descent and hurried to take her place at a desk just as a knock sounded at the front door.

"Gretchen, let our guest in," Mistress Swanson said before she turned and pointed a long finger at each of them. "No trouble!" It was almost a growl from low in the woman's throat. It made the hair on Nat's arms stand on end.

Each girl pulled out a slate from under their desk's lid and copied the math equations the headmistress wrote on the blackboard at the front of the room. No one made a sound, and no one let their eyes wander to the man with Gretchen.

Mr. Hideman was a short man compared to the few men that Nat had ever seen. He always wore a dark suit with a bright red bowtie, and his shirt seemed more yellow than white. The pants of his suit puddled on top of his cracked black shoes.

"Mother, Mr. Hideman is here for an inspection."

Mistress Swanson turned with a bright smile that she only used with him or people coming to hire one of the girls. "Good day to you, sir." She turned to the girls. "Ladies, what do you say to our city inspector?"

They all stood, curtsied, and spoke in unison. "Good day to you, Mr. Hideman."

The odd little man looked at them with no expression. "I know you aren't due for an inspection for another few weeks, but I was in the neighborhood ..." he shook his head and muttered the next few words, "though I have no idea why." He sighed and squared his narrow shoulders. "Figured now was as good a time as any."

For some reason, the words he said sounded to Nat like they weren't his own. Like an unseen force made him say these words and be here to do this. It reminded Nat of a puppet a woman brought when she interviewed one of the girls.

"We are always ready to be reviewed at The Stepping Stone for Wayward Girls. You will find everything in order as always, Mr.

Hideman," Mistress Swanson said, bowing her head toward him.

"Yes, well, let us begin." He put his case on Nat's desk and pulled out a long clipboard before searching the bottom of the leather container. After several seconds, he pulled out a pencil. He looked to Nat. His eyes ran from the top of her head to the bottom of her feet. "How is it you are still here, child?"

Nat could only stare. She didn't want to say the wrong words. As always, Mistress Swanson spoke for her. "Oh, this dear girl, I'm afraid I just can't part with her. After all these years, she is near like one of my own girls now."

Mr. Hideman scribbled something on his chart. "If you think of her as family and she is no longer adoptable, then she will be removed from the city's list as a ward, and you will take over the cost of her care, Swanson." He turned on his heel as Mistress Swanson narrowed a hateful glare at Nat. "Come, girl, you will assist me today."

"But Mr. Hideman—" Mistress Swanson sputtered as she picked up her hem to hurry after him.

The man continued to walk and waved the mistress back without a glance back at her. "Teach your lesson, Swanson. I'm sure the girl can show me the things I need to see."

The housemistress seized Nat's arm and squeezed so tight Nat bit her lip to keep from crying out. "So help me, you little brat, if I don't get a good report it will be your hide," she growled in Nat's ear.

Nat nodded and ran to catch up with Mr. Hideman in the kitchen. She opened the doors he told her to, and answered his questions with as few words as possible and as honestly as she dared. They inspected the dining room and then moved to the workroom and supply area. Mr. Hideman wrote furiously on his paper, the scratching of the pencil like blowing sand against her skin.

Nat clasped her hands around her back as they climbed the stairs to the girls' dormitory.

He wrinkled his nose as he entered. "It smells terrible in here."

"Sorry, Mr. Hideman. We had a minor mishap with the chamber pot in the middle of the night. We've cleaned but will work on it again after lessons."

"You could open a window."

"Yes, sir."

When Nat didn't move, he turned and stared at her, one fat black eyebrow arched high.

"Now, sir?" Nat struggled to hide her shaking as she swallowed loud enough for him to hear.

"I am here now, and that stench is worse than a barn."

"Yes, sir." Nat still didn't move.

"Oh, for all the love of money, are you stupid, girl?" He stomped to the nearest window and tried to raise it. It didn't budge. He stared at it for a moment and moved to the next and the next. After the fourth one that would not open, he turned and looked at her. "Do any of them open?"

Nat stared at the floor; tears filled her eyes as she shook her head.

Mr. Hideman's pencil scratched on his clipboard as he stomped past her, muttering, "I can't believe she's hidden all this from me."

Nat was not going to live to see the sunset once he gave Mistress Swanson his report.

Chapter 16

"Lad, are you up there?" Olrog called.

Jer crawled to the edge of the hayloft and looked down at the owner. "Yes, sir."

Olrog smiled and waved him to the floor. Another man stood next to him. Not as tall or muscled, with his hands behind his back, the newcomer considered Jer.

"Am I in trouble, sir?"

"Not at all, lad, not at all." Olrog patted Jer roughly on the shoulder. "I'm right glad to see you sleeping here some nights. I know that gang of thieves has their sights set on you, but you'll always be safe here." He waved his hand to the other man. "That's why I wanted you to meet my friend. This is Knob. He works at the Rusty Nail."

Jer rolled his shoulders and swallowed a yawn as he reached for the man's hand. The first rays of light brushed the morning sky as Jer shook the man's hand and looked at him. Jer struggled to figure how a guy from the tavern on the other side of the market square could help him with Shark and his gang.

"Knob here keeps the Nail peaceful. I've asked him to show you how to defend yourself."

Jer considered Knob again. He didn't look like he could fight off Olrog let alone keep troublemakers out of a tavern.

As if reading his thoughts, the man spoke. "Size isn't always an advantage," Knob said, his deep voice rumbled in Jer's chest. His hands came out from behind his back and he passed a pair of tall black boots to Jer. "My boy's outgrown these. They'll serve you better than them old shoes—both in keeping your feet dry and your pant legs clean as you work, and in hiding any coin from those rotten pickpockets."

"Thank you." Jer whispered the words as he took the boots. They were barely worn. He plopped down on a stack of hay and pulled them on. They were a little big, which meant they'd last him for a long time, but they were best thing he had ever put on his feet. Olrog handed him two leather pouches on long strings for his coins. Jer dropped one inside each boot and secured the strings over a hook at the top of each boot, then laced the new footwear up his shin. Jer stood and took small steps in them. He rocked his feet and flexed his ankles. "Thank you, sir. I've never had anything so fine."

"I hope they serve you well. Now, let's get started with some basics."

Olrog nodded to them as he stepped away to feed the animals.

Knob took his time instructing Jer where to place his feet and how to hold his fists in order to block different types of blows. They practiced in slow motion for a while as the rising sun spilled more light into the stables.

"All right, you've got the basics. Let's see how you do. I'm gonna come at you. Defend yourself, boy." Knob had barely finished speaking when his right fist came full force at Jer's head. Jer's left arm came up to block the blow and protect his face, but it took him a moment to remember to step closer to his attacker, duck below his arm, and slip behind Knob.

Jer smiled at his victory but missed the foot that swept his legs and dropped him to his back. Soo leapt from where she slept, ears back, and gave a threatening growl as Knob dropped to a knee to smash Jer in the face.

Knob held his punch and slowly turned to look at the snarling beast over his elbow.

"Soo." Jer reached out his left hand for the dog. "It's all right, girl.

Knob, here, is a friend. He's helping me. I'm fine." He sent the dog a calming message, which made the back of his right-hand tingle and itch. After a moment she inched forward.

She sniffed Knob and gave him a full inspection as Jer sunk his fingers deep into her fur and reassured her again through the connection he had with her. She licked Jer's face once and ambled off to sleep in a patch of sun coming through the now-open doors.

"You can't celebrate your wins too early, kid," Knob said as he stood and offered Jer a hand up. "Get too full of yourself and it will cost you."

"Yes, sir."

Without warning this time, Knob swung a fist at Jer's ribs. With his wrists crossed, Jer slammed down on the fist and pivoted out of the way, though this time he remembered that he should never put his back to his opponent. Knob drove him back with a series of swings, but Jer blocked, ducked, or slipped away from all of them.

"Good. Use your smaller size and speed to keep out of my reach. When you're up against a bigger threat, you may wear him out before he even lands a blow."

They trained for about an hour, moving from how to block or avoiding a blow to how to get out of various holds if Shark or the gang got their hands on him.

"You've made good progress today, kid. I'll be back same time tomorrow. We'll work more on this and then on some simple attacks. I can't say I'm a fan of teaching you how to beat up a guy for the basic reason the constables in town don't much care who started the fight. They'll throw you both in a cell without question if you're caught doing much more than running away. Even then there's no real guarantee. But …" he yawned, "the gangs roaming the streets will not be ones to play by any rules or any code of honor."

"No, sir. Thank you again—for the training and the boots." Jer rocked back on his heels and looked down. "They are really comfortable."

Knob mussed his hair as he yawned again. "Time to get this body to bed. See you in the mornin', kid."

It seemed odd to go to bed as the sun came up, but the Rusty Nail didn't open until the afternoon and a crowd wasn't usually there until the sun set. It meant Knob worked some weird hours. Jer turned to his own work and kept at it hard until mid-day when Olrog approached him again.

"I've got to head to the market, lad. Thought you might want to accompany me, get a bite and maybe that change of clothes you talked about."

Jer glanced around at the work which still needed to be done.

"The boss is giving you leave to take a break, lad," Olrog laughed. "I'll not think you're slacking for it. Come on." Olrog waved, and Jer set aside the shovel and raced to follow.

Jer walked between Olrog and Soo. He found safety with them. Olrog left Jer at the tailor's with a promise to swing by and walk back with him in about a half an hour.

"That beast ain't allowed in here," the tall man ordered from behind the counter. He was close to Olrog's height but so skinny he looked more like a post. Jer wondered if he had trouble walking in a strong wind.

"She's not a beast, and I can't leave her outside."

"Of course ye can. Shop ain't no place for animals."

"I'll only be a couple of minutes and then we'll both leave, unless you don't want my coin for your clothes?"

"Like ye have any coin to spare, let alone buy what I'm sellin'."

Jer reached into his pocket and jingled the coins he had there.

The shopkeeper raised one brow over his hard, dark eyes. "Ye steal 'em?"

"No! I work for Olrog in the stables. I've earned every coin from my hard work."

The man crinkled his nose, which made his lean face smash up in an odd way. "No wonder ye stink so, boy. Let's be quick about this. Tell me what ye want, I'll measure ye, then ye two can get out of here."

"Oh, you don't have anything already made?"

"I do custom work, boy. Ye think I'm some cheap mercantile?"

Mercantile? Jer had forgotten about that place. It sat far on the other side of the market square, but if the clothes would be cheaper, *and* he could get them now, that would be better. Could he make it there without running into Shark or any of the gang? Even with the training, he wouldn't be able to stay in town forever and hope to avoid them. "Sorry to have bothered you, sir. Have a good day." Jer turned and reached for the door.

"Wait." The tailor looked around as if to reveal some deep secret he didn't want anyone else to overhear. But as there was no one else in the shop, it was silly. "Don't ye go tellin' no one now, but I got a set of pants and a shirt might fit ye. Young man shot up over a foot taller before I had 'em finished. Ye finished growing?"

"I hope not," Jer said with a groan.

They agreed on a price, and the man wrapped them in heavy paper and tied it with a string. Jer slung it over his shoulder and stepped out of the door. Soo snarled. A flying fist raced toward him. Without thought, Jer stepped out of the way and blocked the blow. The hand slammed against the window beside the door. Burt cursed as his fist rattled the heavy pane. The shopkeeper shouted as he stomped toward the door.

A shadow passed overhead and with it came the presence Jer had experienced last time he ran into Burt. Whatever creature that was—and he wasn't sure how he knew it was an animal and not a person—it seemed to be there to protect him. But if that was true, why couldn't Jer see it?

Soo barked and lunged at Burt as Jer stepped away from the building to have more freedom of movement in case Burt tried again. Jer kept his back protected against the shop and watched for Burt's next move.

A blade flashed in the light as Burt tried to keep Soo away.

Jer called for her. Her hair stood on end, her teeth showed, and Soo growled with such fierceness she couldn't hear Jer's command. Jer stepped between the two and watched the knife closely. "Get out of here." He drew strength from the unseen presence like he did from the voice.

Burt leapt forward and aimed for Jer's ribs. With crossed wrists, Jer smashed the hand away with such force Burt cut his own leg right above the knee. It wasn't deep, but blood colored his tattered pants.

A whistle rang through the air, and Olrog jogged to Jer's side. Burt melted into the crowd, and Jer released the breath that had been trapped in his chest.

"Thank you, sir—for coming back just now, and for asking Knob to train me. I'd be a bloody heap now if not for it."

Olrog smiled and pounded on his shoulder again. "Let's grab something to eat and get back to the safety of the stables."

"Yes, sir." As they walked through the market, Jer noted Burt at a distance and the glare on his face. At least four of Shark's gang stood nearby and watched his every move. Shark leaned against a wall at the mouth of a narrow alley. He stared at Jer for a long time before he pulled the watch on the long chain from his vest pocket and glanced at the time. A smile spread under his narrowed gaze when he looked up again.

Jer got the message. It was only a matter of time before Shark took him out.

Chapter 17

Cay's feet dragged on the ground as he trudged to the back of Kint's house and took his rations for the evening. He wiped sweat from his forehead and turned with his food to go back down the steps. A hand reached out from between the wood planks and grabbed his ankle. Cay fell forward, missed the last two steps, and landed hard on his stomach. His chin slammed into the ground and tears filled his eyes.

A shadow darted out from under the stairs, sprang forward, and grabbed his spilled food.

"Stop!" Cay could hardly make out the muddled shape of his attacker through his watery vision.

"I warned ye, kid."

"Wart!" Cay tried to get to his feet, but his ankle hurt and he plopped on the bottom step.

"Ye get me in trouble one more time," Wart warned as he ran away, "and I'll do more than take yer supper."

Cay put his arm on his knees and dropped his head on top of it. He gritted his teeth so he wouldn't cry like a baby. His stomach growled. He couldn't go a whole day out in the fields without eating. It just wasn't fair.

Something brushed against his leg and the step creaked as more weight joined his. "That creep is going to get whipped to death before he ever lays another hand on you."

Lor sat beside him, half of her dried meat in her outstretched hand.

"I can't take yours." Cay rested his chin on his fists. "It's not right."

"I'll be fine for one day. Tomorrow, you make sure not to get your food until I'm with you. Wart wouldn't dare take you on with me there."

Cay tipped his head and looked at her.

Lor's face beamed with a rare smile. "He tried to kiss me in the milking shed."

"Yuck." Cay crinkled his nose.

Lor nodded. "I wrestled him to the ground and punched him a couple of times in the ribs. He'll think twice before messing with me again."

Cay took the offered meat and chewed slowly. It was definitely better than nothing, but his belly still grumbled.

The wagon rumbled back into the yard, and Kint stepped down on shaky legs. He staggered a couple of steps one way and then a few another. He lurched forward and grabbed one of the horse's bridles. The horse jerked its head away with a snort. Kint mumbled under his breath about dumb horses and useless kids as he wove his way to his house on unsteady feet.

Cay and the others—all except Wart, who was nowhere to be found—waited for Kint to disappear inside before they led the horses to put the wagon to its place. Then they unhitched the animals. Cay brushed the white one, and Lor did the same with the black. They didn't have names—not officially—but Lor called them Snow and Night when no one else was around.

When they were finished, Cay and Lor put the horses in their stalls in the stable.

Lor tapped him on the shoulder and waved for him to follow. They stayed in the deepest shadows and inched their way silently to the milking shed. With the milking done and Kint in his house asleep, the lanterns were out. Without the moon or stars to help, Cay couldn't see his own feet.

A warm hand took his and pulled him inside along the wall until they came to the back of the shed. They sat in the hay listening to the cows breathe and munch on their feed. Cay's stomach growled again.

Cay didn't know how long they sat there, but he woke with a start.

Lor elbowed him and clamped her hand over his mouth. Something brushed his face. It was soft and wet with prickles. It wasn't until the thing inhaled and blew out a hot breath that Cay realized a cow was inspecting him in the dark. He wiped the cow snot from his face onto the back of his arm and felt Lor ease away from him. A moment later, there was a zinging sound and a small splash.

Lor came back and felt for his hands. He took hold of the cup she handed him, and she pushed it to his lips. Warm, thick milk splashed over his tongue and slid down his throat. He coughed and sputtered. If a cow hadn't kicked the milking pail over making it clatter, Cay would have been heard. Lor pushed up on the cup several more times until he finished all the milk.

They waited a little longer, still and silent, before she led him to the ladder and up into the small loft above the cows. They dug a spot in the hay, curled up back to back, and pulled hay over the top of them. Cay listened as her breaths became slow and deep. She'd looked after him again. Was this what it was like to have a family? He liked it.

His stomach stayed quiet for now. Cay rested his head on his arm. He liked this safe, warm place with his friend.

Kint squinted under the morning light. He groaned. One of the older boys said Kint had been drinking something called liquor. It made him walk funny and have trouble getting up in the morning. With a moan, Kint rubbed his face and head. Cay never wanted to try the drink if it would make him feel as bad as the big man looked.

"What's your job for the day?"

That was an odd thing to ask. Kint usually told him what to do. "Water the rye. Weed the corn. Check the wheat for bugs. Milk the cows, brush the horses, and feed both." Cay tried to list every chore he'd ever done. He didn't want to forget one and end up on the receiving end of the belt.

Kint grunted and turned to leave. He swayed a little. "See to it then." He made it a few steps. "That other kid, the skin condition."

"Wart?"

"Yep, him. He needs to work in the back rye."

Was Cay supposed to tell Wart his job? That wasn't going to happen. Cay had made it his goal not to cross paths with that kid for a good long time—if ever. But if he didn't tell Wart what Kint had told him, and Wart got in trouble for it … He just couldn't win.

Chapter 18

Mura monitored her charges. The living situations grew increasingly dangerous for each of them. She couldn't move them while locked in her cell, and she couldn't always get to them to help when trouble showed up. Surely their guardians had taken note of the rising threat and were ready to reveal themselves.

The cold from the stones she knelt on seeped through her filthy, tattered dress. Her fingers rested laced together in her lap. Her head bowed; her eyes closed. Mura pulled all her attention to the dark behind her eyes. Rather than releasing her spirit out of her body, she turned inward to the only strength she could find.

The Almighty had come into her life at a young age. He seemed always near to her. It was part of her heritage as a descendent of the Truefaith line of kings. But it was more than that. Mura trusted in the Almighty to never fail her or leave her alone. Her entire world had fallen apart. Her father—her rock—was dead, and she'd been asked to lead. She'd failed so profoundly. The kingdom was in the mess it was now because of her.

A tear splashed on her hands, followed by another.

She deserved to be in this cell. A ragged breath struggled into her lungs.

These dark thoughts couldn't overtake her again. The children needed her for a little longer. Mura had to see they were safe. She would not fail them again.

She refocused on her Source of strength and pushed the past

mistakes far away.

After her time in prayer, Mura rested in the peace she found in the Almighty's presence. On her stone bed, she loosed her spirit. She came to a corner out of sight of the guards standing in front of her dungeon doors. With the strength of the powerful Savior Stone she'd been gifted, she made her image visible. The watchmen would never recognize her as a short maid with light hair dressed in a simple dress and apron.

As she prepared for her future escape, Mura let her false image stroll around the corner and pass the two guards. Down the hall and out of sight of them. With no more need to be seen, Mira released the image and became vapor, then floated through the corridor and out of the palace. Her spirit sailed across the ward, over the battlements of the inner wall, and through the bailey. Beyond the outer wall, she drifted through the city. Like the palace and the kingdom's citizens, the city of Palace Glen had seen better days. The cobblestones were either broken or missing, which made all travel difficult. Thatch on many of the homes was either black and rotting or had gaping holes. Some homes leaned to the point they were in danger of falling. Others had light showing through cracks in the walls.

Mura's spirit ventured through the streets and in search of a safe haven. Were there none left in Palace Glen who still loved her family? Had Brax killed all the believers?

"You wretched child!" Mistress Swanson's finger pointed at the end of Nat's nose. "This is all your fault." She shook a paper in her other hand. "Violations! That is all Hideman found. Oh, once I fix every one of these and he completes his follow up, I'm done with you. He'll look for marks on you when he returns, but after that—" Her eyes narrowed and her words hissed. "You. Will. Pay."

Nat held tight as a violent tremor started in her feet and filled her entire body. She couldn't swallow and her heart struggled to beat.

Jer looked up from shoveling the corral. He wiped his forehead on the tail of his shirt. A form in the shadow of the alley took shape in the growing morning light. Jer stared for a few seconds longer until Burt stepped into the light. He spun a knife in his fingers. Two more of the gang came into view from the shadows of other shops around the cow pen. They carried blades too. Then Shark strolled forward. He rested his arms on the top rail of the corral and put one foot on the bottom rail. "You can't always hide here with these animals. I'm a patient man. You *will* give me everything you have made working here."

Jer didn't move. He didn't argue either. There was no point. He knew if he ever fell into the gang's hands, they would take every cent he had on him. Jer would fight to defend it, but against so many, no amount of Knob's training would overcome four against one.

Two of the cows turned and charged at the fence where Shark stood. Shark jumped back and yelped as the animals rammed the posts.

Jer tried not to laugh.

"How'd you make them do that?"

Jer was sure the simple beasts read something from him, but he hadn't purposely sent them to defend him. "I didn't do anything. I've been standing here silently keeping an eye on all of you. Besides, you can't make these dull creatures do much of anything on command. They aren't dogs." At that, Soo came to his side. She lowered her head and growled.

Shark straightened his vest in an attempt to cover his shudder, but Jer noticed it. "There will come a day—very soon. You can't escape me forever."

Cay stood and stretched as tall as he could. He arched his back to release the aching tightness. A clod of dirt slammed into his shoulder and sprayed his arm and cheek with tiny bits as it broke up. He turned in time to duck the next flying clump.

"I'm going to kill you." Wart reached down to pick up another wad of dirt when Lor came up behind him and grabbed him by the hair. She jerked him in an awkward backbend until he could look at her face.

"You try that again, and you'll be the one laid out on this earth feeding it your blood." She released him and kicked him in the behind to send him away. "Come on." Lor waved to Cay. "Let's get to the house before he does."

They ran, but Cay's shorter legs let Wart get to the house first. They'd have to wait until he left to get their food so they didn't have another confrontation.

Mura reunited her spirt and her body in time to answer another summons. She stood before Brax. His blade raised her chin. She couldn't swallow without suffering another cut.

His awful breath washed over her face. "Will you join me?"

Her nose wrinkled. "I've already done my kingdom enough damage where you are concerned. I'll not make things worse by turning my back on the truth."

The sword pressed tighter against her skin. "Then I can see no further use for you." He removed the weapon and stepped back. His stare, cold and hard, never left hers. "The anniversary of the day the Truefaith thugs stole the throne of Purlan from her rightful kings is two weeks away. As proof that the Everblood line rules once again—and forever more—it is fitting that I put an end to the usurpers." Though Brax continued to glare at her, he spoke to his guards. "Make the preparation for a royal execution. Make sure all the kingdom knows that in fourteen days, Mura, the last of the Truefaith line, will meet her end. All the nobility must attend. I will take it as rebellion to not show up. Anyone not here will meet Mura's fate."

Mura inclined her head and was returned to her cell.

Chapter 19

Mura settled on her stone bed with a deep breath. In eight-and-a-half days, Brax planned to kill her. But she had no intention of dying at his hand—at least, not until the children were safe. She'd spent much of the previous day in prayer. It had been almost a week since she last visited her charges, but she monitored them daily. Their relocation was of greatest importance, but she couldn't see to it from inside this dungeon cell.

After another deep breath of the cool damp air, she focused on the continual drip in the corner which always came with the rains. *Plop, plop, plop.* Another breath, and she gathered her spirit tight inside her. The Savior Stone she carried allowed her to look into another's heart. Was the ability to separate her spirit from her physical body supposed to also be part of the stone's function, or could this peculiar ability be a side effect of being kept a captive for so long? Either way, she needed to do something more.

As a wisp of air, her spirit floated between the bars of her cell and passed through the metal door of her chamber. She drifted up the steps to the wooden door at the top and gave herself form again. As she peeked through the barred opening at the top, she considered the two guards. They faced away from her. The blond on her right yawned. His coworker, a man with black hair and a beard, elbowed him.

Once they stilled again, Mura passed her spirit hand through the door and reached for the key on the dark-haired soldier's belt. She concentrated on making her hand solid, and not just an illusion. Though she attempted to grab the key several times, her hand could not grasp it. *Please.* Her eyes squeezed closed. If she could have cried in this form, she would have. But Mura hated to shed even one tear.

To give her spirit strength and substance, she tightened it around the object she desperately needed. The key wiggled. She wrapped all of her spirit around the key, not just what she thought of as her hand. If Nataline were in her place, she'd already have the key. Jeremicum would have a mouse or some other creature get it. Calebus would cause an earthquake and be set free. Mura's concentration wavered as Zane came to her mind.

His deep brown eyes that always looked at her with such care, gazed at her again. From the first time they met, he believed in her and said she could do anything she set her mind to. Zane had received the Savior Stone that allowed him to control fire. He would have melted the locks to be free. But he wasn't free. He was in the grave, killed by Brax, and it was her fault. She'd brought the two men together but hadn't detected the danger. Thankfully, she wasn't in her body just now because thoughts of Zane always brought tears. She couldn't cry for his lost life anymore. The children needed her.

The energy it took to separate her spirit and body always drained her for hours. The effort she used now to get the key consumed even more energy. This was her last chance before she needed to join herself together again, rest, and try again later. As all of her spirit surrounded the key, it moved. She focused all of her thoughts on the slim piece of brass.

It rose. After a few attempts, Mura freed it from the hook on the guard's belt. Mura fought to hold the key. Exhaustion filled her. Rest— she needed to rest. The key rose up to the window in the door and slipped between the bars. Her spirit hurtled back to her body so fast that when the two slammed together, she coughed and sputtered.

Mura lay still until her frantic breathing calmed and her head stopped pounding as if the black smith were using it to make a new sword. After several moments, she managed to raise her head high enough to see her hands clasped one on top of the other over her stomach. Slowly she lifted one, then opened the other fisted hand. The key to her cell lay inside her palm. She'd done it.

Her eyes closed as her head dropped back with a dull thud. Sleep, all she wanted was sleep.

You worthless girl! The inspector returns tomorrow. If you don't finish, I'll beat you until you take your last breath and tell that bothersome official, Hideman, the mine masters came and purchased you.

Nataline needed her.

Chapter 20

Nat rotated her hand in circles as she tried to work the soreness out of her wrist. She'd been scraping at the paint-sealed windows of the dormitory for days.

"You worthless girl! The inspector returns tomorrow. If you don't finish, I'll beat you until you take your last breath." Mistress Swanson raised the stick she used for punishment and slammed it on the metal frame of the bed nearest Nat. The clank of wood against metal echoed through the large room.

Nat tightened her muscles so she wouldn't flinch. There were twelve windows around the room. She'd been left to work on them alone as the other girls were given tasks in different parts of the house to meet the inspector's deadline.

"I don't think I can explain so your dumb brain will understand, just how much it will cost you if you fail me."

Nat had finished six of the windows and was working on the seventh. But she didn't know how she'd finish in time—even if she missed dinner and worked through the entire night.

She's wrong you know. Surviving in this place as well as you have, proves how brilliant you are.

Nat took a deep breath and let it out slowly as the voice comforted her with words and the sense of peace that it always brought.

You will be safe. Don't fear her. There is a purpose for you far beyond what this poor, small-minded woman can see. I won't let anything happen to you, and there are others watching over you.

Others? Nat often felt alone, but the voice kept telling her she wasn't. She had to believe—though she never saw anyone else.

Clang! The staff slammed against the bed again. "You brainless girl, why are you just staring off at nothing?" Mistress Swanson raised the stick again and moved closer to her. "Why aren't these windows open yet?"

"The paint has been cleared, but they won't stay open. I'm afraid—"

Mistress Swanson thrust up the window closest to her and released it. It instantly fell closed. The glass shattered on impact. She yelped.

"—that if we aren't careful, they will break." Nat finished under her breath.

"You did that. You broke that window."

Nat forced her lips closed and sucked them between her teeth.

The staff waved over Nat's head. "You did something as you cleaned them to make them not stay open, and now one is broken. I won't be able to get it replaced before morning. You do nothing but cost me money. I should just be done with you now." The headmistress stepped closer to her.

Nat braced for the blow that would most likely kill her.

An odd roar—almost two garbled roars together—came through the broken opening. Another piece of jagged glass shook from the window frame and shattered on the floor next to Mistress Swanson's toes.

The headmistress stared at the window, at the pieces on the floor, at Nat, and then back at the window. She shuddered and the staff lowered to her side. "The rest of these windows better be done before Hideman arrives tomorrow." With one last glance at the window, Mistress Swanson hurried from the room.

Jer gripped the shovel handle so hard his fingers ached. He wanted to throw it across the barn like a spear.

"You all right, lad?" Olrog stepped inside out of the sun.

"I feel like a prisoner. I can't leave without being attacked by Shark and his thugs. It's only a matter of time before they figure out a way to get to me. Then they'll steal everything I have and no doubt leave me for dead."

"Perhaps it's time you think of moving on to another town. Don't see much keeping you here."

It wasn't like Jer hadn't thought about it. But the voice had always told him to stay.

But the time is now right. You best prepare to leave.

He hadn't expected her to answer. "Where would I go?" Was he asking Olrog or the voice? He didn't know for sure.

Olrog shrugged, "If it were me? I'd go someplace cooler." He wiped his face with his sleeve.

Jer laughed. "Cooler would definitely be better."

Yes, head north.

A hand slammed down on his shoulder.

Jer had gotten used to the rough pounding of the stable owner and thought now how hard it would be to leave his one friend and the only place he'd ever thought of as home.

"I'm going to miss you something awful, lad. Don't think I'll find another who'll work as hard. But keep being that kind of man, and it won't matter where your feet take you. You'll do just fine." Olrog thumped his shoulder twice more and strolled away.

North? Could he really leave here? He had steady income, food, a place to sleep.

Soo raised her head and looked at him with her ears pulled forward.

"Not just now, girl, but soon I think."

Soo rested her head back on her paws as Jer returned to his job.

The thought of leaving made him almost as nervous as the fear of the inevitable attack by Shark's gang.

"Where is that other worthless kid?"

Cay glanced up from the bucket of water he dragged to the field. While the canal watered the furthest fields, those closest to the stream still needed to be watered daily by hand. He shrugged at Kint.

"I told ya both to see these fields are watered."

"He was here in the beginning but left after putting one bucket of water in the field." Cay knew telling the truth was best, even if it meant Wart got in trouble. Better that mean kid than him.

Kint stomped away. "Useless, good for nothing, pain in my neck. Got to be a better way to make a living …" His words faded in the distance.

Cay waited until he couldn't see the big farmer anymore before he called the water out of the stream straight into the channels between the rows of wheat that had already grown waist high. Like a serpent rising out of the depths, the water rose and slid above the ground until it splashed down where Cay wanted.

Careful.

Cay glanced around. He couldn't see Mura, but Wart lumbered toward him. As he got closer, Cay could see his eye was already swollen and red.

"I told you what would happen if you ratted me out again, you dumb kid."

"Cay!" Lor called from the edge of the field behind Wart. "Kint wants you in the tomatoes. Says the worms are at them again."

He tossed his bucket at Wart's feet, slowing the older boy's progress, and ran in the wrong direction just to keep out of reach. A stone hit him in the shoulder. He leapt between the corn stalks that were taller than him and raced back toward the house and the tomato patch on the far side.

Lor stepped beside him as he took the last few steps. "I don't know if I can keep watching out for you and still get my own chores done."

"I know. Wart spends all his time skipping work—"

"Then he blames his punishment on you."

"Lor, why won't he do what Kint tells him?"

"He ain't that kind of kid. Has to rebel. It's in his nature." Lor stopped for a moment and gazed off in the distance toward the town, which they had never seen. "It never works out well for the strong-willed ones like him. They always come to a sudden and mysterious end." She turned back to the milking shed.

"I'll hurry and then come help you."

"Don't miss any of those worms. Kint's in a bad enough mood already, and you know he eats most of the tomatoes himself. I can manage."

Cay dropped to his knees on the edge of the garden.

As Lor walked away, she called out behind her. "Keep your eyes open. Wart probably won't stay out there long."

He pulled up a bright green leaf and wrinkled his nose. A fat blue-green worm with multiple sucker feet and gray spots down its sides clung to the back of it. Cay shuddered. He didn't care that the others kids made fun of him for being scared of a worm. These things were nasty. If he could only talk to bugs like he did the earth and water, he'd forbid them to come anywhere near this farm.

He pinched the squirming thing between his first finger and his thumb and pried it off the leaf. He dropped it in a small pail beside him with another shudder. These bugs were so gross it almost made his hunger go away.

Chapter 21

Mura sat on the edge of her bed waiting for the bars to stop wiggling like they were made of Cook's pudding. She had never been this weak. But it wouldn't be safe to rest until she was out of the city. And she couldn't get out of the city until she got out of the palace. And that required getting out of this cell.

She pushed to her feet and fell against the bars, the key almost slipped from her grasp in the process. "Almighty, Abba, You have said, 'My grace is all you need. My power works best in weakness.' Well, I am beyond weak. Only Your strength will see me through now."

She clung to the bars a moment more before inserting the key and turning the lock. With a steadying breath, she stepped out. Though her legs quaked, they held her as she locked the cell behind her and moved to the door to unlock it. Her eyes closed and she fought tears after she glanced at the steep, winding stairs. She knew this would be the worst part until she left the palace. As weak as she was now, the mountainous climb looked impossible. There was nothing but the wall beside the steps to support her as the narrow stairs twisted around three times before they reached the top. Another deep breath, and she approached the first step to begin the climb.

Mura leaned against the wall where it met the door at the top of the stairs. She didn't dare sit like her trembling legs begged or she'd never get up. With no idea how long the climb took, she was grateful to sense others still moving about in the halls outside the dungeon.

She waited until three servants were in the passageway leading out of the palace. With all her might, she hurled an image of a large, hairy beast into the minds of the two women and the man.

They screamed and dropped the items they carried. The noise filled the long corridor as it bounced off the bricks.

The guards outside her door looked up and then at one another. She nudged their minds as well. *Best see what is the matter. If something comes any farther into the palace, we'll get blamed.*

The blond turned and stalked toward the noise. "Better see what's going on. I like my head."

The dark-haired man agreed.

When they rounded the corner out of sight, Mura unlocked her last barrier, locked it again, and placed the key on the ground in a dark hollow near the door. As fast as her weary legs would go, she hurried out of sight in the opposite direction. She waited only long enough to catch a deep breath and pushed the illusion of the slave she'd played the last several days over her skin. As tired as she was, she struggled to hold the image. Then she walked back around the corner, past the dungeon door, the returning guards, and the servants who gathered their scattered items. No one even glanced her way.

Barely able to breathe, she exited the palace and crossed the bailey before the gates of the outer wall closed for the evening. Thankfully, the rain had stopped, but the hold on her image wavered as she braced herself against the first shop she came to.

A woman in a long, hooded cloak passed her, and Mura pushed a thought into her mind. *She doesn't look well. Perhaps my cloak will help.*

The woman did as Mura wished. "Thank you," Mura said as she pulled up the hood of the cloak which now covered her.

The other woman stood dazed, no doubt trying to figure out why she just did such an odd thing as give up her own garment. She shivered and brushed her arms before she continued on her way.

Hidden inside the fabric, Mura let the illusion of the maid go and lumbered down the street to the far east side of town. Here the tiny houses stood so close together they shared back walls with the homes behind them and their roofs touched the houses on either side. At last, she came to a run-down home set back from the main street. She knocked once.

A plump woman with a round face and gray hair braided in a loop around the back of her head cracked open the door. Candlelight bathed Mura against the dark night.

"Gwynn, do you remember me?" Mura raised her head enough for the woman to see her face.

The door opened wide and she was waved inside before it latched behind them. "Land sakes, you are a fright," Gwynn whispered. "We all thought you were dead." Gwynn led Mura toward a set of shelves that stood a head taller than her. Gwynn pulled one side of it from the wall to reveal a space cut out just large enough to stand in if the shelves were slid back in place.

Mura stared at it, not knowing what to do.

Bam, bam, bam. "Open up in the name of the king."

Mura stepped into the hideaway. The shelf slid closed and sealed her in total darkness.

Chapter 22

Mura hid in the wall of Gwynn's home. She'd made it out of the dungeon cell and out of the palace. Jeremicum and Calebus slept quietly while Nataline continued to work on the windows. If the children could stay safe for but a few more hours, Mura hoped she'd have the strength to help them. For now, the wife of the former royal baker stood talking at her door with the city guard. Their muffled words leaked through the crack between the shelves and the wall.

"Someone was witnessed coming into your home," a gruff voice said.

"A neighbor bringing me a bit of onions not fit for the inn to serve." Gwynn's answer was calm, and Mura knew it was truthful.

"Where is she now?"

"Gone home."

"There is no one inside with you?" A creak, as though the door had been opened further, filled the silence.

"Not since the king saw fit to kill my husband."

Mura shuddered. That was a bold statement.

"Watch your tongue, old woman, or you'll be next."

Mura strained to listen as she leaned against the wall within her hiding spot. It was quiet—too quiet.

The floor near the shelves squeaked. "We'll give them time to wander off," Gwynn whispered.

Mura's head dropped against the wall and her eyes closed. The weight of her exhaustion sat on her as if a great knight's warhorse had landed on her.

Mura startled awake as the shelves were moved, which almost caused her to fall. One low candle remained lit, but even that minimal light hurt her eyes after being in such utter darkness.

"Come," Gwynn whispered.

Though her weary and stiff muscles protested, Mura did her best to make them cooperate. She followed the woman to the back of her one-room home. Other than the bookshelf, there was a table with one chair and a slender bed. Beside it against the back wall stood a ladder made out of leather and fat sticks.

Gwynn now wore a cloak too, as she climbed the ladder into the ceiling beams. She pushed through the thatch, and they soon stood in the home directly behind Gwynn's. With a finger to her lips, the older woman worked her way two beams to the right and across the length of the next. From there, she stepped down to the top of shelves like Mura had hidden behind. Then she set her foot next to a wash basin on the table beside the shelves, and finally Gwynn stepped to the floor in her neighbor's home.

Mura wrapped the dangling sleeves of her gown around her arms and tucked in the ends to keep them out of her way. Near exhaustion from the key retrieval earlier, she found keeping her balance nearly impossible. While looking at the narrow logs used to hold up the roof that she was expected to cross, a tremor raced through her.

Gwynn stood in the shadows, but she waved for Mura to follow. The encouragement grew more frantic as Mura delayed.

She slid her hands over the thatch above her for more stability. Mura stepped from one beam to the next. Loose reeds caught on her fingers, and some fell on her and then to the ground. With the stalks came years of dust. Her nose tickled. She pushed her arm against her face and prayed she wouldn't sneeze. She tried not to touch the thatch overhead as much, when she stepped to the next log. With only one foot on the wood, her balance wavered, and she reached to grip the reeds. Once again, dust and debris showered over her. Desperately fighting to regain her balance, she sneezed against her shoulder.

Gwynn disappeared deeper into the shadows, and another movement came from below Mura.

She worried her lip. Could she make it to the other side? Would she fall in this dusty room after escaping the castle? Her legs trembled even more. Afraid to move, a tear slid down her cheek.

Gwynn at last stepped a little into the candlelight and waved at her to continue.

Mura balanced and stepped to the last beam, then inched her way along it, arms straight out at her sides, hands tipping and raising for added stability to keep her on the log. She had no desire to end up on the hard floor. When she arrived at the other end, she wanted to hug the wall, but she couldn't take the time. With one foot, she reached down until she finally found the top of the shelves with a thump of her toe. Mura paused to see if she had awakened the homeowner this time but no other sound followed. She brought down her other foot and stepped to another shelf. Next, she placed her foot on the top of the table. When she added her other foot, she bumped the washbasin. It scraped across the top. She stilled.

The person in the bed behind her rolled over with a mutter.

Mura stood like stone, breath held in her lungs, willing her heart to slow its beat. She couldn't think of any thoughts to push into the person's mind to keep them asleep.

The homeowner wiggled and muttered a moment more, then settled again.

Gwynn brushed Mura's skirt, and she nearly yelped. The older woman offered her hand, and Mura at last stepped to the ground. She wanted to drop to her knees and kiss the rough floorboards, but with a wave of her hand, Gwynn urged her to follow, and they stepped outside into the last moments before night gave way to day.

With hood-covered faces, they strode to the city stables. "My daughter and I wish to hire a small coach for a trip west," Gwynn said.

Mura could only see boots since she kept her face hidden.

"Do you now?"

"Mummy," Mura whined like a child as she played the role of a simpleton. Though, in fact, she was sure even young Calebus couldn't sound this immature. "Mummy, we ride now?"

"Shush, dear. Mother is talking to the nice man." Gwynn fell into her part easily.

The man's feet shifted a little, but he didn't move. "Two passengers, a coach, this early in the morning before the gates even open, and how far west will you be going? It will not be a cheap journey."

Mura failed to hear the exact words which followed as her attention turned again to growing danger around Nataline.

Chapter 23

Nat finished redoing one of her braids as she hurried down the stairs late the next morning. Mr. Hideman had been spotted walking toward the home, and everyone scurried to get to a desk. On the last step, Mistress Swanson grabbed her so tight around her upper arm, Nat jerked to a stop. Her fingers tingled. She would have bruises and cuts left from the headmistress' nails come tomorrow—if she lived that long.

"Did you finish?"

"There are two still painted shut."

"You worthless—"

Nat rose up on her toes as the grip on her arm tightened even more. "They are behind the stove. You can always say they were left closed on purpose because you feared one of the girls would get burned if they tried to open them so close to the heat. Also, if they are opened, the air through them would cool the only source of warmth in the room too quickly."

Mistress Swanson released her with a shove toward the classroom. "Sit on the far side and keep your head down. You will *not* be assisting Hideman again. Do you hear me?"

"Yes, ma'am." Nat slid into a chair next to the wall in the middle row and pulled out her slate and chalk to copy the math problem from the board at the front of the room.

"Why, Mr. Hideman, it is so good to see you again." The headmistress turned and bowed as he came in. Her tone was sweeter than syrup and her smile overly large. Did the inspector know it was fake too? "The girls were just finishing their morning lessons and about to retire for some lunch."

Lunch? They never had lunch. A slice of bread and a glass of watered-down milk in the morning and a bowl of mush in the evenings —if they were lucky—but never lunch.

Mistress Swanson caught her mistake as the words came out of her mouth. Her face grew pale and her eyes wide. "I, ah … Why don't we, ah … Why don't we do the inspection as the girls finish here, then …"

Nat kept her head down and hid her smile behind her braids. The headmistress couldn't say they would go eat; there was nothing prepared. The table wasn't set and there was no one working in the kitchen. She couldn't even say the girls would prepare the meal, because none of them knew how or even where the supplies were in the kitchen to put something together.

"I'll take your new daughter with me."

"New daughter?" Mistress Swanson nearly choked, and Nat held her breath.

"Yes, the one older girl who accompanied me last time who you said was as dear to you as a daughter and you couldn't give her up."

"Yes, well …"

"She is still here, isn't she?"

Mistress Swanson glanced her way, as did all the girls. Nat rose to her feet but kept her head down.

"She is still dressed like one of your wards. I thought I told you to take her off the rolls of the home."

"I, ah … We have been working so hard to …"

Mr. Hideman's case banged down on the nearest desk. "The girls have been making the repairs and improvements that I pointed out last week?"

Mistress Swanson shook as she waved her hand out. "You did not provide us proper time to hire workmen for the tasks."

"You are blaming me, woman, for your inability to maintain this home in a satisfactory manner?"

"No, I … Of course not, sir."

"Come, girl. Let us see how well a bunch of children brought this run-down home up to standards. No doubt you will be needed for the cooking soon," Mr. Hideman said with a sneer at the headmistress.

"We might today. I believe the cook is ill." Nat tried to help. She knew she would pay for everything that happened and as much as she wanted to trust the voice, it was only a voice and not really here to stop Mistress Swanson.

"You actually have a cook?" Mr. Hideman looked doubtful.

Gretchen stood and came beside Nat. "Of course, we do. Beatrice prepares all our meals. Poor dear didn't feel well this morning and went home so none of us became ill too." She used the same sweet tone her mother had when the inspector entered. Gretchen looped her arm in Nat's and smiled. "Why don't we both help you, sir? We know you have more businesses to check than just our little home." She pulled Nat down the hall, and Mr. Hideman followed.

From room to room, they showed the inspector everything they had changed, repaired, and rearranged since his last visit. He scribbled furiously on the paper on his clipboard but never said a word. Gretchen didn't give him time to speak as she babbled away, talking about all the girls had done. Nat didn't think it was a good idea to give him so much information, but she didn't dare stop the headmistress' daughter.

As they entered the dormitory on the third floor, Mr. Hideman instantly took note of the one window with the cloth tacked to it. "Is that broken?"

"Yes, sir." Nat stepped toward it and pushed it open. "After the paint was removed, they do open, but they won't stay that way. I slid it open and it fell closed so quickly the glass shattered."

"You broke it?" His gaze narrowed as he looked at her.

Nat lowered her head, "Yes, sir, last night, as I showed Mistress Swanson the problem. There wasn't time to replace the glass before you returned."

He walked to several of the other windows, sliding each open a little before lowering it gently again. "It's a common problem in these older buildings. The casings expand and don't hold the windows tight enough anymore. A piece of wood can be cut to place under the window when it's open to keep it up."

Nat didn't know what a casing was, but he didn't seem upset, and he didn't write anything on his paper.

They returned downstairs. Mr. Hideman called Mistress Swanson, and they walked into the meeting room and closed the door. The girls started to mutter and ask Nat questions. She stepped to the front of the room and wrote words on the board. Best to keep them busy and quiet until the adults returned.

"Who can read these words?"

"Can you?" Violet crossed her arms.

"As I wrote them, of course I can read them." She pointed to one word. "Read this one, Violet."

"You're not Mother. You can't tell me what to do."

"As it is best to keep doing lessons until she returns with Mr. Hideman to prove we are good, obedient girls, I suggest you follow along." Nat's whisper was harsh.

"Read it, Violet," Gretchen said.

"Why don't you?" Violet snapped.

There was a long silence. Nat forced her mouth closed. They couldn't read. Mistress Swanson had not only failed to teach any of the girls assigned to her home, she hadn't even taught her own children. Nat's gaze rose to look at the closed door of the room where the headmistress had gone to talk with the inspector. Did *she* even know how to read?

Nat shook off her surprise and turned back to the chalkboard and then the students before her. "Who knows their letters?"

A couple raised their hands.

"Can either of you read these words?"

The older of the two, Alice, pointed. "That says *the*, and that one says *dog*. I think that one is *was*. I don't know the other."

"Everyone, copy *the* onto your slates. T-H-E spells *the*. When T and H are written together, they say *thhh*." She pressed her tongue between her upper teeth and bottom lip and exaggerated the sound. "Most words you can figure out if you know the sound the letters make. But there are some words, like *the*, that don't follow those rules. You just have to remember that T-H and E together say *the*."

She had them copy the word *dog* and taught them the sound of each letter. Next, she explained the sounds of each of the letters in the last word and waited to see who could put the sounds together.

"*Happy!*" Rachel shouted. "That word is *happy*."

"Good. Now if you remember the other words, and the one we didn't practice, who can tell me what they all say together?"

"*The dog was happy.*" Alice sat up a little straighter.

"Do another, Nat. Do another," Margy said, and the other girls agreed.

She wrote another sentence, teaching the girls the sounds of the letters they didn't know.

"Happy dogs sit," Gretchen and Violet said almost at the same time.

Nat had time to write three more sentences and teach a few more letters before the door opened and Mr. Hideman exited the other room. He stopped and looked at her with his head tipped to the side. Nat took a deep breath and wrote several random words on the board. "Now use these to create a sentence. Don't say it just yet. Write it down and when everyone has a sentence, we'll share them."

Behind Mr. Hideman, Mistress Swanson stood with her mouth

gapping open.

"It's good to see them reading and writing. I have only ever observed them doing math." He pulled his watch from his vest pocket and popped it open. "They should be having lunch by now. With the cook ill, Swanson, you'll have to get something prepared for them." He waited until she bowed and scurried down the hall. But he didn't leave. He leaned against the doorframe and nodded for Nat to continue. "I'll stay until lunch is prepared."

"Maybe I should go help Mother." Gretchen stood, and Mr. Hideman, again, inclined his head, giving his agreement.

Nat had the girls each read the sentence they had made as she walked around and looked at their writing. She helped a couple form their letters better and showed little Edith how best to hold her chalk in order to write. When she looked up again, Mr. Hideman smiled at her.

"Well done, young lady."

After a few more sentence creations, Mistress Swanson swept into the room. Sweat dripped from her brow, and her cheeks were redder than normal. "Come girls. Put your slates away for now. It's time to eat."

The girls exchanged glances, but they remained silent as they followed instructions. In a single line, they walked down the hall to the dining room and took their places around the table.

A pot filled with a thick brown mass sat in the middle of the table. A burnt smell filled the room. A slice of bread lay over each spoon, and Mistress Swanson scooped the lumpy substance into the bowls before them. Again, the girls looked at one another, but no one dared say a word.

Nat had no idea what Mistress Swanson had attempted to make, but it wasn't their normal mush. After missing last night's dinner and breakfast this morning, her stomach growled repeatedly, but the smell of the odd mixture led her to believe she'd be better off going hungry until Beatrice arrived to make their supper.

Mr. Hideman shook his head and turned to leave. "Farewell, Swanson." He said it like the girls did when one of them left the home. The headmistress startled. Did he mean that he wouldn't be back again? That seemed unlikely. Nat glanced at Mistress Swanson. Her eyes were wide, and her face had no color. It looked like she wouldn't be here next time Mr. Hideman came for an inspection.

Chapter 24

As soon as the front door closed behind Mr. Hideman, Mistress Swanson burst into tears and ran from the dining room. Gretchen, Rachel, and Violet hurried after their mother. The rest of the girls stared at their bowls. All ate the bread, but few were brave enough to try the brown goop.

"What do you think is happening, Nat?" Alice whispered.

"I don't know. But it seems like bad news, and you know that means Mistress Swanson will take out her troubles on us." Nat stood and dumped the untouched contents of her bowl back in the pot in the middle of the table. "Best we see to our chores and stay out of her way."

The others copied her. Nat carried the pot back into the kitchen. Alice and Margy followed with stacks of bowls. Edith brought all the spoons. "Thank you." Nat glanced around the kitchen. Food bits and spills covered every surface. Large spots dotted the floor. "I'll see if I can't get this mess cleaned up."

"We can help," Alice said.

Nat shook her head. "She's maddest at me. Best not be around when she comes out of her room again. I don't want anyone else to get hurt."

"We don't wan ya hurt neither," Edith said, hugging Nat's leg.

She patted the girl on the back as the other two came to her and hugged her tight. Tears filled her eyes.

"You're the only one who makes this place bearable, Nat," Alice said with a sniffle.

The voice had been right; she wasn't really alone. "Thank you. That means more to me than you will ever know. But again, it's best that you stay clear of me until we know more of Mistress Swanson's mood."

"But—" Margy clung tighter to her.

"I'll be all right. Don't worry. Best get your chores done."

As the girls left the kitchen, they glanced back at her. Nat offered Wolf and Bane, Mistress Swanson's dogs, the leftover meal, but they wouldn't touch it either. Nat dumped it all in the large trash bin in the alley behind the home. She scrubbed the pot of the thick layer of burnt material in the bottom, then got on her hands and knees and scrubbed the floor clean. She had just moved to the counters when Beatrice arrived to begin dinner.

"What'cha doin' in here?" She wasn't much taller than Nat, and about as skinny, but her face held a mass of wrinkles. Yellow hair, too thin to braid, stuck out all over her head.

"Mr. Hideman returned for his follow-up inspection. Mistress Swanson accidently said we were finishing our lessons before lunch."

"She don't feed y'all durin' the day."

"True, but that wasn't what she told Mr. Hideman."

Beatrice shook her head, her hair waved as she clicked her tongue. "That woman's her own worst enemy, she is."

"Well, when Mr. Hideman got upset that us girls might be making our own meal, Gretchen and I said you were out sick. Then he waited around after he was done until Mistress Swanson made us something to eat."

"She were in me kitchen? Land-sakes. Could ya eat it?"

Nat covered her snicker as she shook her head.

Beatrice laughed too.

"I was trying to clean up the mess she left behind before you arrived."

The cook patted her hand. "Always such a good girl, ya are. Always liked ya best."

Nat stared at her.

Beatrice waved her out of the kitchen. "Ya got yar own tasks to be doin'. Off with ya, now.

Nat staggered from the room. It had been a very confusing day. Maybe it wasn't so bad here. People liked her. The cook, the other girls—she mattered to them. How did she not know this before now?"

Nat climbed the stairs, not minding where she was going or who was around. Something long and dark flew through the air and slammed into her stomach, doubling her over. Pain exploded throughout her body, and Nat dropped to her knees. A wild shriek filled the second-floor landing as Mistress Swanson's staff crashed over Nat's shoulders. It nearly flattened her to the floorboards.

Nat turned over on her back to escape another blow.

The headmistress had the staff raised above her head in both hands—her grip so tight her fingers turned white. "It's all your fault." The staff smashed down onto the stairs leading up to the dormitory. Nat lurched out of the way in the nick of time. "Dismissed!" Nat rolled the other way as the staff banged against the railing above her head.

Something crashed on the roof with such force, dust from the third floor above them showered down on them both. Nat covered her face with her arm. She couldn't afford to be blinded while Mistress Swanson tried to kill her. That same garbled roar Nat had heard after the window broke followed the thud on the roof. The headmistress paused before she struck again.

"I've been dismissed. Hideman is replacing me." The staff crashed onto the stairs as Nat tried to scoot up them backward. "It's all your fault." She swung and missed again, which only increased her rage. "My girls and I—thrown out in the street all because of—"

The confused roar filled the upper floors again, and a shadow passed over Nat. No, not a shadow. It had color. A woman in a red flowing gown with black hair that blew as though she stood in a strong wind. But there wasn't any wind, and the woman wasn't *really* there. Nat could see right through her.

Mistress Swanson screamed and her staff tumbled down the stairs behind her.

The calm and assuring presence that always accompanied the voice surrounded Nat. But there was more. Tangled with the peace was anger —no, rage. Mistress Swanson cowered under it. She crumpled to the floor and covered her head as she cried for the ghost not to hurt her.

The shadow turned and looked at Nat. Blue eyes gazed at her with such love, and a gentle smile turned her lips. *Time to go, Nataline.*

Nat stared. The voice in her head had a body.

There is not time to discuss who or what I am just now, love. You have to go.

"Mother?" Gretchen poked her head out of her door and screamed when she saw the ghostly woman standing over her mother. "Witch! I knew you were a witch."

Now, Nataline. You must go now.

Nat pushed to her feet, but she couldn't stand straight after the two blows she'd taken from the headmistress.

Nataline, you really must hurry. I'm weak and won't be able to remain this close to you much longer.

Nat raced down the stairs as fast as her sore body would allow. She put her hand on the door, but she couldn't turn the knob. She didn't remember ever being outside—other than in the back alley.

The ghost woman floated down the stairs and through the door. *Time to be brave, my love. Come.*

She looked back at the hall, the classroom, the library she loved. Could she leave this place just when she learned that the others cared for her—needed her? What awaited her outside? At least she knew how things worked here—and they were getting a new headmistress. Surely everything would be better now.

Nat glanced up the stairs to see Mistress Swanson rise. She turned and glared at Nat. "Don't you dare think about leaving, you horrid, retched child. You will pay for what you have done to my girls and me."

Now, Nataline. The voice was faint.

Nat jerked open the door. The headmistress stomped down the stairs and bellowed for her to stop. Nat stumbled down the front steps and across the sidewalk. A horse reared in front of her.

"Watch where you're going, girl," the rider yelled.

"Get back here," Mistress Swanson screamed from inside the home.

Nataline, this way.

A shimmer of light across the street caught Nat's attention. The ghost woman waved for her to follow. Horses, carts, and people filled the street between them. Nat looked for an opening.

The voice filled her with calm. *You are smart and brave, my love. Come, you need to be away from here.*

With halting and weaving movements, Nat dodged the traffic and soon stepped onto the sidewalk on the other side of the street. She turned and looked back. How had she made it across without getting trampled? She followed the woman, who seemed to be getting fainter and fainter, down the alley. Now she could barely see any of her image. Nat jumped at every sound. She didn't belong here. It was scary outside the home.

They moved through alleys and across street after street until they came to a wide lane four times as large as the one outside the girls' home. The many carts, people, and riders didn't look so cramped now because this street was so big.

A wagon pulled to a stop in front of her, and a bent old man struggled to get down. He lumbered to the back of the wagon and reached for a bundle of papers tied with twine.

Help him, love.

It took Nat a moment to move, then she reached and pulled the stack she now recognized as newspapers down with the old man.

"Sophie, girl, there you are. Where have you been?"

Nat opened her mouth to correct him, but the voice stopped her. *He thinks you are his daughter. Let him. Go with him and help him. He will take you to the city gate where I will have someone help you continue on your way.*

As the old man went around the far side of the wagon to climb back into the seat, Nat walked to the front of the wagon on her side. "Where am I going?" she whispered.

I'm still working on that. You'll have to trust that the Almighty will provide for us all.

Us all?

Chapter 25

Mura inhaled as her spirit joined with her body once more. She'd fallen asleep with her head on Gwynn's thigh hours ago, but Nataline had needed her.

"Oh, praise the Holy Father above," Gwynn muttered as the coach bumped along the road.

Mura yawned and looked up at her.

"You gave me such a fright, child. Thought you were dead for sure."

Mura had never separated while in anyone else's presence. She really didn't know how her body behaved without her spirit. By the horrified look on Gwynn's face, it wasn't good.

"I think I am beyond exhaustion, my friend. But I am sorry I frightened you."

Gwynn gave her a curt nod as if to put the whole thing out of her mind. "Rest a little longer: we should be there in a bit."

"Where are we going?"

"Someplace where there are others who will help you continue on your journey."

"Time to wake, dear. We are here." Gwynn's gentle words pulled Mura from the depths of sleep.

Mura managed to sit and pull her hood far over her face as they jostled to a stop. Someone jumped down from the seat at the front of the coach and the door opened. Gwynn stepped out first. "Come, child. We will get something to eat before we continue on our way."

Though confused, Mura followed. They had stopped in front of a long wood single-story structure. A stable with several horses stood to the right of it, and a few saddled animals stood tethered out front, their reins looped over a single beam held up by two posts.

Gwynn and Mura stepped up onto the porch and pushed open the door. The majority of the space was filled with round tables surrounded by chairs. There was a bar on the left side and what sounded like a kitchen behind it. Several men sat at tables scattered around the room.

Gwynn led them to a table in the corner, where she sat facing the door and put Mura with her back to everyone else.

A maid in a light blue dress covered in a once-white apron came to their table. A long dark blue strip of cloth covered her head and wound around her long hair. "What can I get you two?"

Mura sensed the recognition between Gwynn and the bar maid, but neither woman acknowledged it.

"Stew and some cider, if you please."

"A silver for each." The maid held out her hand.

A silver for both together would be robbery. Had things changed so in the time she'd wasted away in the palace dungeon that travelers were cheated at every inn along their journey?

Gwynn pulled out two coins and placed them in the woman's hand. The maid held onto them for a moment too long, and again, Mura could feel the strong connection between the two women.

Once the maid left, Mura whispered, "I will see you repaid soon—"

"Shh now, child." She spoke loudly enough for those closest to make out her words. "The food will be here soon. Don't you worry now." After a few moments of silence, Gwynn leaned a little closer to her. "Just get back to where you belong and any debt will be well repaid, dear."

But Mura didn't have the heart to speak the truth—she would never sit on the throne after all she'd done. But maybe by saving the children, they could take their rightful place and put right what she had so destroyed.

By the time they finished the best meal Mura could remember ever having, most of the other guests had left. The maid led them to a back room where a tub of steaming water sat in the middle of the space. The maid entered the room with them and closed the door. She unwound the cloth from her hair and revealed blond curls kissed with red.

Gwynn handed it to Mura as she reached out her other hand. "Give me the cloak, dear."

Mura hesitated.

"Ruth is going to wear it and continue with me. You are going to take her place here and work the rest of the evening. Someone will be waiting behind the inn to escort you when you leave. The Holy Father bless your journey."

Mura took the cloth and passed the cloak to Ruth. "The Almighty bless your journey as well. Thank you."

Chapter 26

Jer leaned on his shovel and wiped sweat from his face. It was only early spring and already the heat—especially inside the barn—was stifling. Soo's head came up from where she panted in the far side of the space. Her ears flicked as she stared at the door out to the street.

Olrog's office was out front. The kind owner had gone to the market each day before it closed to get Jer something to eat. Olrog didn't want Jer anywhere near Shark and his gang could get to him. But it was still a couple of hours before Olrog was due to make the trip.

Soo stood, and Jer sensed her unease. He leaned the shovel against the wall and crept toward the door. He thought he picked up the sounds of men fighting, but it was faint. Either he was jumpy or Soo was spooking him.

As Jer stepped out into the afternoon sun, its rays flashed on a strip of metal thrusting at his gut. With the instinct that Knob had spent the last couple of weeks training into him, Jer blocked the knife with the back of his left arm. He hit most of the weapon on the flat portion of the blade, but the edge still made a shallow cut below his rolled-up shirt sleeves.

Jer took a step back and he brought his fists near his face to guard his head. Before Shark could charge at him again, Jer swung his left leg forward, planted it on the gang leader's chest, and shoved him away.

Knocked off balance, Shark's hand slammed into the open door of the barn. He lost the grip on his knife. It dropped and sank deep into the cart full of manure Jer had shoveled all morning. Shark didn't try to retrieve it.

Jer kept his defensive stance as he pivoted to look for the others.

Shark called to his gang. "Get him. The one that brings him down can have anything he wants."

A blond boy, only a year older than Jer named Nichols, charged him with a leap in the air. His right arm was drawn back, elbow high, his fist near his cheek. Had Knob not spent so much time training him, Jer might have thought this was good form. Now Jer knew better.

Her bent his knees a little deeper and ducking under the thrown punch. Using Nichols' falling momentum, combined with the power of his own punch, Jer landed his left fist in the boy's right side just below his ribs.

Nichols screamed. He crumbled to the ground and curled in a ball on his side. The rusty blade in his other hand landed beside him, broke, and skidded over the dirt. He didn't move again.

"Take him out! I want him dead!" Shark screamed.

Soo kept Shark from joining the fight with a vicious snarling bark. Anytime he tried to move, she growled and snapped at him.

The weight of an attacker landed on Jer's back and forced him to the ground. Another knife broke beside his head and dropped from his attacker's hand. The boy punched Jer twice in the ribs before flipping him to his back. Burt sat over Jer's hips.

A shadow passed over them, and a roar vibrated the ground.

"You got him, Burt. Kill him, and half his money is yours." Soo kept Shark glued to the wall of the stables. He couldn't do anything other than yell instructions.

Jer laced his finger bend his head and used his forearms as a shield. His elbows stuck out in Burt's way. Though he tried, Burt couldn't make contact with Jer's face.

Burt leaned forward to grab Jer around the throat.

Jer couldn't stop smiling. He bent his legs until his heels were next to his rump. With a quick movement, Jer thrust his hips up and sent Burt vaulting over Jer's head. Jer shoved Burt's legs aside, arched his back, and popped up to his feet.

Soo barked.

The roar rumbled nearby.

Jer kicked Burt in the rear as he tried to get up.

The head of Jer's once-comrade rammed into a barrel full of feed grain. Burt slumped flat and didn't move.

A dark-haired boy Jer had never seen before ran at him on his right. As Jer turned to defend himself against another knife attack, the boy slid to a stop. He stared wide-eyed at Jer for two heartbeats, then dropped his knife, turned, and ran until he disappeared in the shadows.

Jer straightened a little, thinking his skill had scared the boy off, before he remembered Knob's early lesson on claiming victory too soon. He spun. Only Shark remained with the two unconscious boys on the ground.

"You think you're the king's pudding taking Nic and Burt down like that." Shark kicked weakly at Soo, trying to get past her. "I *will* kill you. Maybe not today. But ..."

A shadow of a woman floated toward Shark.

He squealed like a piglet.

Soo stepped aside with a whine as the shadow placed a hand on either side of Shark's head.

Shark thrashed in her hold. He screamed like nothing Jer had ever heard before.

Everything stopped except Sharks shrieking.

Time to leave this town, Jeremicum. The ghostly woman turned and looked at him with a gentle smile.

"What are you doing to him?"

Filling his mind with the pain he wished to inflict on you, my love. I don't possess the strength to hold him much longer, though. You must leave now.

"But …"

Olrog stumbled from his office a few feet beyond the gang leader. The stable owner's shirt was covered in blood.

"Olrog." Jer leapt for him as the woman vanished and Shark collapsed on the ground in tears.

The stable owner's nose was no longer straight, and the skin around his eyes was already darkening. He held his side. "Lad?"

"I'm here."

"No. No, you can't be. Time to go."

"But you're hurt."

"He'll be fine." Knob came up behind Jer. He gave a quick nod when he looked at the fallen attackers. "You did well, but the constables are already on their way. They'll lock you up as the only one standing."

Jer moved to the cart and retrieved Shark's knife, then washed it and his hands in a nearby bucket. "I was defending my—"

Knob's hand rested on his shoulder. "Of course you were, but do you really think the wicked king's lawmen care?"

Olrog reached out and dropped a bag the size of an apple into Jer's hand. Coins jingled inside. "Go, lad. Hurry."

Jeremicum, the constables are almost upon you. I can't save you from them. You have to leave the city now.

Jer opened his mouth to say his farewells, but Knob shoved him away. "Get, kid. I didn't spend all that time training you for you to rot in the city dungeon until they hang you."

Loud marching steps drew closer. As fast as possible, he and Soo dashed for the first alley to get out of sight, and then they wove around the many dwellings leading to the city gate. He paused in the shadow of the last building before leaving Dimward forever, then held out his hands in front of him. Soo sniffed at their contents. One held Shark's blade, and the other a bag of coins. It had to be as much as Olrog had paid him the entire time he'd worked for the man.

Jer leaned back against the wall and tried to organize his thoughts.

There will be time to think later, my love. Now, you should hide the money and the knife, then leave. If you hurry, you can catch up to a large group of traveling merchants on their way north. Stick close to them. Help where you see a need, as you always have, and they will keep you safe. They know the roads and where to stay.

He closed the knife and dropped it in his pocket. Jer spread the money out in his many hidden pouches. Finally, he walked calmly to the city gate. At last, he glanced one last time at the city behind him.

The merchants, Jeremicum.

Jer took a deep breath and walked through the gate. A short distance outside, he patted Soo's head. "Come on, girl. We have to catch up with a caravan." Jer ran as faint shouts called out behind him.

Chapter 27

Nat shivered as the wagon with the old newspaper deliveryman bumped along the stone street. When the driver reigned in the horses, she hopped down and placed another bundle of stacked papers on the curb. She rubbed the back of her right hand against her hip as she drew on some of her ability to help with the heavy load.

"Hurry, Sophie. We got lots more deliveries before the gates close us in tonight."

A hand grabbed her arm. The same arm Mistress Swanson hurt earlier. A man with a fat black mustache that curled at the ends pushed his face so close to hers it was all she could see. "Who are you? I know you're not Sophie." The man shook her. "What do you want with Fredd?"

"Nothing, sir."

He shook her again. "Why's he think you're his dead daughter?"

"He's old. I just wanted to help. I don't mean any harm." Nat didn't want to cry. If only she had left the home once in a while, maybe the world outside wouldn't feel so scary.

The man straightened and lightened his grip. He was tall, dressed in dark tan pants and a lighter shirt tucked into his waist. His black hair was wavy. He glared down at her.

Fredd waved at the man, forgetting about her, and popped the reins to get his horses moving again.

"Please. I just want to help. I won't take anything from him, I promise."

"I'll find you if you go back on your word." The man released her, and she ran to rejoin Fredd.

The wagon stopped a few blocks away. When she caught up, she leaned on her knees, panting for air. Fredd hobbled down to move the next papers to the sidewalk.

"Sophie, girl, there you are. Where have you been?"

It was like he hadn't seen her only moments before. They set the sack down as a boy came to collect it.

Back in the wagon, they rode down the street toward the gate.

When all the newspapers were delivered, they joined a long line of wagons, carts, and horses waiting to leave the city. Fredd mumbled something beside her, but she couldn't understand him.

Nataline, time to leave Fredd. Head for the street there on your right.

Horses neighed. Wagon drivers shouted at one another. People hurried along the streets, their heads lowered—most moved away from the gate Fredd waited in line to exit through. Nat hadn't remembered a wall around Fairlight. She could just make out the gray, blackened top of the wall at the end of the line of still wagons.

Nataline, please move. The wagons are searched. Dressed as you are, they will know you belong to someone and will stop you. Please, love.

Her stomach growled. She'd only had a single slice of bread since breakfast yesterday.

Fredd turned away from her, and she slid from the seat beside him. He never noticed. No one looked at her as she crossed to the sidewalk and turned down a side street. She kept walking, waiting for the ghostly woman to appear again or the voice to tell her what to do. She crossed two streets before she received any direction.

Turn left at the next alley and do what the boy says.

When she turned, she found a wagon waiting. It was half the size of Fredd's and pulled by one red-colored horse. A boy, about her height and age, leaned against it, with crossed ankles and head down. He had long straight hair that was darker than hers. It hung so she couldn't see his face.

Nat didn't know any boys. Rarely had one come to the home to deliver something. She didn't know what to say to him.

He looked up and tipped his head to the side so she could see one eye and part of his mouth. Though he held a long piece of straw in his lips, he still managed to smile at her. The one dark eye she could see winked. But he still didn't say anything.

He straightened, reached into the back of the wagon, and pulled up a board inside. Then he tipped his head toward it.

Nat stepped closer and saw a long box hanging under the bottom of the wagon. The boy held the lid open and reached out his hand to help her climb up. He wanted her to crawl into the hidden box?

Yes.

Nat didn't take his hand but put both hers on the top of the wagon wheel and used the spokes to climb up, and wiggled into the secret compartment.

The boy smiled at her as he put his finger to his lips and then closed her inside. There were slim openings between the boards so she could see faint light through them. At least she could breathe. The wagon rocked gently from side to side before it lurched forward. It bumped over the stones at a slow pace until it stopped, only to move forward a little later. They must be back in the long line of wagons waiting to exit again.

Nat dozed when the wagon was still and startled awake when it moved again. Finally, she heard voices.

"Where are you headed?" a deep voice asked. It was strong and serious, though not quite angry.

"South to my home in Creek's Bend," a quieter voice answered.

"What was your business in Fairlight?" the first spoke again.

"Delivering my goods to the mercantile on Eighth Street."

There was a grunt, and heavy steps walked around the wagon. Flames of a torch passed under her and licked through one of the slats of her hideaway. Nat put both hands over her mouth. She squeezed her eyes closed, held her breath, and thought about one of her favorite stories so she wouldn't scream.

"Be on your way," the gruff voice said at last.

The wagon lurched forward and rumbled along at a steady pace. It bumped over the rough road. Nat braced her arms and legs against the sides of her hideaway as she was jostled about. Her stomach and shoulders still hurt from the strikes Mistress Swanson had delivered earlier. This ride added more bruises.

The wagon pulled to a stop and tipped side to side. Footsteps came beside her. The hatch over her scraped open, and the boy peeked in.

He smiled. "You can ride up front with me now. It's safe." He reached out his hand to help her.

Nat hesitated for a moment before she took it. It was rough and scratchy. Once she climbed out of the box, she stepped over the bench seat from the back of the wagon as he climbed up beside her.

He put his hand out sideways toward her. She'd seen men greet one another this way out on the street. She put her hand out and loosely took his. His grip was strong as he pulled her hand up and down a couple of times. She watched the movement. "Jay-Kob. Nice to meet you."

"Thank you. I'm Nat."

His clicked his tongue at the horse, and the wagon moved again. "Gnat? Like the little flying bug?"

"It's short for Nataline."

He nodded and reached into the dark cloth bag at his feet. He pulled out an apple and handed it to her.

"Thank you."

"Yep."

She had never heard that word before. The fruit was sweet and crunchy, and the juice ran down her chin. "Where are we going?" Only a sliver of light shone out on the horizon, making the trees look like black shadows. Nat didn't remember much about living outside the home and the city, but she'd read about forests and farms before. Is that where she was?

"We'll stop soon, sleep, and then leave again early tomorrow."

"Why are you helping me?"

"Was the right thing to do."

"Thank you."

"Yep." He put the piece of straw back in his mouth. The conversation ended.

Nat rubbed her arms. Her thin, tight dress was no match for the chill evening outside the girls' home. She blinked away tears. The home hadn't been the best place, but it was the only home she remembered well. Was she doing the right thing? Could she trust Jay-Kob and the ghost woman?

She sniffled and wiped her nose on her sleeve.

Chapter 28

Mura startled as her spirit again joined with her body. She shivered. The water in the tub where she sat had chilled while she helped Jeremicum escape Dimward. She'd left him when Nataline needed help to leave Fairlight. Once Nataline was safely with Jay-Kob, Mura had finally joined her spirit with her physical form.

She quickly exited the tub and dried by the fire. A pair of dark trousers, tall boots, and a long shirt with wide cuffs that would cover most of her forearms were draped across a chair. She put these on first before covering them with a maid's simple rough dress and Ruth's apron she'd left behind. Mura loosely braided her hair and folded it over a couple of times. Then she wrapped the length of blue fabric around her head. She only stopped when she couldn't see any of her distinctive hair in the small hand mirror. Her pale skin made her look like the ghost the children thought her to be. Years without sunlight had drained all the warm tan from her flesh.

Mura exited the chamber and went quickly to the bar. The owner filled a pitcher and handed it to her with a nod. Like Gwynn and the original maid, Ruth, she could sense that he knew who she was, but he did nothing to bring attention to her as anyone other than the serving girl.

Mura moved among the tables, carrying pitchers and trays of food throughout the afternoon. Good thing she had stayed fit while locked in her cell. Had she lain on a slab all day, she would have collapsed after the first hour.

Even with all her exercising in the cell, the efforts of retrieving the key, escaping the dungeon, finding her way to Gwynn, fleeing with Gwynn to the stables, separating from her body to rescue the children, and getting very little sleep were quickly catching up with her. If she dared stand still, she'd start to nod off. When she reached her appointed destination, she feared she would have to sleep a week to regain her strength. And they weren't going to have that kind of time.

As each new customer arrived, she greeted him or her. "Welcome to the Wayward Hawk. What can I get you?"

Fortunately, most only ordered a drink and the stew. Mura admitted that among her many shortcomings was a terrible memory. It made taking orders without writing them down a great challenge.

But she was supposed to be a simple serving maid, and very few of the common people knew how to read—even though her mother had tried for years to encourage the instruction of all children. How would reading help tend crops or bring in the harvest? Mistress Swanson was a good example. She'd risen to her position without ever learning the skills that she promised to teach the girls under her care.

"Girl." A man stuck his mug up in the air. "You going to bring me more or stare off at nothing all night?" The empty metal container *thunked* down on the table. The man continued to mumble at her poor service as Mura hurried to the bar for a pitcher.

"Sorry," she told the owner.

"Don't let old Kev get to you. He hasn't had a kind word to say to anyone in the five years he's been stopping here. He's a silver merchant, and not many can afford his goods anymore."

Mura returned to Kev and filled his mug. When she looked in his eyes, she saw a sadness that was as deep as the Bottomless Sea west of their kingdom. "Forgive me for my delay. I shall pay for this one."

He sighed his thanks and downed half his drink in one gulp.

Mura continued around the room, bringing food, clearing away dishes, and wiping down the tables, just to do it all over again when the next person entered.

On either side of the door, the sun thrust its rays through two square windows. They were not any bigger than her forearm, and divided into four panes. There was more wood frame to them than glass, yet the sun still managed to blind her every time she turned in that direction.

Soon the light coming through the windows turned orange, then purple, then finally disappeared all together. The costumers disappeared with the light. Mura returned the last of the dirty plates to the kitchen and wiped down the tables. She picked up chairs and set them upside down on tables and swept the floor. Her yawns grew more frequent, each one bigger than the last.

One time when she looked up, the owner tipped his head to the back door and gave her a single nod. She tried to give him all the coins she'd been paid throughout the evening but he shook his head with a smile.

"Thank you," she whispered before returning to the room where she'd taken her bath earlier. Mura removed the apron and serving dress and hung them on a peg, then she collected a short cloak. She wound the belt from the dress over her long shirt and pulled up the hood of her cloak.

Outside the back door, a man on a black horse held the reins of a dark brown one. His hood was up, too, so she couldn't see his face, but she sensed he intended to protect her, even if it cost him his life. He passed her the reins and she mounted. They plodded through the deep wood following well-worn hunting trails in the dim light of a half-moon.

Mura jerked awake when she almost fell from her saddle. The moon was now overhead. A clearing only about two wagon-lengths long appeared between the trees. A hut not much bigger than her dungeon cell sat on the far side.

Her guide led her to it, dismounted, and went inside. Soon the light of a fire flickered in the glassless window. He came out and spoke to her for the first time. "Sleep for an hour, then we must be on our way again."

Mura stepped down from her horse and almost collapsed. She had never been this tired, and she hadn't ridden since Brax stole the throne. After a moment of grasping the halter of her horse, she staggered toward the door. "Are you going to rest also?"

"No. I'll keep watch."

Mura took three steps inside and dropped to the thin mat of hay in front of the fire. She was asleep in before her next breath.

Chapter 29

Nat startled awake when the wagon stopped. They were in front of a small wood structure with one window beside the door.

"Squirt," Jay-Kob called out.

Nat straightened. She'd been leaning against his arm. Her cheeks were hot as she lowered her head, glad it was too dark for him to see her.

A girl who reminded Nat of Alice stepped outside the shack. She appeared to be a few years younger than Nat with the same long straight hair of Jay-Kob. She yawned and rubbed her eyes.

"Take care of her, 'kay?"

"Yep," she said yawning again as she reached for Nat.

Nat stepped down, and the girl looped their arms and led her into the small structure. A rough wood table with three chairs were near the door. A stove sat against the right wall like the one Nat had filled with coal in the dormitory. A pan lay on top. There was a long board mounted on the back wall with a square basin set in one end, and a hand-pump next to it to bring up water to fill the basin. To the left sat a bed as wide as three of the girls' beds from the dormitory put together. A ladder leaned in front of the bed against a shelf near the ceiling.

Squirt led her to a chair. "Here, sit a minute. I'll fix you something to eat."

"Is this where you live?" Though she'd read about them, Nat had never seen a home before, just the tall buildings of the city from girls' home windows.

"Yep." Squirt went to the long board, pumped three times with the handle over the basin and filled the pot from the stove with water. Next, she cut up some things Nat didn't recognize—round purple items, long orange sticks, and curved green stalks—and put them all into the water. She stepped onto a box and cut a slice from the long soft red stuff hanging above her. Squirt chopped it into small squares and put it in the water also. She sprinkled something from shaker jars and added a couple of leaves from plants on the windowsill, then she put the pot on the stove and sat beside Nat. "We don't get many our age."

"You mean Jay-Kob often brings people out of the city?"

"Yep. Says the Almighty leads people to him who need help. He hides 'em in his wagon then brings 'em here before taking them the rest of the way."

"Rest of the way?" Nat bit her lower lip.

Squirt got up and stirred the pot that quickly filled the room with the most wonderful smell.

Nat's stomach growled.

"It will only be a couple more minutes," Squirt sat down again.

"Is your name really Squirt?"

The girl laughed. "Probably not, but Daddy died before I could walk, and Mother's been gone a few years now. It's just my brother and me now—and our farm hand, Uncle. That's not his name, either, but the names are what we've always been called." She shrugged and got up, then stirred the food again.

Nat had trouble thinking of anything but the gnawing pain in her middle. The silence felt awkward. "Jay-Kob's your brother?" It was a silly question to get Squirt talking again.

"Yep." They talked for a time as the room filled with tantalizing smells. The contents of the pot bubbled as loud as Nat's stomach.

Squirt pulled a bowl off one end of the board she'd used to cut up the food and scooped some of the contents from the pan into it. She placed the steaming dish in front of Nat and turned away, then returned a moment later with a spoon. "Blow on it a little first. It's hot."

The brown squares and orange, green, and purple bits bobbed in the thin dark liquid. It didn't look particularly good, but the smell made her want to try it anyway. She scooped some on her spoon, watched the steam rise off it, and blew gently. Nat slid the spoon into her mouth, a little afraid of what to expect. It was nothing like she'd ever tasted before. The crunchy bits each had their own flavor, and the squares were easy to chew and full of tastes that made her tongue want to dance. "This is wonderful. What is it?"

Squirt tipped her head and her eyebrows pulled together. "Haven't you ever had stew before?"

Nat shook her head and enjoyed another mouthful. As she continued to fill her spoon again and again, she told Squirt of her two daily meals.

"That's awful." Squirt pointed out each of the bits. "Carrots, celery, and onions make the meat taste good."

Nat nodded again, appreciating the last bite, and Squirt refilled her bowl. She was surprised when Squirt poured the last of the stew in her bowl for a third helping. They never got seconds in the girls' home, and who would have thought of thirds? "Aren't you going to eat any?"

"Oh, I had my dinner before you got here." Squirt put the pan in the basin and added the bowl and spoon when Nat finished. "Now, let's see what we have for you." Squirt opened a trunk at the foot of the bed and pulled out men's and women's clothing of all sizes. "Like I said, we don't get many kids here—at least not on their own."

Squirt held up a dress much like the simple one she wore. She gripped it by the shoulders, turning to compare it to Nat. It dragged on the floor, so she shook her head and dropped it on the growing pile. Next she pulled out a long blue blouse. "Maybe." She draped it over the open lid of the trunk. "I think we have a skirt in here somewhere …"

After a few more items, Squirt pulled out a green skirt with rows of ruffles at the bottom. "Yes!" She brought it over and held it to Nat's waist. It pooled on the floor. "I can cut off the last three rows of ruffles and take it in a bit around the waist. It should work." Squirt put the skirt on the table, then she returned the clothes to the trunk after folding each item. "You can go up and get some sleep. I'll work on this and join you if I finish before Jay-Kob wants to leave again."

Nat glanced at the ladder. She climbed it slowly to find a bed, not as big as the one below it, but bigger than what she had slept in the dormitory. The space above the rest of the dwelling had its own floor where the bed sat tucked under the slanted roof. There were two thick blankets and a fat pillow. She couldn't stand straight because of the roof that came to touch the floor on the far side of the bed, but it didn't matter. The bed was warm and soft. She should have asked where Jay-Kob was taking her tomorrow and what would happen once they got there, but she was so very tired.

Chapter 30

The sun peeked into the sky as Cay walked toward the fields. Watering and weeding, weeding and watering, that was all he did this time of year. Lor was doing the same on the opposite side of the farm in the millet field. Millet always made Cay itch, so he worked the wheat and corn instead.

The bucket clattered over the ground behind him as Cay made his way to the stream.

Someone slammed into him, knocked him to the ground, and pinned him there with their weight. A fist hit his left side and then his left ear, and something hard dug into his back.

"I told you I'd kill ya." Wart let his spit drip on the side of Cay's check, then grabbed his hair, jerked back his head, and slammed it into the dirt.

The dirt caved, making space for his face, and cocooned softly around him so he didn't get injured. Wart yanked Cay's head back again.

A shadow passed over them, and a noise that sounded like a mix of a bird's caw and a roar filled the air.

Wart jerked and released him. "What was that?"

Cay wiggled and managed to flip over, but Wart pinned Cay's legs before he could escape.

A splint held Wart's right arm bound to his chest. The bully's focus returned to Cay. Wart drew back his left fist. The weird caw-roar came with a gust of wind, making the corn wave and sending dust into their eyes.

Wart squirmed and tried to wipe his eyes.

Cay wiggled out from under him as he blinked away the tears and dirt. He struggled to see what happened as he scrambled to get up.

Mura passed through him, her image even fainter than most times. But she wasn't wearing a dress. She had on tall boots, men's pants, and a long shirt. She stomped toward Wart, who crawled backwards on his rump and one arm to get away from her. *Time to go, love.*

Cay stared through one watery eye.

Run, Calebus.

The normal love and calm that came with her image and voice in his head also held anger today. "What about Lor?"

You have to get away from here right now.

"I can't …"

Wart didn't seem scared by Mura anymore as he stood and walked through her image. He stalked toward Cay, swinging his fist. "I'll deal with your little girlfriend next."

The roar-caw and gust of wind flew through the corn again. Wart turned to it, and Mura moved in front of him between him and Cay. When he tried to walk through her again, he cried out in pain.

Now, Calebus. Across the stream and through the field. I can't hold him, and Kint's coming.

Cay could make out the farmer's bobbing hat in the distance over the corn. But Cay shook his head. "I can't. Lor—"

Will be fine for now. We will get her another time. Calebus …

Something tingled in his head with her voice. It made him turn, but he tried to stop. He stumbled forward, forced to move against his will. "Stop it."

Will you go on your own?

"We'll come back and get her?"

I promise. Just not right now.

If she weren't forcing him in the opposite direction, he would have raced to the other side of the farm to get his friend. Lor had always looked out for him. He didn't want to leave her. Not with Kint *and* Wart *and* all his chores too.

Calebus, please.

Kint was almost at the corner of the field. Another couple of steps and he'd turn and see them.

Cay wouldn't be able to escape then. He grumbled. "Fine." The force she used to make him move left, and Cay dashed for the stream. The water parted before him even though he hadn't touched it and didn't think he requested it to do anything. Four stones pushed up through the deep mud and made a path for him. He bounded from one to the other and crossed to the opposite bank. Steps formed in the steep dirt, and he climbed as fast as he could, and leapt behind a boulder.

Cay held his knees to his chest and pushed his face against them. Scary things happened to kids who ran away from the farm. Maybe it would be best to go back and take his punishment. Everyone said the farm wasn't a bad place to work compared to the mines.

Come, Calebus. Time to go.

He heard her but didn't see her. Kint roared and Wart screamed.

"Is he going to kill Wart?"

No, love. Not today anyway.

Low to the ground, Cay crept from rock to tree to more rocks. Kint always spoke of clearing the land on the other side of the stream and planting more crops, but he was afraid to because the land belonged to someone else. If anyone caught him farming it, he would be charged with stealing. Right now, Cay was glad, because he had many bushes, boulders, and trees to hide behind.

A bunch of trees stood on the far side of the unused land. Cay slipped behind one of them and leaned against it, then closed his eyes. Sweat made his shirt stick to him and his heart beat hard enough to thump in his ears.

Calebus, Mura shimmered in front of him, *you have to hurry. Go to the other side of this grove of trees.* She pointed behind her. *There is a young man with a wagon there, but you have to hurry.*

Cay paused for a moment to look at the farm across the stream. It was the only home he remembered. He didn't really like it there, but it was what he knew. And Lor was there.

Calebus.

He turned back to the trees and ran.

The morning sun blinded him as he stepped from the deep shade of the trees. A dirt road stretched out in front of him to the right and left. A wagon pulled by two black horses stood on the far side, the back of the wagon tipped toward him. Its bed held enough full cloth bags to fill it to the top of the sides. Grain maybe? Nothing on Kint's farm was ready to harvest yet. Cay couldn't see anyone who might be driving it.

In the next moment, the whole wagon lurched and dropped level. An older boy stood and brushed off his hands. "That should do it. Can't believe the wheel came off." He shook the cart. "Looks good for now. Going to make me late though. Won't be able to get to town and back now. Have to find a safe place to stay."

The boy didn't seem to be talking to Cay. He hadn't looked up yet. Did he even see Cay standing there?

The wavy brown-haired boy wore a dirty white shirt and tan pants much like Cay's. Still brushing off his hands, the boy walked around the end of the wagon. "Best get back on the road. Places to go, things to do, people to—" He jerked to a stop and stared at Cay. "Well, hi there. Didn't see you." He looked around. "Where'd you come from? One of the farms, I imagine. Lots of kids work the farms hereabouts. Hard work farming. I'm taking my family's sweet peas to the market east of here. Too many farmers sell here in Quickwallow. Can't get a good price for our crops. Have to take them to the city where there are fewer farms nearby."

The boy never seemed to take a breath. Words came out of his mouth faster than water flowed into Kint's canals. Cay stepped toward him.

"Heading up to Lake Side. We get pretty good prices there. Better if we want to cross the lake to the homes of the rich, though not as many live there as use to. King Brax has—well, that isn't really something good folk talk about, now is it? Not without fear of losing their heads, anyway." He reached out a hand. "Good to meet you. I'm Gan-Nonin. Happy for the company if you're interested in a ride." He shook Cay's hand quickly.

"Cay, thank—"

"Sure, of course." Gan-Nonin turned toward the wagon and climbed up onto the seat. "It's a long ride, but it should go faster with someone to share it with."

Cay had barely sat before the reins popped and the wagon lurched forward.

"Have you ever been to Lake Side?" Gan-Nonin didn't wait for a reply before he described the city they were headed and then all the places they'd pass on the way. He continued in an endless flow of words.

On a rise, Cay looked back. He could see the roofs of the house and barn on Kint's farm, with the silver line of the stream peeking through the trees. His heart flopped oddly. Would he find something better where he was going? Would he ever see Lor again?

Chapter 31

Mura squinted against the light that flooded through the window of the inn. The noise of people doing business in the street below and the constant traffic of horses and carts filled her room. She pushed up and sat on the side of the slender, sagging bed. After a moment, she found the strength to stand and lumbered to close the curtain. At least it blocked a little of the light, if not the noise.

She'd stumbled into the room in near darkness a few hours earlier. Now she saw it contained only the bed, a rickety square table that would barely hold a tray of food, and a chair. Her feet dragged the four steps back to the bed, and she dropped more than sat. Mura didn't bother to remove her boots. She fell back and waited for sleep to return as she recalled how she arrived in this place.

The guide, who had led her from the Wayward Hawk to the hut in the woods, had allowed her a short rest before he woke her and they continued westward. The first rays of sun were lighting the sky when they turned out of the woods and onto a road. He reined in his horse. The silhouette of city walls could just be seen in the distance. "You will find the Hairy Goat Tavern and Inn near the center square of Plain View. It is two streets east and one north of the main thoroughfare. Take the horse to the stables and ask for Yen. He will board the horse and show you to the room reserved for you. Another will meet you in the stables before the gates close tonight to lead you on the next part of your journey."

As the sky's glow grew, she'd found the Hairy Goat and the young stable hand Yen easily enough. He was a boy about Jeremicum's age with tan skin and long, black hair he wore in a braid. After he led her up the back stairs, he gave her a key to a room in the back corner of the two-story inn. It was quiet this early in the morning, but the tavern on the first floor would be crowded later.

She only had time to lock the door before Wart attacked Calebus. She flopped on the bed without thought and her spirit went to him. When he was safe with Gan-Nonin, she'd joined herself together again.

Now the light irritated her and kept her awake. It would only be a few hours before she needed to send her spirit back to her dungeon cell. The appearance that she remained a captive when they delivered her daily meal was key to their success. She hoped to go to her execution and make Brax believe he killed her. But the exhaustion hammering her drained her of any strength she had left.

She needed to sleep now and worry about the next challenge when it came. Just sleep. It's what she needed most.

"Squirt?"

Nat woke at the call and the movement beside her.

"She ready to leave?" Jay-Kob called up to them.

The person beside her wiggled again and groaned. "Give us two minutes," Squirt said. She yawned as the door below creaked open, closed, and the latched clicked. "You awake?"

"Yeah," Nat said with a yawn of her own.

Squirt slid out of the bed they shared and crawled to the ladder. Nat followed.

"Put those on." Squirt pointed to the blouse and skirt draped over the chair Nat had used last night. Squirt continued to the board at the back of the room.

When Nat finished dressing and came back toward the table, Squirt carried three bags. Two were wet and round with a bent neck and a cork in the end. The other looked like the dark bag Jay-Kob had in the wagon last night. It bulged with lumps. Squirt looked at her new clothes and frowned.

Squirt put the bags on the table and went back to the trunk. She pulled out a smaller box and set it on the bed. Metal clanked inside, and she pulled out a long strip of leather with gold-colored metal on one end. "Let's see if this belt helps." Squirt tipped her head as the belt drooped between her hands. "Try tucking in the shirt first."

Nat did.

Squirt slung the belt over her shoulder and took hold of the waist of the skirt, rolling over the fabric twice to bring up the hem so Nat could see the toes of her shoes. The door opened, and Squirt tipped her head to the bags on the table. "Water skins are filled and there's lunch for you both. We'll be out in one more minute."

"'Kay." Jay-Kob scooped up the items and went back out the open door.

Squirt wrapped the belt around Nat and fed the end through the metal, then pulled it tight. She made a mark in the leather with her fingernail, removed the belt, and took it to the shelf where she'd made the meal last night. She hammered something into it and returned. The belt pulled tight again and Squirt pushed a skinny strip of metal in a hole that hadn't been in the leather a moment ago. The girl took the long loose end of the belt and wrapped it around Nat, then tucked it in at the back. Squirt came in front of her again and looked her over. "Better. Not perfect, but better than what you arrived in."

She led Nat outside. Only a widening purple area broke up the blackness of the sky to her left. Now parked in front of the house, the cart faced the opposite direction from last night. Jay-Kob sat on the bench, waiting.

Squirt hugged her.

Yesterday in the kitchen of the girls' home was the only time Nat remembered being hugged. It seemed so very long ago.

"You take care." Squirt gave her one more squeeze.

"Thank you."

"We need to get moving in order to reach Bottom's End before night fall." Jay-Kob stretched out his hand to help her up.

The wagon bumped along the road as the sun rose on their left. When the sun sat overhead, Jay-Kob offered her two pieces of bread with meat inside.

"What is it?"

He looked at her as he chewed his similar meal. "Haven't you ever seen a sandwich before?"

Nat knew a lot from the books she read when she sneaked into the library at night. She had read about people eating sandwiches before, but she'd never seen one. Just like she'd never had stew or a belt. She was lost in the world outside the girls' home. "I've heard of them. Never had one though."

"Enjoy," Jay-Kob said with his mouth full.

They ate apples out of the bag as the sun slipped down on their right. Soon the walls of another city came into view. Nat squirmed in her seat.

"Don't worry. No one will bother you here in Bottom's End dressed like you are now. I'll deliver my goods to the mercantile here, then we'll find a safe place to sleep for the night. You'll be fine."

Nat tried to take a deep breath as she nibbled on her lower lip.

Chapter 32

Jer woke as the others started to stir. The caravan of merchants had walked until almost sunset before they turned off the main road and pulled their many wagons into the shelter of a ring of fat trees. Jer went with the younger men to collect firewood while the older men guarded the camp, cleared a place for the fire, and collected stones to surround it.

The flame burned bright when Jer returned. Edward waved him over to sit near his wagon. Jer was glad for the quiet; the constant clanking of the man's pots had grown annoying throughout the afternoon. Edward's hair was white and sparse. His skin, likely tanned from his many journeys through the land, looked more like worn leather than flesh. His two front teeth were missing. "Sit, my boy."

"Thank you." Jer plopped down and Soo curled beside him. Jer had worked hard in the stable every day for months. How was it that walking had tired him so much? His feet and back ached. Soo put her head on her paws and closed her eyes. Within moments, her breathing deepened.

"I'll make ye a deal, Jer," Edward said. "I'll let ye ride with me and share me meal if—"

"Yer not snatching the lad, are ye, Ed?" Albert, another of the older merchants, waddled up. One of his legs didn't move quite right. He dropped a three-legged stool on Jer's other side, almost setting it on Soo. The dog snorted and scooted behind Jer.

Edward crossed his arms. "What business is it of yours if I be makin' a deal with him? He seems a good strong lad, even though he's skinny."

Albert took the pipe out of his mouth. It wasn't lit and didn't seem to have anything inside. His bushy gray beard and long hair waved as he pointed the pipe at Edward. "I was plannin' on makin' me own deal."

"I offered him first." Edward spit on the ground. "Yer always stealing my customers, Al. Ye can't have the lad."

It was a little odd to have the men talk over him. Did they forget he sat there between them?

"I wager, like the customers, I can offer him a better deal." The pipe returned to his mouth, and he leaned back on the stool.

Jer glanced at both men. "Maybe I should hear what both of you are offering."

"I'll give ye—" they both said at the same time.

"In all fairness, Edward did approach me first. He should probably give his offer before you begin, sir." Jer nodded toward Edward, then shrugged.

"Sir." Albert chuckled. "I knew I liked ye, lad."

"I like him just fine, and he said I could speak first," Edward huffed.

"Then be about it, ol' man. A body could die waitin' for you to get to a matter."

Edward growled and raised his fist. "Why, I oughta …" He lowered back down on his rump but continued to glare at Albert, who didn't seem to care. "Ol' man, yer older than me," he muttered.

"Only by a few months, and it's done nothing to weaken me hearing."

Jer drew in a slow, deep breath. This was going to be a long trip.

"So, lad, like I was sayin'—before this buffoon interrupted," Edward spoke again.

Albert opened his mouth, but Edward ignored him and kept talking. "I'll let ye ride with me and share me food, if ye help set up and break down me stall when we get to Beaver Crossing tomorrow."

"I'll do the same and pay ye a copper to boot," Albert said.

Jer thought for a moment. "I imagine you'll set up not far from one another in the open market. I could ride with one of you and Soo with the other."

"Ye want me to carry a dog in me wagon?" Again, both men spoke at the same time.

"She's an excellent watch dog and will help us both tonight and at the market." Jer put his hands on his knees as if to get up. "But if you're not interested, I can always see if one of the other men could use our help."

The pipe dangled from Albert's lips, and he put a hand on Jer's shoulder, pushing him down. Edward grabbed his other arm and pulled him down also.

"No need to go threatenin' to desert us, lad," Edward said. "Al will be happy to carry the mutt."

"And I think you'll be perfect company for her." Albert crossed his arms.

Jer popped up between them. "You two talk it over. I've got to find her something to eat." He wandered until he found Victor, one of the younger men—likely in his mid-twenties. He had short dark brown hair, and his body was oddly shaped with overly skinny legs but a broad chest and fat arms. He was a blacksmith, so maybe his arms were strong from pounding out iron all day.

After he and Soo had eaten from what he purchased from Victor, Jer lay down in the soft leaves between Albert's and Edward's wagons. The men continued to bicker as Jer fell asleep.

The next morning, Soo sat on the bench beside Albert and Jer rode beside Edward. They entered Beaver Crossing as the town was waking up. Edward and Albert set up across the square from one another. Both men yelled at Jer to help as soon as he reached the other's stall. He worked fast and soon both men called for customers to come see their goods, bargaining over prices and chatting good-naturedly with all who stopped.

Jer wiped his brow and wandered the market for a bit. He searched through several vendors to see if he could find anything he wanted to purchase. A dark green shirt caught his eye, but it was made for a grown man and was much too large. He bought a meat pie and an apple, then found a quiet place to sit and watch.

Jer noticed a boy slipping between the shoppers. He grabbed a woman's coin pouch and headed toward Edward. Jer leapt to his feet and raced through the crowd. He bumped into the blond boy and put his hand over the boy's, which gripped Edward's coins.

"What are ye doin' there, lad?" Edward said, his eyes fixed on the boys' hands.

"You should really put your coins somewhere out of sight, sir. Never know who might be trying to nick them." Jer spoke up.

The thief jerked his hand away. "I was saving your coins from him." He pointed to Jer.

Jer pushed into him, thumping him in the center of the chest with the heel of his hand. The boy sputtered and coughed while Jer snatched back the woman's pouch. "Excuse me, miss?" Jer called to the woman. She turned. "Is this yours?"

She glanced in the bag looped over her arm. She stomped over to them. "Did you steal that from me?"

"No, miss. I think it slipped out of your bag. This boy here picked it up, but he wasn't sure who dropped it."

Her gaze narrowed as she looked between the two boys, but she took her coins and hurried off.

"Why'd ye do that?" the blond boy asked.

"I gave you a second chance, same as I was given. There is a better way than stealing. This man here," Jer pointed to Edward, who was tucking his coin pouch in his shirt, "and that one over there," he pointed to Albert, "could both use quick strong hands to help them. They travel the kingdom. If you're honest and give up your thieving ways, they might be inclined to let you join them for a meal and a safe place to rest your head."

The boy looked up; his lips twisted in doubt. "Nobody'd trust a thief with their goods."

"Trust can be earned, if you're willing to work for it," Edward said as he reached out a hand to the boy. "Name's Edward."

The boy took it in a weak handshake. "Davie, sir. I swear, I'll never steal nottin' from ye."

"Glad to hear it."

Jer took Davie and bought him something to eat while they waited for the market to close. Together, they helped take down and load the stalls and goods into the wagons.

Soon they were on the road again, still headed north. Now, Jer and Soo rode with Albert, and Davie rode with Edward. Jer sat a little taller. He'd helped someone today. It made him smile. Wherever he was headed, he promised he'd look for others he could help.

Chapter 33

Cay yawned and took a sip of water from Gan-Nonin's container.

"It's a hot one today. We need to drink water. I'll make sure to refill the skin in the next village. It's small, usually not enough people there interested in sweet peas to stop, but they let me use the well when I pass through."

Gan-Nonin's talking hadn't slowed. Cay didn't know anyone could say so much. He yawned again. How'd he get so tired from sitting all day? He never sat and did nothing. Sitting and weeding, or picking worms off plants, sure—but not just sitting. He shook his head as he yawned yet again.

The cart slowed as they passed through the tall doors of a wood fence. As they entered the town, Cay noticed the houses close together surrounded by the fence.

"Sheep Pen is a nice little village." Gan-Nonin waved and greeted a few people they passed as they moved to an open area in the center of the dwellings.

It looked similar to the three villages they had already passed through this morning. And like those places, the older boy seemed to know most everyone in town. But, instead of passing through, they stopped and Gan-Nonin stepped down. Cay did too. He stretched and wiggled his arms and legs, which were stiff from the lack of movement.

"Whatcha got today?" a woman with a big belly called.

"Sweet peas, Olive. Interested?"

Olive's fat black braid swung over her shoulder when she turned and yelled to another woman with red hair on the other side of the open area. "Rae, want to split a bag of sweet peas?"

Rae was not very tall and, though not skinny, she wasn't overly round. "What are ye offering to pay Gan?"

"I can give him a couple meat pies," Olive called back.

Now Rae looked to Gan-Nonin. "I can add a fist of raspberries and two fists of strawberries."

The older boy walked over to her red fruit-covered table. "Throw in two of those late-season apples, and you two fine ladies have a deal." Gan-Nonin stretched out his hand toward Rae, who glanced at Olive. When the black-haired woman smiled and nodded, Rae shook Gan-Nonin's hand. "Cay, take a bag of them peas to Olive and fetch our lunch."

After Gan-Nonin collected the fruit, he waved Cay over to a bench by the well. He spread out the cloth full of red berries between them. "Help yourself." He reached for one of the pies Cay carried.

"This is better than sneaking a bite in the fields." Cay smiled. "Wheat, millet, and corn aren't really good picked right off the stalks, anyway." He watched Gan-Nonin bite into the side of the pie and then tip it back to keep all the dark contents from falling out while he chewed. "I've never had one of these before." It looked like a pocket covered in hard bread-type stuff. He bit into it. The outside was softer than he thought it would be, but it tasted really good. Some of the gooey insides spilled into his mouth too. Soft meat—not the dried tough stuff he normally ate—carrots, and peas. "Ummm."

"Olive does a good job on her pies." Gan-Nonin looked over his shoulder at her. "When I'm old enough, I hope I find someone to marry who can cook this well."

Cay didn't really know what being married was, but Lor talked about finding someone to marry her and take her away from the farm. If Lor could cook like this, maybe Cay would marry her, whatever that meant.

Then they'd both be happy.

The berries exploded with flavor-filled juice when Cay bit into them. He rubbed his bulging stomach. "Thank you. I'm so full it hurts." Cay licked his lips.

"No problem, kid. Thanks for coming along and keeping me company."

They finished the strawberries, raspberries, and pies. "Why don't we save the apples for a bit? We should probably get moving again. It'll be almost the end of the day by the time we get to Lake Side, and we'll need to find a place to sleep before we get some dinner." He handed Cay the apples and filled the two skins with water before they walked back to the wagon. They waved to Olive and Rae as they left. They headed through another tall door on the opposite side of the village and moved out onto the road.

"See, told ya Sheep Pen was a good village. Nice people there."

"And good food," Cay said quickly before Gan-Nonin continued.

"Ab-so-lutely! We should be set until we get to Lake Side now, and the apples are an extra bonus. We used to grow apples on the edge of our fields when I was little, but the fruit kept getting worms. Dad got tired of feeding the pests, so he cut down the trees, and planted carrots and squash there. The squash has taken over in recent years, but we still get a few carrots."

The boy talked in a steady stream again. Cay yawned and considered the many thick clumps of trees broken up occasionally by a lone field of some crop, or a hill, or a pile of large rocks. Mura hadn't given him any directions, and he worried about Lor.

He shouldn't have left without her.

Chapter 34

Mura sat on the side of her bed in the Hairy Goat, forearms on her thighs, head hanging. The children had spent the day traveling, and were just reaching their destinations for the night. Her spirit had made an appearance in the dungeon when her food was delivered. The numerous rats would clean the plate of the meager food; she needn't worry about it appearing like she wasn't eating.

She sighed again. Everything in her screamed for her to drop back onto the bed and sleep for the next week. But the guide from last night and Yen had both told her someone would come for her before the gates closed tonight.

With great effort, she raised her head and looked toward the window. If she didn't move soon, she'd have to light a candle or open the curtains again.

Tap, Tap.

She pushed to her feet, lumbered to the door, and drew it open a crack.

"I've a small meal for you." Yen raised the tray in his hands. "He waits in the stable when you're finished."

Mura pulled the door open all the way, and Yen handed her the tray. A tankard, half a round loaf of dark bread, three wedges of different types of cheese, and a small steaming bowl of stew filled the wooden surface. "Thank you."

Yen nodded and pulled the door closed. Mura blew over the stew to cool it, ate, and drank all that she'd been given. She found a small patch of fabric, and put the bread and cheese in it, and bound it closed with a piece of bootlace she broke off.

She picked up the tray and tankard and went down the back stairs. Her horse from last night had been saddled, and Yen exchanged her reins for the tray and cup. He pointed to the man on horseback just outside the stable doors.

This guide was larger than the first one, but other than that, she couldn't see any of him since he was in the shadow of the inn.

She led her horse out and mounted, then adjusted her hood to ensure her face was covered. They rode silently through the city and out the gate. After they were well out of sight of the city walls, they turned off the road and rode through the woods.

"May I ask how you knew to fetch me this evening?" Mura asked when they came to a place in the trail where they could ride side by side.

"There is a network that keeps watch. We eagerly wait to join the battle to set things right. We send coded messages by pigeon when aid is needed throughout the kingdom."

It was an ancient way to communicate over long distances. They were wise to bring it back now in their time of need. But these people came to her aid in hoping she was the one they would rally behind. She couldn't bear to disappoint this man—and all the rest—by telling him she couldn't be trusted again. "Where am I going?"

"I only take you as far as Widow's Marsh. Only one person knows your final destination. If our network is ever uncovered, and we are captured and threatened for your location, we'll not know it."

The trail narrowed again, and she slipped behind him. She pulled a wedge of cheese from her bag, nibbled at it, and looked at the moon poking through the thick trees. They were heading west. She noted the direction of the children. They would all converge in Lost Worries. Mura squeezed her eyes closed against the tears.

Nat squirmed on the hard bench seat. Their bag of food and water skins were empty when Jay-Kob pulled the wagon to a stop in a town called Bottom's End. Nat was not used to sitting for long periods of time and eagerly climbed down from the wagon.

The sun she rarely saw in Fairlight had blared down on them all day and now sat low on the horizon. Nat was glad to see it go. Her face and hands were hot and stung.

In the growing shadows, Nat glanced around. Bottom's End appeared much smaller than Fairlight. None of the structures looked taller than two floors, and most looked more like Jay-Kob and Squirt's house rather than the tall, fat buildings of her city.

"Give me a minute to see if I can make this delivery now. It's late, and the owner may ask me to come back in the morning." Jay-Kob took a couple of steps away, paused, and turned back. "You'll be all right here. No one will bother you. Just don't wander off."

She nodded.

He walked up a couple of steps to the wooden sidewalk. From there he strode to a door that sat beside a large window displaying pots, a dress, an arrow, a bag of flour, and many things she couldn't name. A bell jingled as he pushed the door open.

Nat watched people walk by—mothers with children skipping behind them, men walking or riding with eyes straight ahead, intent on where they were going. A few wagons rumbled down the road. She breathed in a deep lungful of the clean air. How different than what she experienced inside the girls' home or even in the city of Fairlight.

Nataline, you need to head to a town called Lost Worries.

Nat jumped when the bell jingled again as Jay-Kob came out of the shop. He leapt off the steps and raced to the back of the wagon.

"If you'll help me unload quickly, he'll wait for me to do it now."

He dropped down a flap on the back end and pulled out a wooden box, then held it toward her. "Can you handle that?"

She took it and, using some of her ability to compensate for what her arms couldn't do, she nodded.

"Good. Take that inside to the counter on the right. Empty the contents onto it."

She turned to the stairs as he reached for another box. With her thoughts, she turned the doorknob, and she pushed open the door with her foot. Despite the window, it was still hard to see inside. Shelves full of all types of items covered every wall from the floor to the ceiling. Nat wound her way between boxes, barrels, crates, and tables burdened with goods in the middle of the room until she reached the counter on the right. A stove sat at one end, but it wasn't lit. She took several deep breaths before she pulled the lid off the box and pulled out a decorative blanket, setting it on the counter. She added two more blankets to the counter before pulling out the last items.

The man behind the counter wore a white shirt with a black apron over it. She'd never seen a man wear an apron before—but then she rarely saw men at all. His thin face revealed pointy cheekbones. One long brow arched over both dark eyes, and his bushy hair looked like a cat slept on his head. Two round bits of glass set in wire perched on his nose. She'd read about spectacles before but had never seen any.

Like Mr. Hideman, this man scribbled on a pad of paper. "Three quilts, eight skeins of yarn, six spools of thread." His voice sounded like his nose was pinched closed. Nat tried not to laugh.

"Here, empty this one next." Jay-Kob put a new box on the counter and grabbed the empty one she'd brought in.

She pulled out belts and leather pouches engraved with designs.

"Eight belts and five small knapsack pouches," the man behind the counter said as he scribbled on the paper.

Nat took the box back toward the wagon but met Jay-Kob at the door. She put her crate on the floor at his feet and took the one he carried.

She pulled out a long length of rope and set it on the counter. The man took the end in one hand, and with the other, he stretched the rope to touch his nose. "One." He dropped the end and took hold of the spot near his face and brought the next portion of the rope to his nose. "Two." He continued while Nat watched. When he finally got to the other end of the length of rope, he dropped it on the floor with the rest and wrote on his paper again. "Eighteen yards of rope."

Jay-Kob brought in one last box and helped her pull out the contents.

"Twenty horseshoes, sixteen decorative iron hinges, and a two-inch-square box of nails." The man wrote everything before he looked up and handed the paper to Jay-Kob. "I'll be open in the morning for you to collect the items you need. Good day to you."

Jay-Kob put the note in his shirt pocket. "Thank you, Mr. Stewart. A blessed evening to you."

Mr. Stewart waved a hand at them as they each grabbed a crate, then he followed them toward the door. It locked behind the young people, and the curtain drew over the window.

Jay-Kob set the boxes back in the wagon with a sigh. He raised the flap on the back of the wagon bed and glanced around. "Now to find a meal and a place to sleep."

"Will Squirt be all right alone?"

"She's never alone. Uncle's there to watch over her." He walked to the horse and took hold of the bridle. "Come on. I know of a few places we might be able to stay. By the way, do you have a certain place you're heading?"

"Have you heard of a place called Lost Worries?"

"Yep. Still a few days south of here. I don't go that far, but I'll find someone who will be heading that way."

Nat tried not to cry. Jay-Kob was kind to her, but he wasn't going to go with her. She bit her bottom lip. She didn't like being scared all the time, but she'd even been afraid in the girls' home. Who would watch over her now? Would the next person be like Jay-Kob?

Jer yawned and stretched. He tossed his bedroll on the ground for the night.

Head to Lost Worries, Jeremicum.

Jer shared his blanket with Davie as they settled in for the night. "Albert? Will we be heading anywhere near Lost Worries?"

The older gentleman grunted as he tried to find a comfortable position to lie in. "Nope. Use to, but all the rich folks fled when our good ol' king started hunting and killing all the noble families. Now only the servants who were left behind still live there. They don't buy enough to warrant us going that far. Why?"

"I need to head that way. Told someone I'd meet them there if I ever left Dimward."

Victor dropped a log on the fire. Sparks flew into the growing darkness. "We'll be in Rusty Bend tomorrow. From there, we'll head east on to Plain View, and if we still have goods to sell, we'll head on to Palace Glen."

Edward yawned and wrapped himself tightly in his blanket. "There's a road north out of Rusty Bend that'll take ye to Lost Worries. But ye're always welcome to stick with us, lad."

Jer stared up at the twinkling stars between the leafy tree covering. Tomorrow at this time he'd be on his own again. No one to watch over him, no blanket. Maybe …

You are never alone, my love. The Almighty always holds you in the palm of His hand, and I am watching.

But did he trust the one who appeared as a vapor?

Cay yawned and stretched as the wagon slowed and they crept through another gate. This one had a bridge over water that ambled around the bottom of the wall in slow waves. Next, they came to two huge metal doors in the thick brick walls. As they passed through, Cay could see that the wall was wider than he was tall. Inside Lake Side, tall buildings sat so close together a boy his size would barely be able to walk between many of them. The pink of the setting sun shone off windows that were three and four rows high.

The wagon slowed and so did Gan-Nonin's talking. "Lake Side has a lot of people. Good for selling your crops, bad for getting around."

Other wagons passed them on the way out of the gate. The wheels almost brushed each other as both drivers tried to avoid the people walking beside them in both directions. Men on horseback also strained to find space to move. Some people shouted at one another to watch where they were going, while others greeted those they knew with cries of "Hello."

Cay had never been in such a loud place. The cows and few children working the farm, even with Kint's yelling, could never come close to all this racket.

Flickering candlelight leaked through many of the windows long before the boys stopped. How did anyone find their way around this place? All the buildings looked the same. Many had squares of wood that hung over the doors, each painted with something different. One had a thread and needle over a window with a shirt and dress hanging inside;

another had a loaf of bread painted on it; several had mugs painted on them.

Gan-Nonin steered the wagon behind a dark two-story structure with one of these mug signs.

"What do the painted wood squares mean?" Cay asked as they turned down a lane between two buildings. The wagon fit but almost brushed each wall.

"They let a body know what business is inside."

"A needle and thread are a business?"

"A tailor. They make clothes for people."

"So, the bread means they sell bread."

"A bakery. They definitely have bread, but they sell other baked goods as well—rolls, biscuits, tarts, and the like." Gan-Nonin stopped outside a large door at the back of the dark building with the mug. It smelled like the cow barn at home when someone hadn't cleaned it in a couple of days. "Robby, you here?" Gan-Nonin called.

The door slid open, and Cay plugged his nose.

"Yeah. Where else am I gonna be?"

"You got room for my rig and a spot for a couple bedrolls?"

Robby looked a couple years older than Gan-Nonin. His skin was the color of cow's milk, and his long straight hair was green. Cay had never seen green hair before. Robby rubbed his neck and stared at his toes. Several stalls were empty behind him. "I don't know, Gan. Dad isn't really looking to help your kind."

"My kind? Since when have we ever considered our differences? Have I ever treated you less than an equal? I've always paid for my horses' feed and a space in the loft. Is my money not good enough anymore?"

"You know it's not that. But this city is divided. Your kind don't like my kind, and they hate us owning businesses. What will our customers say if we let one of you use our space?"

"Robby, I can't believe you're turning me away. I've always thought of you as a friend." Gan-Nonin clicked his tongue and popped the reins over the horses' backs. The wagon lurched and slid along the narrow lane.

"I wish more people thought like you do," Robby mumbled as he pulled the door closed.

"What was that about?" Cay asked as they came out onto a wider street. He glanced around. Fewer people remained outside now.

"Robby is an Albinus. They were brought here as slaves centuries ago when the Everbloods ruled. When the Truefaith kings came to power they outlawed slavery. But now that an Everblood has stolen the crown, the Albinus fear they'll be made slaves again. Most of us want nothing of the sort, but there are a few who would love to see the fair-skinned people put back in their place." Gan-Nonin spit on the ground. "Stupid, ignorant, small-minded …" His words faded like the morning dew in the fields.

Cay hugged himself and rubbed his arms. Though the night air held little cold, he shivered from deep inside.

Chapter 35

Mura and her current guide rode through the night without stopping. He pushed them as fast as the dark and the thick woodland would allow. Well before sunrise, they passed the small hamlet of Widow's Marsh. With the gates locked tight for the night, they continued around the city, careful of the soggy land surrounding it.

As the first rays of sunlight splashed on the road only feet beyond the forest, he led her to the edge of the tree line.

"The next city lies just an hour's walk to the west."

She knew that. The area was familiar even far from the road. It had been many years, but the landscape had changed little other than perhaps being more over grown.

"I'll leave you here. Best I not know where the next underground helper leads you for shelter."

"Yes, you're probably right." But it didn't make it any easier knowing she would go on alone. She closed her eyes and took a slow, deep breath. She'd faced Brax with all his evil and hate. And how many times had she told the children they were never truly alone? Surely she could handle some long-faded memories.

The guide cleared his throat. Mura opened her eyes. "I will need to return the horse as well. I am sorry."

She lowered from the saddle. "I will blend in better as a traveler on foot than someone rich enough to own such a fine horse. Also, I will be less likely to be robbed on foot."

"Don't be fooled. The roads are not as safe as they once were." He took the reins from her and inclined his head with a small smile. "But the Almighty may soon free us from the darkness that has overtaken the land. Our Savior keep you safe." He bowed his head again and turned back into the woods.

Mura watched as he disappeared into the thick forest, then she waited until she couldn't hear him any longer. Still, she lingered longer. As a youth, she had been the one to sneak around the castle, seeking to train with the sword. When she grew into a young woman, she traveled to distant lands in the name of her father, the king. Nothing had ever stood in her way of what she wanted to do.

Not until Thedo Brax.

Not until Father died and she'd failed so terribly.

If the guide who had just abandoned her knew she caused all their troubles, he'd make sure she died on this road. A hated tear slid down her cheek. She swiped at it with the back of her hand and turned to the road. In order to see if any others traveled this early, and to look for any who might be waiting for an unsuspecting traveler to rob, she loosed her spirit. There wasn't another soul between here and her destination.

Even so, she pulled her hood all the way over her head to hide her face. She stepped onto the road and headed for the last place she ever wanted to be again.

The high city walls of Lost Worries stretched out at the bottom of the small hill where Mura stood. Sunlight sparkled off Hidden Depths Lake on the far side of the old resort town. Once it had been a place for noble and wealthy families to come and relax. It had also been one of the first places Brax sent his troops. Many died rather than follow a king who stole the throne.

Those who helped her get this far hoped she still had friends here. Mura knew better. Any not dead had gone into hiding, like her sister and her husband. They had been missing so long, most believed they were dead as well.

Mura took a moment to note the children's progress.

Calebus waited on the far side of the lake for the next ship to cross. Boats used to carry passengers back and forth and around the lake several times a day. Now only one old ship remained to transport people and cargo from Lake Side to Lost Worries and any other town around the lake. But it only left Lake Side twice a week.

Nataline was in a wagon moving south, still over two days' journey away.

Jeremicum had an equal distance to travel north.

It would have to be enough time for her to regain her strength. Mura wished she knew what she would do once they were all together.

She pushed the thoughts of the children aside and turned from the view of the city to the overgrown lane on her right. Best to face one hard situation at a time.

The willow trees she'd sat under as a young woman were so full of long-hanging branches, she couldn't see the trunks any longer. The uneven stone path would make even a lazy stroll difficult. Weeds grew knee high between them and some stones were missing. Her steps slowed. She didn't want to trip on the old road. But she knew that was a lie. She shook her head. Still, she hesitated.

Though all this property had belonged to Zane's family, a brick wall surrounded the house, gardens, and outbuildings. The massive oak, which once shaded the gate, had toppled and damaged the wall. The gate reminded her of so much of the kingdom, fallen and disrepair. The iron gate was rusted now and, though chained together to keep out intruders, one side bent away from the fallen tree.

Once, golden lions had sat on top of the gate posts and watched over all who entered. They were gone now, like the family who had lived here.

Mura ducked under the chain and squeezed between the sides of the gate. At one time, rows of white bark trees had lined the path to the large home; now weeds grew everywhere, and some of the trees had fallen. She only caught glimpses of the house a few times before she climbed through the branches of one fallen tree lying across the path. Her hood became snagged and pulled from her head. So far away from the main road, she didn't bother to put it back.

The formerly beautiful home looked as bad as the land that surrounded it. She scanned the house—paint pealed, window shutters dangled, the roof sagged and toppled. Cracked, and dry cement made up the foundation in front of the home. She couldn't hold back her tears. Not a single whole pane of glass remained. The stairs to the wraparound porch creaked and groaned as she climbed them. How many nights had she sat with Zane's family on this porch discussing her impending wedding? The one that never came.

She pushed open one side of the double doors. The metal hinges cried as she stepped inside. The grand entry no longer boasted the rugs and tables which had once decorated the space. The massive stairs on her right ascended from two directions and met on a circular landing below a round stained glass window before dividing again, leading up to the bedrooms upstairs. The carpet on the stairs, along with many posts in the railing, was missing. Leaves crunched under her feet with the groaning boards.

This once-beautiful home, was now withered, abandoned, and broken, much like Mura herself. Movement and creaking boards drew her attention to the far end of the long hall in front of her.

Two figures stepped from the kitchen in the back of the home and walked toward her. Mura had been so consumed by the decay of the place that she'd failed to notice anyone else was inside it with her.

A male and female Albinus came into the light of the entry.

"Molly?"

The woman wore her bright pink hair braided on the left side of her head, which hung a few inches onto her shoulder. She curtsied deep. As she rose, a huge smile stretched across her face, and she greeted Mura. "Oh, it is kind of you to remember me, miss."

Slavery had been outlawed in Purlan in the time of her great-great-grandfather. Many of the white-skinned Albinus still worked as paid household servants. But a few, like Molly and her husband Quinn, had worked as valuable employees and had become like family to some of the nobility.

"What are you two still doing here?"

"Oh, we no longer live in the Honorcut's home, miss." Quinn's lime green hair waved against his shoulders. "We heard you might be headed this way and came to attend you."

Again, the tears came. Mura staggered forward a couple of steps. "I don't require attending as much as I desperately need some friends."

Molly and Quinn stared at each other for a moment.

Mura could sense their discomfort. "Please." She'd fallen so low she begged.

Molly took tentative steps forward and opened her arms.

Mura fell into her embrace. "It has been so long since I have felt the comforting touch of another person."

Molly rubbed her back. "There, there, miss. I know you must have suffered terribly, but all will be restored by the Almighty. You will see. For now, we have prepared your room. The water is heating for your bath, and I will prepare a meal."

"Yes, miss. No need for tears. All is waiting for you," Quinn said.

After several more heartbeats, Mura pulled from Molly's arms and wiped her running nose on her sleeve. Not a very lady-like thing to do, but the escape and days of travel had made the tears uncontrollable.

Quinn walked away.

"He goes to bring the water from the fire up to your bath. Why don't you start up? I can bring a tray of food up to you, and then you can rest," Molly said with a smile.

"We will be here as long as you need us, miss," Quinn added as he passed carrying two buckets of steaming water.

Mura took a deep breath. "There will be others joining me."

"Others?" they both said together.

"Yes. Three. Three children. They should be here two mornings from now."

Molly smiled up at Quinn as he turned on the landing. "Of course, miss. We will have everything prepared for them."

Mura turned to the stairs. So much about the house was familiar, and yet even more had changed. Perhaps she had changed the most.

She lumbered up the back stairs and followed Quinn to the room which she used anytime she'd come to stay. At the top of the stairs, an image of Brax came to mind with his pale skin and white hair. But he couldn't be Albinus *and* an Everblood. They were sworn enemies. The Everbloods were responsible for enslaving the Albinus. Obviously, she was beyond the ability to think clearly.

Steam already rose off the water in the tub in the bathing chamber in the corner of her room. After a bath, some food, and a long nap, everything would make more sense.

Chapter 36

Somehow, they managed to find a place to park Gan-Nonin's wagon behind a low row of windowless brick structures far from Robby's place. They'd eaten their apples long ago, and the moon shone down on them as they covered the bags of sweet peas. The sounds of bells rang out from time to time—some loud, deep, and from high in the air, while others almost sounded like a tinkle. Those came with a man's voice. Each time he said a different number. The tinkling bells sounded now. "Hear the bells toll. 'Tis one."

Gan-Nonin finished arranging his bags of peas, stacking them more toward the front and sides of the wagon. "Here, Cay, help me cover as much as we can with these blankets. It'll mean we'll be colder, but thank the Almighty at least the nights are not full of dew and winds right now."

Cay pulled the edge of the blanket tossed to him. "Why do men tell us to listen to the bells?"

"They are the town criers, and along with important news, they tell the town of the time."

"Time?"

The older boy climbed up into the back of the wagon in the narrow open space he'd created by moving all the bags. He offered Cay a hand up. "Yes, the time. It tells everyone when things are happening throughout the day. We'll need to rise by six to get to the market to set up our stall before all the places are taken. Shoppers usually start arriving at half past seven."

They reclined on the blankets against the bags. Both of them wiggled against the mass in order to find a comfortable position. "We got up with the sun and went to bed when the work was done." Cay's stomach growled.

"Sorry about supper, kid. We'll get something as soon as we're set up in the morning."

It wasn't the first time Cay had missed a meal. In truth, he had eaten more today than he did most days on the farm. He lay back and glanced up at the blinking stars above. Did Lor look at the stars and think about him too? Was she angry with him for leaving her behind?

For the last two days, Cay had gone with Gan-Nonin to the area near what he called the wharf to sell his sweet peas. The many men and women who sold items they'd grown and made formed two halves of a circle on either side of a long wooden road that went out into the biggest pond of water Cay had ever seen. He couldn't see the other side. The water splashed against the shore in small waves. Hidden Depths Lake was nothing like the stream or pond found on Kint's farm.

Everyone came to the wharf at some time. They looked for fish from all the little boats that floated to the shore. They shopped for fresh produce, or shoes, cloth, jewelry, and other goods. But there was a clear separation between the sellers and shoppers. The whited-skinned Albinus with their green, blue, or pink hair only shopped at the stalls owned by other Albinus. And those with pinkish skin, or tanned like his, or dark, and even black skin didn't go near the Albinus vendors and what they had to sell. When the crowds grew, it reminded Cay of anytime Kint stormed near the kids who worked his farm. Everyone held their breath and hoped nothing bad would happen.

Cay removed the blanket that covered the now-empty board Gan-Nonin had used for his stall. Few bags of sweet peas remained.

"The Albatross is just coming into port," the older boy said, lifting his chin toward the wooden pathway in the water he called a pier.

Cay turned and looked at the new boat as it neared the shore. It was as long as six of the little fishing boats, and about as wide as four. Black smoke puffed out of a fat pipe in the middle of an upper story. "It's huge."

"Oh, my father says it's not as big as some that used to sail on these waters, and nothing like the battle ships that protect the coast of Purlan out on the Bottomless Sea. But it is the only vessel left that goes all the way to the other side." Gan-Nonin sighed as he placed the blankets in his wagon with the last of the peas. His hand thumped Cay on the shoulder. "I really do hate to see you leave, kid. You've been my good luck charm. I sold my crop faster and for more money than any trip before." He winked at Cay. "You are good with people, and the ladies all think you're cute."

Cay didn't know what to say to that, but it made his cheeks hot.

"Now I promised you passage on that ship for helping me, but I'd be just as glad to give you the coins and have you stay with me. We could find a place for you on my family's farm. Then we could travel together after each harvest."

"Nah, I have to keep going. The farmer I worked for will kill me if he finds me."

A low, drawn-out horn sounded, and Cay turned to see the Albatross stopped next to the pier. It looked even bigger than it had a few minutes ago.

"Well, best get your passage purchased before all the places are taken." Gan-Nonin sighed again and walked beside Cay down toward the water and onto the pier.

Many people passed them headed to the shore on the other side of the wooden path. They came to a man with dark pants and a striped shirt. "Two tickets?"

"No, just one for the kid here."

The beady-eyed man looked Cay over from head to foot. "Must be brave or desperate to travel alone so young." He looked to Gan-Nonin again. "You vouching that this kid has leave to travel freely about the country?"

Gan-Nonin took one of Cay's arms and pushed up the sleeve, then turned it so the man could see. Then he did the same with the other. "No slave brandings or markings. He's meeting someone in Lost Worries."

The man shrugged. "Ten coppers."

"Ten! He's half the size of a grown man, won't take up more than a place to sit, and he's traveling with his own food."

Cay held up the bag of bread, cheese, and fruit Gan-Nonin had collected for him.

A couple passed the striped-shirt man and dropped several coins into his hand. He nodded, and they walked up the steep ramp onto the ship. "Eight is as low as I'll go, and he'll have to sleep on the deck tonight."

"I'll give you six, and he'll help swab the deck. He's very helpful and not afraid of a little work."

The man looked Cay over, a little longer this time. "All right."

Gan-Nonin gave the man the coins. "See you around, kid. Stay out of trouble."

The man tucked the coins in the pouch at his waist and called up to another man on the deck. "Vern."

The man with light yellow hair turned and looked down at them.

"You have help." The man they'd paid put a hand on Cay's shoulder and gave him a little push. "Put him to work."

"You got it." Vern waved him up. "Come on, lad. Lots to do before we sail in the morning."

Cay glanced back and watched Gan-Nonin's wagon disappear with the rest of the vendors. He was alone again.

Chapter 37

Nat shifted her position again as the wagon bed she rode in jostled over the rough road. Jay-Kob had found a family traveling south who was willing to take Nat along with them if she agreed to look after their children—three wild boys who didn't seem to mind. Behavior like theirs would never have been tolerated by Mistress Swanson. Nat glanced out the back of the wagon at the dust swirls that floated behind them. She wondered what had happened to her, Gretchen, Rachel, and Violet.

Today was the second day with the Inis family. Since she had not grown up as part of a family, Nat found it rare to meet someone who had two names. Mistress Swanson had another name and each of her girls were Swansons too. What had her name been when she still had a family?

"Waaaa!" The wail from two-year-old Toby Inis, reminded Nat she needed to keep them entertained. He grew impatient faster than five-year-old Abner and seven-year-old Frank. All three boys looked like their father—lean in the face with a long pointed nose, thick brows, and hair the color of muddy water.

Nat found the little box Toby had dropped. She'd put a couple of rocks in it to make a rattle. She shook it to get his attention and his short chunky fingers opened and closed for the invented toy. Nat handed it to him and restarted what she'd been doing with the older boys.

With a bit of yarn she'd found, she'd cut a length about the size of her arm, tied the ends together, and hooked matching fingers from each hand through it. With the string stretched between her hands in a loop, she used each of her fingers to pick up the string on the opposite hand and made patterns for Abner and Frank to marvel at.

She gave the string to Frank when Toby tired of his homemade rattle. Nat wiped the sweat from her face. It never got this hot in Fairlight. Four metal poles arched from one side of the wagon to the other, high enough for her to stand and covered in a heavy cream-colored cloth. Still, the sunlight bore through it.

Toby fussed and Mistress Inis turned and glared at her. The back of the woman's dress was wet, as was the hair around her face.

Nat took a large button and strung another bit of yarn through it and tied the ends. With the button in the middle, she twisted the ends in opposite directions. Holding each end, she pulled them apart. The button spun wildly. She released the pressure and the string wound itself, ready for her to do again.

Abner snatched it, and the string tangled before she could stop the button. With the wagon bouncing around so much, Nat struggled to get the string unsnarled and wound once more. She handed each end to Abner. With her hands over his, she pulled apart slowly and brought them together in a rhythm to keep the button spinning.

Nat yelped as they banged over a big bump, and one of the stacked crates tipped. Her ability kept it from hitting her or the children before her hands could catch it. The children didn't notice, and their parents didn't bother to turn around. But a book tumbled from the crate, grazed her head, and landed in her lap. She secured the box and then opened it to see what it was about.

"Whatcha doin'?" Frank asked.

"Reading the title of this book."

"You can read?" Mistress Inis looked at her with a narrow gaze.

"Yes, I can read."

The woman snorted.

Nat turned to the first page. "Sing to me of the man, Muse, the man of twist and turns driven time and again off course, once he had plundered the hallowed heights."

Mistress Inis' eyes grew wide. She stared unblinking as the wagon jostled down the road. "Teach them," she said and turned away.

Nat sighed. "I will need a piece of slate and a hunk of chalk."

"The town of New Well is just ahead. You'll have what you need." It was the only thing Mister Inis had said to her in a day and a half.

Nat glanced at the squirming boys. Toby was far too young to learn his letters. Abner might be too. But even if he wasn't, it was going to be hard to instruct them when Nat couldn't keep their attention with games for more than a few moments. And what did it matter anyway? She'd be leaving them in another day. How much could she possibly teach them in the time she had left with them? The memory of her one fleeting lesson with the girls flashed through her head.

Nat sighed and wiped the sweat from her face again as the wagon slowed. The sounds of another town tickled her ears.

"I don't like this. Reading's dumb. It's just a bunch of silly scribbles." Frank scrunched over so that Nat could only see his back.

"Yeah, it's dumb. Tell us the s'ory about the knight who fighted the king," Abner added.

"If you learn your letters, you can read that story and hundreds more for yourself. You won't need me."

"I don't want to read myself. You do it," Frank mumbled.

"I won't be with you much longer—"

"You'll stay as long as I say." Mistress Inis glared over her shoulder. "Them boys'll learn to read—even if it takes ya a year or more."

Nat bowed her head over the slate in her lap and let her eyes close. In the morning, she was supposed to leave them. The voice had said so, and at the moment, she favored whatever the voice had planned for her over staying with these whiny boys and their harsh mother.

"Well, get back to it," Mistress Inis said. "And you boys had better listen, or I'll box yer ears."

"But ma," Frank and Abner whined.

"Listen to your mother!" Mister Inis' loud voice boomed. Toby woke from his far-too-brief nap and cried out.

Great. Nat pulled in a slow, deep breath. Now she'd have to keep the little brat happy and try to teach two boys who won't even attempt to grasp the simplest of things. "Let's begin again. Tell me the name of this letter," Nat said as she pulled Abner into her lap.

Nat stared up at the last of the stars. The new day leaked into the dark sky, driving back the night. While the Inis family slept, she'd moved farther and farther from the wagon. The parents bedded down inside with Toby. Nat found it hard to believe anyone could sleep over Mister Inis' snoring. The two older boys slept under the wagon, but Nat was still supposed to watch over them.

"If anything happens to my precious children, you'll be to blame," Mistress Inis had said, her finger shaking at Nat's face.

"But what if I fall asleep?"

"Don't."

Mistress Inis expected Nat to watch them all night and keep them entertained and educated all day. Nat was better off in the girls' home. There she only had to work during the day.

She pushed from the tree she leaned against and slipped behind it. With just enough light to see the shadows of the trees, she moved away from the wagon. Careful not to trip or make too much noise, she sneaked from tree to tree toward the growing light.

"Girl!" The roar of Mister Inis slithered through the trees, but she was too far away for him to follow her.

Nat stayed in the shelter of the trees and skulked as fast as possible, but no less quiet—just in case.

Chapter 38

The clouds blew across the sky, bringing a cool breeze with them. The sun played hide-and-seek behind the puffs of white as Jer and Soo climbed a large hill. He'd passed a couple of travelers earlier in the morning, but the road was empty now.

After a day of selling in Rusty Bend, he'd parted ways with Albert, Edward, Victor, Davie, and the rest of the caravan and continued north. Soo remained ever alert at his side. Jer sensed the strong presence he'd first noticed in Dimward even closer now, but one look at his big dog and no one dared bother him.

Jer and Soo ambled across a large stone bridge over a fat river, and through the town of South Bridge on the other side. He purchased some fruit and a small cooked hen in the market—which they didn't stop to eat—then they continued through the town and beyond.

When the sun began casting long shadows, Jer and Soo strolled off the road into the thick trees. He found a log near a small grassy area big enough for them to stretch out and plopped down. They shared the meat and fruit. Jer left a sweet peach for the morning, then lay down in the grass.

Soo rested her head on Jer's chest, ears alert to scan for sound.

Snap, crunch. Someone moved through the woods. Whoever made the sound was still a ways off because Soo wasn't up chasing him. And it wasn't an animal because Jer would have sensed it.

But then Soo stood, head down, ears back.

Jer sat up.

A roar rumbled through the darkness, followed by the yelps of at least two men, and then everything went silent.

Soo shook and flopped back down beside him, closing her eyes. Jer lay there trying to think of who had been in the woods with them and what had happened, but he fell asleep. Nothing bothered them the rest of the night, as it hadn't during their long walk yesterday or during last night.

Now as they neared the top of the hill, Jer's nerves tingled. He wanted to know what would happen next. Certain it was good, Jer couldn't stand still. His hand tapped out a rhythm on his thigh, his heart beat faster, and he bounced with each step. "Something good is about to happen, Soo. I can feel it."

They stopped at the top of the rise and looked down to the left at a large town. "That must be Lost Worries," he told Soo, rubbing her head. Her tail wagged lazily.

Beyond the buildings inside the tall wall, rays of sunlight broke through the clouds and sparkled on a huge lake. "Everything's about to change." The rhythm he tapped out spread to his toe as they stood there.

Movement caught his eye. A young boy with long straight hair a little lighter than his walked up the hill toward him. From this distance, his clothes looked dirty, torn, and tight. He trudged upward with his head down.

Before the boy could spot him, Jer continued on his way. But when he turned back to the road, a girl about his size walked toward him. She wore her light brown hair in two braids. The blue top and green skirt she wore looked too big. The morning breeze ruffled all the extra fabric around her. She looked at him, but her expression didn't change.

Jer could see the narrow lane the voice had shown him in his dreams early this morning. Overgrown with branches and weeds, it was almost hidden. The girl wouldn't be able to see it from where she was, and by the time she got to the spot where he now stood, he'd be out of sight.

Hopefully, she wouldn't investigate where he'd disappeared to.

When she put her head down, Jer and Soo slipped through the brush. He'd only gone a few steps when he heard the rocks crunch behind him. The girl walked up the lane. Jer stopped as she neared. "Where are you going?"

"That's really none of your business." She stomped past him.

Jer came alongside. Soo didn't seem to mind her presence.

The girl walked faster, and Jer matched her pace. She increased some more, and so did he. "Why are you following me?"

Jer looked at her, then at the gate across their path. "I turned this way first, so it's you who are following me," she asked.

She slipped under the chain and between the iron gates.

Jer followed.

"Now, who is following?"

Jer hurried past her. She passed him at a jog a moment later. Jer trotted faster. Soon they ran as if in a race. They didn't slow until they came to a tree lying across the brick path. The girl climbed through the branches at the far side of the road while Jer and Soo scrambled over the fat trunk. They landed on the other side first and ran for the tall castle-like structure. The girl caught up with him, and they climbed the three stairs together. Normally he would have knocked, but the girl grabbed the door on her side, so he did the same with the one on his side. Both doors flew open and banged against the walls behind them. They stopped and stared. Their heavy breathing reverberated off the bare walls. No other sound met them.

Soo ambled forward, her tail swinging slowly. Whatever this place had been, it was in need of a good cleaning and many repairs. The dry wood creaked under Soo's weight. The huge window above had a few pieces of colored glass missing. Jer could see through the holes to the tree branches and clouds outside.

The girl slipped from his left toward the first room off the entryway.

Jer followed her. Soo stopped in the doorway and looked in; her tail wagged faster.

Inside the near-empty room, that looked no better than the space they'd just left, sat a table covered in trays of steaming food, bowls of fruit, platters of cheese, and piles of sliced bread. A stomach growled, and Jer wasn't sure if it was his or the girl's.

They both stepped forward at the same time. Their shoulders pressed against each other as their outer shoulders banged into either side of the door frame. They became wedged in the opening as neither would let the other go first.

"Stop." This time the voice was in his ears, not in his head.

Chapter 39

Jer couldn't move. It was as if the voice that had commanded him to stop controlled him somehow. It must have been the same for the girl because she stopped and didn't try to wiggle past him into the room. Even Soo sat still next to the table full of food.

Movement high and to his right caught his attention. A woman walked slowly down the stairs. It was the same ghostly person he'd seen during the fight right before he left Dimward. But now she looked as solid and real as the girl stuck in the doorway with him.

The only thing able to move was his head, so he turned it and followed the woman's movement down the stairs. Her long dark brown hair held streaks of purple and lavender. It was braided into one fat rope that sat on her shoulder before hanging down to her waist. Her dark blue dress wasn't like any he'd seen the women in Dimward—or anywhere else in the kingdom—wearing. The sleeves were tight around her arms with wide cuffs much like his own shirt. It had large shiny silver buttons that secured it from the neck to the waist like a man's coat. The skirt wasn't whole. A huge piece of the front of the skirt, in the shape of a triangle, was missing. Because of the large gap in the skirt, he could see she also wore black pants and tall gray boots that laced up past her knees. Jer had never seen any woman in pants before. She stopped on the circular landing in the middle of the stairs almost directly behind him.

Jer still couldn't move, and he could barely see her now. Thumps, which sounded like steps, and crunches made him turn his head the other way to look past the girl out the doors they had left open. The younger boy he'd seen walking up the hill now climbed the outside steps up to the porch and joined them inside.

He looked at Jer and the girl first, then his head turned toward the woman. "Mura," he shouted, running across the entryway and up the stairs to her.

The woman knelt and took the boy in her arms as he wrapped his around her neck. "Calebus, it is so good to see you."

"Calebus?" the girl beside him whispered.

"I didn't think I'd ever get here." Caleb's said as the Mura let him go.

The woman stood, took his hand, and came down the rest of the stairs. "Well, we are all here now. Nataline, Jeremicum, are you ready to join us like well-mannered people?"

"Yes, ma'am," Jer said.

"Jeremicum?" Nataline whispered again.

Jer jerked forward and almost fell as whatever held him let go. He righted himself and joined the line behind Nataline as they followed Mura and Calebus. They walked to the back of the house and turned left into a small chamber with a cabinet. On top of the cabinet sat a bowl and a pitcher. Mura poured a little water over one hand into the bowl, took a piece of root, and rubbed it between both hands in the water until bubbles formed, then she rinsed and dried her hands on a towel she took from the cupboard. She stepped aside and Calebus did the same, then Nataline, and finally Jer.

Nataline was staring at him when he stepped out of the little room. Mura smiled like she knew a secret but wouldn't tell. They walked back toward the first room and moved around the table, each standing behind a chair.

The girl looked back and forth between them. "Jeremicum. Calebus," she whispered. "Jer? Cay?" Her head tipped as if she were trying to solve a puzzle that was missing some of its pieces.

"Do you know me?" Jer asked.

She shook her head, but Mura smiled. "You all know each other."

"What?" all three kids said at the same time. They started to argue, but Mura raised her hand, quieting them.

Mura pulled out a chair between her and chair. It had part of the back missing. On the seat part was a bowl full of food. Soo stood and sniffed it, and her tail picked up speed. "Let's say grace, start eating, and see if the food doesn't fuel your memories a bit." She reached one hand across the table to Jer and the other to Nataline. Jer took it and Calebus' beside him. Nataline had to stretch over the table to take the younger boy's other hand.

Then Mura bowed her head. Jer tried to concentrate on her words, but the smells from all the food on the table and the thoughts that they knew each other were distracting. "Dear loving Father, Protector, and Giver of all good things, we thank You for watching over us on our long journeys and bringing us together here in this place of safety. Thank You for the large meal before us and those faithful friends of Yours who provided and prepared it. May it give us strength for the days ahead and remind us of Your loving care. Help us to be strong in our troubles, kind to those who struggle beside us, and fiercely protective of those who are hurt by evil. We ask all these things in the name of Your precious Son. Amen."

"Amen," Jer repeated. The other two didn't say anything as they raised their heads.

"Now, there is a great quantity of food before us." Mura pulled out her chair and lowered into it. "Far more than we could eat right now, no matter how hungry we think we are. It will not be the last meal we eat together, so please only take a little and see if you like it. You can always have more." Mura picked up the bowl of white fluffy mounds in front of her and put a small scoop on her plate. She passed the bowl to Jer and picked up a cup with a spout that contained a thick brown liquid, then poured some over the white mounds.

The dishes were passed around the table, and they each took a little until Jer couldn't see his plate any longer. Nataline didn't take as much, but she continued to stare at the boys.

Mura ate silently, watching them and smiling between bites.

"You said I know them?" Nataline asked without a glance at Mura.

"Yes, of course you do. You just have to let yourself believe that the dream was in fact a memory."

"Dream?" Calebus said before biting into some corn.

"Memory?" Jer looked from Nataline to Mura. "So, we know each other from a long time ago?"

Mura nodded.

Jer looked at Nataline again. The faded memory of a little girl with short curly hair danced through his thoughts. "You were sitting on the lap of a man with dark hair and a short beard." The words came before Jer could stop them.

"The woman beside him had long hair with streaks of gold in it. She held a baby in her arms," Nataline said as they both turned and looked at Calebus. "Cay," she whispered again.

"Nat." Jer stared at her for a few minutes, his food long forgotten. "So, if we were all little together with the same man and woman, what does that mean? Were they looking after us before we were sent away?"

Nat shook her head. "I think those were our parents."

Cay coughed. Food flew from his mouth. "Wait. What? *OUR* parents? That means we're …"

"Brother and sister," Nat finished for him.

Jer's knife dropped from his hand, clanged against the plate, then *thunked* on the table. "No, it can't be true."

Mura raised a bite of food to her lips and smiled. "Oh, but it is very true."

All three children spoke at once.

"How can we be brother and sister?"

"Who are our parents?"

"Why were we split up?"

"Are they dead?"

"Who are you?"

The food—which was the best Jer had ever tasted—was pushed aside as the children leaned forward. Questions hurled at Mura faster than she could answer.

Chapter 40

Cay had seen Mura in her ghostly form many times. But now here she was eating a huge meal with them. There was something even more amazing than that, though. Cay had a brother and sister. And they were eating with him too. He'd often thought of Lor as a sister, but this was his real sister. Did he look like Nat? He didn't think he looked much like Jer, who had darker hair.

Mura put up her hand again. "I know you have many questions, but I also know you have each had a long hard journey. I am going to ask you to be patient for a little longer. I will answer all your questions this evening."

The kids groaned. Maybe they were alike.

"Now, you'll be able to understand better once the food has had time to strengthen you and rest—real rest—has had time to restore you. It'll only be a few hours, and those will fly by. I promise. Right now, you can go up the stairs on the right. The three rooms just above us have been prepared for you. Nataline's first, then Jeremicum's, and then yours, Calebus. A bath and a bed wait for you." Mura stood. "I'll meet you here with answers when the sun goes down."

Cay slid from his chair, passed behind Jer, and headed toward the doorway. His brother and sister—that sounded so weird to say, even in his head—stayed and tried to convince Mura to give them some answers now. Cay knew better. Mura wouldn't do anything until she wanted to. He wondered why they don't know her as good as he do.

He had just turned the corner at the top of the stairs, which led to the side of the house with their rooms, when Jeremicum and Nataline stomped across the entryway below him and to the stairs. They didn't look like they moved willingly. Cay sighed. Mura had made him do things before too. Not really against his will, but definitely not what he really wanted to do. He figured she could control people the way he controlled water and dirt.

Cay passed the first two doors and opened the third. He stood there and stared as the other two joined him at their doors. A wide, fat bed sat in the middle of the room.

"My own room," Nat said.

"A bed," both he and Jer said at the same time.

Nataline stepped inside. "Do you have a washroom inside your rooms too?" she called through the open door.

"If that is the little room on the side, yes. And a huge bucket full of warm water," Cay called back.

"That's a bath, not a bucket," Jer corrected.

Cay stuck his head out into the hall again. "You mean I'm supposed to clean myself indoors? Won't my clothes get everything all wet?"

Jer's head poked out and looked down the hall to him. "You take your clothes off first. I have new ones laid out on the bed; don't you?"

Cay looked back over his shoulder. There was a new shirt and pants on the side of the bed.

"Towels are by the washbasin," Nat said as her door closed.

"See you two at dinner," Jer said as his door closed too.

Cay stepped back inside and went to stand beside the bath. He'd cleaned himself in the stream when he couldn't stand his own stink any longer, but he'd never removed more than his shirt and usually not even that. His clothes smelled as bad as he did, so didn't they need to be cleaned too? Kint's clothes sometimes hung on a line from the house to a post in the garden to dry, but the farmer had more than one set to wear. Cay looked back at the new shirt and pants, then down at his dirty ripped clothes. He rarely got different clothes to wear, only when his old ones were too tight or torn. But he'd never had anything new. He didn't dare touch them even though he'd washed his hands before they ate. The tan pants and light green shirt were sure to show every speck of dirt.

Cay yawned.

You're tired, love, and the water is getting cold. Best take a quick bath, then climb into bed.

Somehow, he hadn't expected Mura to talk in his head when she was downstairs, but he knew better than to disobey. She'd make him do it anyway just like she made Nat and Jer come upstairs. His brother and sister. He had both a brother *and* a sister. That was so weird. Brother and sister. Cay shook his head

"I still miss Lor though. I hope she's okay. Can we go get her soon?"

We'll get her as soon as possible, but first, a bath and rest.

Though it felt strange, he enjoyed the warm bath. When it started to cool, he dried himself and walked to the bed. He couldn't stop thinking about Lor. He hoped she was okay and that Wart—if he was still on the farm—didn't bother her now.

Chapter 41

Cay stirred at the movement in the next room. Why was Jer banging around? Cay yawned and stretched. He wanted to know more about the family he just met, but that meant getting out of his bed, which was like sleeping on a cloud. Never in his life had he ever experienced anything so comfortable.

"You coming?" Cay thought that was Jer's voice, but it was hard to tell through the door.

"Coming," Cay groaned. Someone else said something, but he couldn't hear it well enough to make out the words.

The shirt and pants were the finest he had ever had—though a little big. At least he could grow before they became too tight. He brushed his hands over them as he stepped out into the hall. Jer had pants just like his, but he wore a yellow shirt. Nat wore a dress that fit her better than her old clothes and ended above her shiny black ankle boots.

"Well, we look better." Nat smiled.

"Should we go down now?" Jer turned to the window of colored glass across from them. "The sun is setting, and she said this evening." He shrugged.

Cay walked past them. "She's not stopping us. I got out of a fluffy bed, so I'm going down now."

He could hear the others behind him.

"How is it I've eaten more today than in most weeks, and I'm hungry again?" Jer said as he jumped over the last two steps and landed on the floor. The wood groaned and cracked.

"Food's good," Nat said.

They headed back into the room where they'd eaten earlier.

"Go wash your hands first." Mura walked down the other stairs.

Cay could feel the nudge to do as she requested and went.

Jer turned to her. "I washed before eating the last meal, then took a bath and climbed into a clean bed."

Nat paused too. "Seriously, how dirty could we have gotten while sleeping?"

Mura joined them and walked with them to the washroom. "It is part of good manners and a sign of being a civilized person."

Cay passed them as he left and they entered. He waited for them behind his chair. Some of the food on the table was left from earlier. Breads and cheeses and fruit. But there were a few new dishes as well. A pot of steaming brown liquid sat at one end, and there were bowls beside their plates.

"Is that stew?" Nat asked when she entered.

"Yes, I believe it is." Mura took her seat. The others followed.

"What's stew?" Cay asked.

Mura smiled at him, but her eyes didn't sparkle. They looked sad—like she might cry. "A thick soup with vegetables and meat."

Cay was going to ask what soup was, but Mura's eyes closed and her head bowed. She prayed again. Mura talked about the Almighty and all He did for them all the time. She said that everything depended on Him and that Cay should ask the Almighty when he needed anything. Cay had never seen this Being Who controlled everything, and he wasn't sure he liked the Almighty. If He was indeed as powerful as Mura claimed, then why was his family split up, and why did he have to live and work on Kint's farm? But when Mura prayed, he wanted to believe and trust, since her words said that she did.

"Amen," Jer said when she finished.

"Now, Nataline, would you hand me a roll?" Mura asked. The

crooked smile she wore told Cay Mura was up to something.

The breads were all at the far end of the table out of Nat's reach. She pushed back her chair to stand.

Mura put her hand on his sister's arm to keep her still. "No, just pass one to me."

Nat stared at her, glanced at her brothers, and back to Mura. After a nod from Mura, Nat looked at the bread basket. A roll near the top lifted off the rest and floated in the air. It dangled there a moment before it glided to Mura and dropped in her hand.

"Thank you, my dear." Mura tore the roll in two and stuck a knife in a lump of yellow stuff in front of her. "Calebus, could you fill my glass?"

He lifted his brow and tipped his head as he stared at her. He was afraid to ask his question out loud. *You want me to make the juice move to your glass?*

Mura nodded, her smile growing.

Cay put his fingers on the pitcher, and a second later, a stream of juice rose out of the top, floated across the table, and dropped into her metal mug.

"Thank you, my good man."

When Mura didn't ask Jer to do anything, Nat did. "So, what can you do?"

The big dog (or maybe it was a small shaggy horse) stood from where she sat eating. The dog spun twice in one direction, then once in the other. She barked before she sat again. Then a small brown bird with a bright blue spot on its wings zipped into the room and perched on the back of the chair the dog's dish sat on. It chirped and flew to Jer's shoulder. He offered it a small bit of bread before it flew away.

"Okay, that's cool," Nat said. She turned to Mura. "So, we all have powers. Is that because we're related? Does everyone in our family have some special ability?"

"Yes and no." Mura paused to eat her roll. "Let's finish our meal and retire to the parlor?"

"What?" Cay and Jer both said.

Mura smiled. "Eat, then we'll go into the sitting room next door and talk."

Cay held a spoon heaped with stew. He'd never used silverware until a few days ago with Gan-Nonin. "But we are sitting now. Why do we have to move someplace else to sit and talk?"

Mura wiped her mouth with a cloth beside her plate. "Oh, indeed, we are sitting and dining, so this is the dining room. The next room is the sitting room or parlor."

Cay still hadn't taken a bite. "This house has a room for just eating and another for just talking?"

Mura nodded at him with a funny smile. "I see how that sounds odd. But it is thought bad manners to speak with one's mouth full. Add to that," she nodded at his full spoon, which he still held in the air, "that food tends to get cold if the discussion is long and involved. It was decided that mostly eating would be done in one room and mostly talking in another. Also, those who work to make the food and clean up afterward don't have to wait as long to see to their tasks if we are out of the way."

"So, if we can't talk here, we should hurry up and eat so we can go to the talking room," Jer mumbled as he dipped his spoon in his food.

"We could have talked first." Nat blew on her stew.

Cay smiled at her. "She's Mura. She does things her own way. I've tried to ask her why. She only says it makes me grow."

"At the moment, I don't care about growing or even eating. I want answers." Nat dropped her spoon into her bowl. She sat with her arms crossed, but her stomach growled.

"Right." Jer put his spoon down. "Like, what's going on? Why were we split up? Where are our parents? What's going to happen now?"

"Pouting is not attractive on you, Nataline, and demanding is beneath you, Jeremicum. I have promised to tell you everything when we have all finished eating."

"You best eat. Mura doesn't change her mind." Cay took another bite. "Don't you know that?"

"It would seem you know her better than we do." Nat picked up a bit of cheese and broke off a piece. She popped it in her mouth and then turned to Mura. "Why is that?"

Chapter 42

Jer didn't eat as much this evening as he had when he arrived. He felt like Nataline, or Nat as he remembered. She'd eaten even less, and his demand to know things now and not when Mura was done eating had left them eating in silence.

"Well," Mura tapped her mouth with the square of fabric that had sat next to her plate. "As it seems you don't plan to talk to me until I tell you the whole story, I guess we should move to the solar."

"So—what?" Cay slipped from his chair and behind Jer before he could get up. "I thought we were going to talk in the pillar."

Mura chuckled as she rose. "Parlor, my sweet. A parlor is a room where there are lots of places to sit and talk with guests who come to visit. It is usually on the bottom floor near the dining room so that if your company comes for a meal, you can move between the two rooms easily. A solar is similar, but it is usually upstairs and only for the family to sit and talk together. So, since you are family, this room could serve as either the parlor or the solar."

They strolled to the next room between where they ate and where they washed their hands. Like the rest of the house, the paint and decorative paper on the walls had chipped and peeled. The floorboards were uneven, dry, and rough. There weren't any chairs here, but a blanket with large pillows on it sat near the fireplace.

Mura crossed her ankles and sat. Jer had never seen a woman sit with her legs crossed. She was a strange woman. But he was eager to hear what she had to say, so he plopped on a pillow next to her. Nat and Cay took the other two pillows, and they sat still, watching and waiting.

"I am quite sure this will make you unhappy, but I feel I must start with a bit of history to help you understand why things have happened as they have."

Jer didn't really care as long as she told them everything. Cay leaned forward with his elbows on his knee and chin on his fists. Nat sighed and shifted on her pillow. This might take a while.

Instead of fire, several fat candles burned in the fireplace. Odd shadows danced across Mura's face. She'd looked ghostly when Jer had first seen her, but now she looked a little spooky.

"To begin, your five-times great grandfather lived the quiet life of a fisherman near the Bottomless Sea. Before he married, he learned of a very special man from long ago. This man was fully the Almighty and fully man and came to live in our world to save us. The man called fishermen to work with Him and spread the good news of what the Almighty had done for them. Your five-times great grandfather, Liam—later known as Liam the Pure—loved the Almighty and hated the evil he saw around him. The enslavement of people—"

"Like the Albomables?" Cay sat up straighter.

"Like the Albinus, yes." Mura was gentle in her correction. Jer liked that about her. "There were others, too, outsiders from other kingdoms who were also made slaves. But it was the sacrifices of people to the statues of stone that hurt Liam's heart the most."

Nat wrinkled her nose. "They killed people?"

"It is sad but true. The kings of the time didn't see that each and every life was created in the image of the Almighty."

"So, what did Liam do about it?" Jer wanted to get her back on track so she could finish her story.

"Nothing at first, but as more and more people who felt the same way gathered around him, they chose to go to war against their king. It was a terrible decision for Liam to make. How could he make the killing stop with more killing? He and the army that followed him gave the king of the Everbloods and all his followers a chance to change. When they refused, Liam's army surrounded the palace and, again, gave them the chance to leave of their own will. They would not. The battle between the two armies lasted almost a year, but finally Liam's army defeated the Everblood king and his followers. Now that the evil ruler and his court had been removed, Liam hoped to return to the sea and his fishing. But the people made him king. The first of the—"

"Wait." Nat sat on her heels with her hand braced on her knees and leaned forward. "You're saying that our five-times great grandfather was a king?"

Mura grinned big, and the flickering light sparkled in her eyes. "Yes, as was his son, and his son, and his son, and his son—your grandfather."

Jer and Cay also spun and sat on their knees. "Our grandfather was the king?" Jer repeated. "That makes our father…"

"One of the noble families, but your mother was the king's daughter."

Nat whispered, "A princess."

"If mama was a princess, then what are we?" Cay asked.

Mura looked at each one of them. "You are the princes and princess of Purlan."

The three of them all spoke at once, making it hard to hear what the others said. Mura put her hand up and waited for them to hush, which took a while this time.

"You're getting ahead of the story. Let me finish, and then if you still have questions, you can ask them—one at a time. Now, where was I?"

"Liam was made king," Jer blurted, hoping she would hurry.

"Yes, Liam. He cleaned the land of all the statues where sacrifices were made. Then he built places for followers of the Almighty to meet and learn of His good and gentle ways. When the Everbloods who were still left wouldn't stop their wicked ways, Liam banished them from the land. Because of his goodness, he was given the title the Pure, and our kingdom became known as the Pure Lands."

"Purlan," Nat said.

"Yes, over the centuries the name was shortened. Now, each of Liam's descendants who ruled after him was as good to his people as Liam had been. They all loved the Almighty and followed in His ways. But by the time your grandfather, Jonnus, took the throne, the people he ruled didn't follow the Almighty as they once had. Few went to the meeting houses, and not everyone believed in the Almighty or remembered all the things He had done for them.

"One day, the high priest came to King Jonnus. 'I have had a vision from the Almighty of terrible times to come,' he told the king. The high priest and King Jonnus spent many days together talking about the vision and how best to protect the people.

"Now, the high priest wore a special breast piece over his sacred robes. It held twelve precious stones representing the tribes of the Almighty's chosen people." Mura made a circle with her first finger and thumb and put it over her other palm to show them the size of the stones. "Each of these Savior Stones, as they are now called, was different. They were very rare, and no two were alike. The high priest believed the only way to keep them safe until the time of trouble had passed was to remove them from the breast piece and give them to those the king trusted.

"There were six noble families who were descended from the first men to follow Liam long ago. Each of these families had two teenage children. King Jonnus called these twelve together Your mother, the king's daughter, was one of them, as was your father, the man she was promised to marry. All were faithful followers of the Almighty and righteous in their ways. Each swore a holy oath to protect the stone they were to be given. The high priest placed one of the Savior Stones into the right hand of each of these good people."

Mura sat straighter. Her smile grew. "Now, here's where things get interesting. No one knew what was going to happen next. But as each closed his or her hand around their stone, it vanished."

Cay gasped. "Where'd they go?"

"No one knew for a time, but soon they figured it out. The stones were within their right hands. And not only that, but in a short time, those who carried the stones were able to do amazing things. Fire would come from fingers; another saw visions of the future—"

"Or they moved things with their thoughts," Nat said.

"Or the earth and water listened to their wishes," Cay said.

Jer sunk his fingers deep into Soo's fur. "Or animals of all kinds obeyed them."

"Yes, each person was given a tiny characteristic of the Almighty. He gifted them with a little of His power."

"But we weren't one of the twelve given the stones." Nat shook her head.

Jer nodded. "Right, so how are we able to do these things?"

"It was five years before the terrible times came upon us. King Jonnus died. Thedo Brax stole his throne, then hunted and killed many of the nobles before they found out his plans to take the kingdom back to a time of idol worship. At first, Brax didn't know about the stones or their power. When a noble was killed, the Savior Stone was released from his or her hand and someone took it for safe keeping. Which brings the story to you three."

Chapter 43

Cay wiggled. Mura finally finished telling of the whole country's history, but when she came to how they received their powers, she stopped. Mura rose. "All this talking is making me thirsty. It has been so long." Again, her words sounded sad. "I'm just going to fill my cup again. I'll be right back." He was going to have to wait some more.

Beside Cay, Nat stared at her hand. She flipped it over to look at the back and then the palm and then back again. "There is no way there is a rock in there. Not as big as she says. I think we got our powers from our parents. I read in a book once that we can get things from our parents when we're born."

"You can read?" Cay stopped looking at his own hand to stare at her.

"Yes," she said with a sigh. "I suppose I can teach you if we end up staying together."

"I can read too," Jer said. "Nat, if we got our powers from our parents, how come we can't all do the same thing? Maybe you got Mother's power, but then we," he pointed to Cay with his thumb, "would have Father's ... so shouldn't we have the same ability?"

"Not every trait in the parent shows up in every child, but we can't have the stones." Nat sounded very sure of herself.

"Of course, you have the stones." Mura returned with her tall metal cup and sat with her legs crossed again. "Nataline, take a hold of Jeremicum's right wrist."

His sister sat up on her knees and reached across the circle they formed.

"Now, Jeremicum, take a hold of Calebus' right wrist."

The hold on Cay's arm wasn't hard when his brother's hand closed around his arm. Cay didn't get touched much on the farm unless it was for a beating. This felt good and weird at the same time.

"And Calebus, take Nataline's right wrist to close the circle."

As Cay's hand took hold of his sister's, warmth and the tingle that made the back of his hand itch filled his skin. It didn't take long until light grew and brightened under their skin. "Do you see that?"

The children gasped and struggled to keep their grip tight on the other.

"We have stones?" Cay said.

"The light looks like a symbol of some kind," Nat said.

"But they're all different." Cay's was blue. "Mine looks a little like a wave."

Nat's was more green than blue. Cay laughed. "It looks a little like a bunch of worms or snakes wiggling in a ball shape."

"Yuck!" Nat crinkled her nose. "Now I'm going to think of snakes every time I see it. Thanks for that."

Jer's was red.

"It *kind of* looks like an animal. Maybe a goat with a big curling horn," Nat said.

"It looks like a bird to me," Cay said.

"How'd we get them?" Jer finally released Cay to turn to Mura. Cay let go of Nat also. The glow in their hands faded until it disappeared.

"Those stones, recovered from the murdered nobles they were originally given to, came to your home. There your parents, as the highest-ranking family of the Truefaith line, decided who they could trust with the most precious treasures. The three stones you carry all arrived at the same time. Your parents and a couple of trusted friends were busy arguing about who would get them. You three had been playing in a nearby room and slipped out when your nanny fell asleep. You entered the room without anyone noticing. Then the stones were gone. It took almost a day before your parents figured out what had happened to the stones."

"Were our parents mad?" Cay asked. He hated to picture either his mother or father screaming or beating them like Kint.

Mura shook her head, looking at him. "Your mother cried for days."

Nat sighed. "Cried? She didn't want us to have powers like her?"

"She didn't care about the gifts that the stone would allow you, or the honor of the Almighty choosing you as worthy to carry the stones. By the time you had the stones, Brax knew about them and was hunting for them. Your mother and father were already in great danger. But with all of you carrying a stone, they knew you couldn't remain together any longer. You had to split up if there was any hope of survival. You were too young to protect yourselves from Brax's hunters." Mura's eyes closed for a moment, then she took a sip of her drink.

"Are they dead?" Jer twisted a thread from his pants around his finger and looked up at Mura.

"I really don't know. I think I would sense it if they died, but I haven't been able to feel them in years."

"What powers did our parents have?" Nat rubbed the back of her hand where the symbol had glowed.

Mura's smile grew so large, Cay smiled too. "Your mother was gifted with the Almighty's creativity. It didn't matter the medium: paint, wood, fabric, metal. She could take anything and make something beautiful. And given a problem, she could come up with an ingenious solution— for everything except how to stay with her precious children. It broke her heart to be separated from you. If you remember nothing else of this sad tale, remember that you were your parents' world, and they fought in every way they could not to be parted from you."

"What of Father?" Jer asked.

"Your father was gifted with the important ability to make the holy words of the Almighty understandable. He could read anything the Almighty had given to men and then share it with someone in a way that they could grasp."

Cay scooched closer to Mura and leaned against her. "What are we going to do now?"

Mura wrapped her arm around him and kissed the top of his head. "I wish I knew. I don't have the gift of prophecy; that stone was lost long ago. I fear bringing you together will only endanger you more, but you could no longer stay where you were. I have been praying for direction, but I don't have your father's ability to understand the leading of the Almighty. I can only promise you I will do everything in my power to protect you as long as we are together."

Nat crossed her arms, and her tone left no room for argument. "I'm not leaving them again. I have wanted a family—a place to belong—my entire life. There won't be any way to keep me away from them now."

Jer reached a hand to Nat and to Cay. "Together. Whatever comes next, we face it together."

"Together," they all said, holding hands.

Mura closed her eyes and bowed her head. "Good Father, watch over Your children. Protect them from the enemy, and hold them close in Your loving arms."

Chapter 44

The last two days—well, nights really—were the best Mura could remember having since she received her stone. The children's presence and being with them, even if they didn't know who she really was to them, made everything she'd suffered worth it. They had a chance to be who they really were. After she'd told them the story of how they got their stones, they'd gone to what remained of the gardens behind the house and practiced their unique abilities.

Mura laughed at the memory of Nataline trying to pick up a branch with her thoughts. It had been a little too heavy and long for her current skill level, but still it hovered over the ground and began to come to her.

It was at that moment that Calebus took her hand. Whether he thought to comfort her in her struggles or he intended to encourage her was unclear—but the effect was instantaneous. The branch flew at them.

Nataline ducked and screamed as it sailed over their heads and smashed into the house, showering Mura with bits of wood. Soo barked as though warning them of some attack. The flying branch gave the children the idea to link their hands and see if they could all do more. Somehow, with the stones linked, their abilities were stronger and more accurate. Calebus called water from the stream ten minutes from the house. Jeremicum had every woodland creature with in a league sitting at his feet. Nataline raised the fallen statue of a mother and child back to its pedestal. The figure had to weigh five times as much as she did.

It had been hard to get them to go to bed as the sun rose. But Mura needed to appear to be in her cell should Brax or the guards come for her. While the children slept, she opened her senses to any movement in the dungeon. Not even a meal was brought to her cell on the night before her scheduled execution.

When the sun set, they rose again, ate, and went out to practice in the overgrown garden.

"Mura, I think we should do more than practice our powers," Jeremicum said as they walked down the hall. "We need to know how to protect ourselves."

It was true, but if they thought they could fight, they'd try to stand against Brax's men. They'd have no chance against trained warriors. But then, she couldn't leave them defenseless either. She didn't know how much longer she'd be able to remain with them.

"I can teach Nat and Cay what Knob taught me."

Mura sat on a broken garden wall surrounded by torch light and considered them. "It is right that you should know a little to help you escape should Brax's men come for you. But you must also be smart. First, you cannot reveal to them that you have the stones. To use your abilities in front of them will make them hunt you relentlessly, and anyone who dares to aid you will be in danger as well. Also, your best option—for now—is escape. If you stop to fight, you will be outnumbered, and they will overpower you. You must remember that escape is always better then standing and fighting."

They agreed to her terms, and she watched Jeremicum train them. He took his time, gave clear directions, and remained patient in his expectations. He would make a very good leader one day.

Mura swiped at a tear even now as she lay on her bed. After training for several hours during the night, the children had grabbed some fruit and bread from the kitchen and headed up to their rooms.

A heaviness filled her. Whatever happened this day, their lives would never be the same. She didn't know how she knew that, but she did. Her palms were damp with sweat. Her heart pounded in her ears. She hadn't eaten much at sunset, but still her stomach rolled like she was on a ship in a wild storm at sea. "Almighty, You are in control of all that will happen this day and all the days to follow. May Your hand cover Nataline, Jeremicum, and Calebus. Fill them with Your strength, love, and truth. Help them return to their rightful place as leaders of this kingdom." Another tear slid from her eye back into her hair. "Please rescue them from my failures."

She loosed her spirit and gave it form and substance a hundred miles away just as the guards descended the stairs. Her plan was to go all the way to the execution. Make Brax believe was successful in killing her, and then return to the children. She would then find a place where he couldn't discover them until the time was right for them to return and challenge him.

With all the strength she could summon, she pushed her arms between two of the bars and made them as solid as if she were really in the cell. Though much stronger than when she'd escaped a week ago, when the shackles were placed around her wrists and ankles of her spirit form, it was all she could do to keep them there. A few steps out of the cell, the restraints fell to the floor.

Mura pushed a thought at the guards. *Nothing. You didn't hear a thing. This prisoner will be dead soon. What do noisy chains matter?*

They paused for a moment. The guard in front glanced down at her hands. She'd added the image of shackles to the illusion of herself in her old tattered gown and messy unwashed hair. Though she didn't really breathe in her spirit form, she held her imaginary breath. One moment. Two. Three.

The guard turned, and they continued until she stood before Brax. The guards left her a little distance from the bottom of the stairs where Brax sat on his bone throne. It still made her shudder—even in this form.

Mura was struck afresh at his pale skin and white hair. So much like an Albinus, and yet her mind would not accept that the Albinus could be a part of the Everblood line trying to take back the throne.

He stood, his smile large and mocking. Step by step he descended, drawing out his approach. She may not have the chains anymore, but holding her image in a solid form was still hard. *Let's get on with this already. I've had enough of you and want this to end as much as you want to put me to an end.*

She knew her thoughts would have no effect on him. They never did. His soul was too consumed with evil to be bent to her will.

Each clomp of his boot heel echoed off the tiles to the empty walls. *Clunk. Clunk. Clunk.* She would have sighed in exasperation if she could have. *Get on with it.*

He stopped in front of her, and his grin made her shiver. "You have to be the most stubborn woman—no person—I have ever met. I didn't ever think I could get you to …" He raised his gloved finger and waved it in front of her. "… but I am getting ahead of myself."

"What are you talking about?"

His hands went behind his back, and he started circling her. The sound of his slow pounding steps hit her like a hammer. "I knew you would never join me." He waited until he came in front of her again. "You are as good as old King Liam the Pure. I knew that the first time I laid eyes on you."

He walked another circle around her. "Oh sure, you were innocent, naïve even. Sheltered here as you were from all the evils of the world. Protected by the beliefs your family forced down everyone's throats for so many generations. Beliefs that kept you blind to my true intentions. But I also knew you were too righteous in mind to ever join me willingly. So, I made your life difficult. Locked you in your chambers." He halted before her again.

She'd stopped following his movements because his circling made her dizzy.

"But you never tried to escape. Moved you to the lowly servants' quarters, and still you remained—as though you believed you belonged there."

"We have been called to be servants of the Almighty," she said, though even in this form the voice she projected quaked.

Brax circled her again while he swatted her comment aside like an annoying fly. He pushed away the thought of serving anyone but himself. "I took away every comfort, nearly starved you, and locked you in the freezing dungeon." He stopped again to look her in the eyes. "You would not budge. I knew you were the key. But I couldn't just let you go. That would make you suspicious and you'd never go to them."

Every part of her—here before this terrifying man, and the part she'd left a hundred miles away in the run-down house outside Lost Worries—froze from head to toe.

"What are you talking about?"

Brax removed the glove from his right hand. A pink Savior Stone sat in an opening in his decaying flesh. It was held to his hand by a thin leather cord that laced in his skin and crossed over the stone. The bones of his hand were exposed, and the dead flesh around the open wound left black trails across his hand that snaked up his arm.

"Oh, it resists me. But with this stone of prophecy, you have finally led me right to them. Children. I would have never guessed."

Mura let go of her image, shrinking to a ball of light.

Brax screamed as her spirit surrounded the stolen stone strapped to his hand and wrenched it free.

Only one thought filled her.

RUN!

Chapter 45

Cay eased his door open. He was supposed to be in bed, but the sun was up. He had a brother and a sister. He'd escaped Kint's farm and had clean clothes and food. And he had special powers given to him by the Almighty because of a stone hidden somewhere in his hand. Who could sleep with all that? Not him. Besides, there was food downstairs, and though he'd eaten more in the last few days than he had in the last year, he was hungry.

He tip-toed toward Jer's door, trying to avoid the many creaky boards, but he froze as his big brother's door cracked open. Jer grinned at him as Soo strolled out, her long bushy tail swinging in slow waves.

"Looks like none of us can sleep." Nat leaned against her doorframe.

"If we're quiet, maybe Mura won't send us back to bed," Jer said.

Cay kept his mouth closed. It didn't matter. Mura would know. She always did. But maybe, if they were lucky, this time she wouldn't care. "I'm hungry. I want one of those fruit thingies."

They walked to the top of the stairs. "You mean the berries? Red or black?" Jer said, taking the lead with Soo.

"No, the round things that are brown on the bottom, kind of like a meat pie, but filled with fruit on the inside," Cay said.

"Mura called them tarts, I think," Jer said.

"That's a dumb name. They're super sweet." Cay really didn't care what they were called; he only hoped there were some left.

As they reached the bottom of the stairs, a low rumble outside vibrated the boards beneath their feet and drew their attention toward the front door. Soo's ears went back, and an intense growl came from deep in her throat. The hairs on Cay's arm stood like dried corn stalks. The noise outside grew louder. Soon the neighing of horses and the shouts of men added to the clatter. Soo looked down the back hall and barked repeatedly.

RUN!

Cay winced at the scream in his head. Nat and Jer must have heard it, too, because one groaned and the other made a whistling sound.

Before they could run down the back hall to follow Soo out into the garden they'd practiced in, steps pounded up the front of the house and shouts came from the back.

Jer's arms went out protectively in front of Nat and Cay. He stepped backward and pulled them into the shadows under the stairs. The front door crashed open. Crouched low behind his brother, Cay could see the tops of helmets over the center landing.

Steps thundered down the stairs overhead. They went silent for a moment as Mura leapt down the last few steps of the upper stairs, landed near the railing in the middle, vaulted over it to the floor, and landed on one knee. Her partial skirt flew out behind her like a cape in a strong wind. When Mura stood, Cay saw she had a short sword in each hand. The weapons whirled as she cut down each approaching solider.

Soo's barks and snarls came from the back of the house. "Be careful, girl," Jer whispered as he rose up on his knees. He turned and looked at each of them. "The way is blocked out front and in the back. Mura's good, but there's too many of them."

Nat inched behind Jer and Cay to get a better view while she still staying in the shadows of the stairs. Soon a loose pole from the stair's railing flew through the air and whacked one of the soldiers in the face.

His nose bled, and he slowed down long enough for Mura to end him. Next, the post jabbed another soldier in the gut, doubling him over. Nat used anything she could pick up with her mind to hit the attackers as fast and often as she could in order to distract them.

"That's a good idea." Cay yanked up a broken piece of floorboard and reached down until he touched the dirt under the house. Soon mounds of soil exploded near the front door under the warriors who kept pouring in. They were thrown off balance, and many were knocked off their feet.

"Thanks," Jer said. A wave of snakes and scorpions scrambled through the holes Cay's dirt created to bite and sting those trying to stand.

A garbled roar of a big animal—or maybe two—added to Soo's snarling and barking at the back of the house, followed by multiple screams. The house shook violently. A roar followed that made Cay shudder. Men and horses at the front of the house yelled and cried. The weird caw-roar added to the noise. Then, like a gong being silenced, the sounds outside fell quiet.

A blast of fire lit the room. Another soldier stomped between the mounds of earth and screaming men, his empty hand raised toward Mura. He wore no helmet, and his black hair blew behind him he walked so fast. Fire came from his dark-skinned hand. It had to be a Savior Stone, but clearly he was not on their side.

"Cay, if I can get the pitcher of water we use to wash, can you make the water put out those flames?" Nat inched farther out from under the upper stairs to see into the washroom.

"Yeah." He took her hand to help her lift the heavy jug.

Jer moved in front of them and drew his knife. So far, no soldiers had gotten past Mura. He stood guard all the same.

The pitcher floated through the air toward Mura as she backed away from the flames. The heat grew in intensity. Though she fought with two swords, Mura didn't have a shield to protect herself. She tried to use the blades, but the fire was too powerful. Still holding Nat's hand, Cay called the water out of the jug. It flew out of the pitcher and surrounded the fire-throwing hand. It stayed there like a mitten, putting the flames out and not letting them start again.

Mura lunged forward and cut off the hand. It dropped with a thud as the water splashed on the floor. She stepped over it and thrust her sword at the soldier hugging his injured arm. As the man fell, Mura back kicked the hand. It slid and stopped in front of Cay's knees.

"That's disgusting." Nat wrinkled her nose and covered her mouth.

She was right. The dull orange stone stuck out of the exposed bones. It had been sewn in place, but many of the stitches had pulled free of the rotting dark skin. The smell made Cay's stomach wobble.

Jer reached for it with one hand, his knife open in the other to cut the stone free.

"Don't touch it." Nat put her hand over Jer's. "I don't know if we can carry two stones, but I don't think we should chance it."

"We can't leave it, but I'm not touching that dead thing." Jer grimaced.

"Here." She pulled up the edge of her skirt, revealing another white one underneath. "Cut a little off my petticoat."

Cay had never heard of such a thing before, but he watched as Jer used his knife to free a chunk of fabric. Then he cut the last of the string holding the stone to the dead hand. The rock floated up and Nat wrapped it in the bit of cloth, then put in it her pocket.

The room went silent. Cay jerked his head up. Only Mura stood. She didn't move as she faced the front door and all the bodies of the soldiers. Why didn't she move? Turn? Look at them and see if they were all right?

Her swords clattered to the floor, startling Cay. Nat jerked beside him too. Mura swayed and dropped to her knees. Jer raced to her side and caught her before she fell on her face.

Chapter 46

Nat ran to Mura's side as Jer laid her down in front of the stairs. Her dress was blackened in places and some of the buttons were melted. A large gash in her side oozed blood. Nat bunched up some of Mura's skirt and pressed it against the wound. Mura squeezed her eyes closed and gasped.

"Failed you again. I'm so sorry, so very, very sorry," Mura mumbled. "Can't get it right." Her head tossed from side to side.

Nat wanted to cry. It sounded like Mura was dying and leaving them alone.

Cay held her hand as he sat on her other side next to Jer. "You're going to be all right. We can go get—"

"No!" Mura took a couple of deep breaths. "Jeremicum, you need to summon your guardian and teach Nataline and Calebus to call theirs." She pushed a pink stone into Nat's hand.

"Guardians?" Jer and Nat said at the same time.

"The Almighty has sent powerful beings to watch over you. But they are fearsome and frightening." Mura wheezed and coughed. "They will come in a form that you can recognize—as animals. Jer, you have felt yours near. And all of you have heard them recently. But now you need them. They will take you to safety." Mura's words slowed as her gasped for breath grew more frequent.

"I'm staying with you. You've always kept me safe." Cay held her hand to his chest. Clearly Mura and Cay had a special bond that Nat never had with her.

Again, Mura's head shook. "I have failed you again and again. You're better off—"

"I'm not leaving you," Cay insisted.

"Jeremicum, go outside and call to the one you have sensed." She stared at Jer until he stood and walked past the bodies and mounds of dirt and disappeared out the broken doors.

Mura's eyes closed. She fought for each breath. It wouldn't be long before she used her mind to make Nat and Cay leave too. Nat pushed the new stone in her pocket with the other one.

"I think we can help her," Nat whispered as quietly as she could. "I know of something—"

"How? What?" Cay whispered back.

"I read it—"

Cay raised up some on his knees. "Do it."

Nat pulled the stone they'd cut from the dark-skinned hand out of her skirt pocket and held it out to him as she continued to press Mura's skirt into her side. It filled with blood. "Can you use your power to make this glow hot? No flames, just super hot?"

Cay pulled back some of the fabric covering the dull orange stone and touched it with the tip of his finger. He looked up at her and smiled. "The stone will do what I ask."

Nat made the stone float in the air and had it hover over Mura's wound a little above Nat's hand. The rock began to glow, turning darker, then red-orange like a hot coal, and finally almost white. The back of Nat's hand felt like she'd moved too close to the stove.

Nat held the stone there as she pulled the skirt away and, using both hands, made the tear in Mura's dress larger. Then she forced the glowing stone into Mura's bleeding wound.

Mura's back rose off the floor. Her mouth opened in a scream, but it was drowned out by a terrifying roar that shook the house.

Nat and Cay looked toward the door. Soo's bark sounded odd.

Finally, Jer's voice floated into the room. "You guys have to come out here. You're never going to believe this!"

Nat turned back to Mura. She continued to breathe. Then Nat made the stone float out and scanned the wound. The bleeding had stopped.

"I'm not leaving her." Cay sat with his arms crossed.

"I don't intend to either, but she has to get out of this house. Clearly the king knows where we are now." Nat stood and stepped to the top of Mura's head. The stone, though still warm, had cooled enough to put back in the cloth and in her pocket with the one Mura had given her. "Let's hope these guardians can carry her."

Nat reached under Mura's arms and, with her physical strength and powers, lifted Mura part way off the floor. "Can you hold her feet?"

Cay picked up one of Mura's ankles in each hand, and they lifted her enough to carry her. Still, they were kids, and Mura was a grown woman. Nat walked backward, trying not to trip over the many obstacles or to look at all the dead men.

They made it out onto the porch when Cay's eyes grew huge and he nearly dropped Mura's feet. Nat glanced over her shoulder and almost dropped her too.

Chapter 47

Jer had left the house partly because of Mura pushing his mind and partly because he knew that she had been right—they needed to get out of this place before any more of the king's men showed up. Mura wasn't able to fight for them now since she was hurt, and even with their powers, he and his brother and sister could never fight a group of soldiers. But mostly he went outside to call his guardian because he was curious. What was this creature sent by the Almighty to protect them that would be so scary it would come in a different form?

Soo trotted up to him from the back of the house, her tail wagged but her mouth and fur splattered with blood. She'd fought hard to protect them too. Jer patted her head. "Thanks, girl."

Jer closed his eyes and searched for the one being that had been on the edge of his awareness for at least a couple of weeks. It wasn't an animal, as it seemed to understand him better than creatures did, but it wasn't like talking to a person either. "Are you there?" he whispered. "We're in trouble. We need your help."

Jer stepped back as a huge gust of wind slammed against him. He shielded his face from the little bits of rock and wood that hit him. Soo barked a warning—deep and loud. Something landed hard. Jer took another step to keep his balance. When he opened his eyes, all he saw was a massive post of red scales. They reflected the late morning light and ranged in shade from the color of lips to the color of blood. Claws, longer than his hand, stuck out on one side.

Jer's gaze rose up the tree-trunk sized leg to the shoulder and across the spine-spikes down the back. Soo's barks were frantic. The red-scaled neck bent, and a massive head topped with horns, wide ears, and large purple eyes lowered. A puff of smoke eased from the nostrils and blew over Jer. It smelled like the forger's coal fire.

"You're a … a …"

"Hello, Jeremicum." A gentle female voice washed across his skin. Was that a smile through her rows of long jagged teeth?

"You're a dragon," Jer finally managed to say.

"I am one of the Almighty's host. I go where He sends to do His will."

"But you look like a dragon." Jer reached a shaky hand toward the spot on the upper lip between the nostrils.

The dragon pushed her head forward so they connected. Then she raised her head and roared a laugh before lowering it and looking at him again. "Yes, I do appear as a dragon most of the time."

Jer never took his eyes off her as he shouted over his shoulder. "You guys have to come out here. You're never going to believe this!" His hand rubbed up her snout. "*I* don't believe this."

"My name is Layla. I am your guardian, Jeremicum."

"Layla." Again, it looked as if the huge dragon smiled.

Layla turned her head away from his hand and looked toward the door. Nat and Cay were carrying Mura from the house.

Both of them nearly dropped her when they saw the huge dragon towering over the broken fountain.

"Layla, can you help her?"

A pure white winged horse landed close to the porch.

"Peryum is Mura's guardian. He will carry her, but I can help." On steps that seemed far too gentle and quiet for such a large being, Layla eased toward the front of the house. She reached out a front foot, picked up Mura in her claws, and gently placed her on her stomach on the back of the winged horse.

"A dragon and a pegasus. That's amazing." Nat said.

"How do you know about these things?" Cay said.

"Late at night, while everyone slept, I'd sneak downstairs to the library and escape from my troubles in books."

Jer brushed some of Mura's hair that had come out of her braid away from her face. "How is she?"

Nat came down the stairs to stand beside him. "The bleeding has stopped, but she hasn't woken up again."

"The Almighty assures me, she will live. You still have need of her, and there are things she still must learn yet," the dragon said as she pulled back to the other side of the fountain.

"She can talk." Cay stared at the dragon with his mouth open.

"My guardian's name is Layla," Jer said. He stood with shoulders back and chest puffed. As Nat understood it, the guardians were assigned to them. It wasn't as if Jer had called a dragon with his power.

"Jeremicum, you must instruct the others how to call their guardians. More soldiers will be arriving soon." Peryum pawed the ground with one hoof, his deep voice vibrated in Nat's chest.

Cay took a step back and looked at Peryum. "The pega … The pearaga … The horse with wing—he talks too."

Jer ignored him and pulled Nat by the wrist into the opening between the guardians. "Close your eyes." She obeyed immediately. It would not be good to be here when more of Brax's men showed up. "Now, Nat, there have been strange sounds or noises lately. They've been close enough you could almost feel them." Nat nodded. "That is your guardian. Tell her that you need help and to come."

"Please, can you help us?" Nat whispered.

"Whoa," Cay called. "What is *that?*"

Nat looked, and for once, she didn't know the answer. It reminded her of a drawing of a lion she'd seen once in a book. But it stood taller than the pegasus, and it had two heads. One had a full mane like a lion. The other was orange with back stripes. A tiger, she realized as she walked closer. She'd never seen anything with two heads. The body had solid-colored places like a lion with striped spots in others. Two wings came from its shoulders, and the tail curled over its back was shinny black with a stinger on the end. A scorpion's tail … on a big two-headed cat with wings.

"A rare guardian indeed. You should be very honored, Nataline," the dragon said. "Your guardian is a chimera."

Nat took slow careful steps toward the front of the large animal. The two heads bowed as the body stretched both paws out far in front and the rump went in the air.

"Jab" the lion head said in a deep male voice.

"Ril," the tiger head said with a voice a higher male voice.

"At your," the lion said.

"Service," the tiger concluded.

"That may take a little getting used to." Nat smiled.

"We are—" The lion tipped his head and raised his nose.

"A bit of—" The tiger shook his head, and a ripple went down the spine to the tail.

"An acquired taste," the lion concluded.

"I think you're beautiful." Nat reached out to touch the outer cheek of both heads.

The left paw reached forward and pulled Nat close as each head leaned against her in an odd hug.

Jer moved closer to Mura. "What'd she say?"

Nat pulled free of JabRil and returned to Mura's side.

"Jer-emi-icum, you must take them." Mura gasped for breath. "Black

Rock Outpost. You must go. Now."

Cay stepped away from the others and closed his eyes. "I'll call my guardian." He tried to think of what he'd heard. Nothing came at first, then he remembered the wind and the caw-roar. "Please, come help us."

A gust of wind washed over him, and Cay opened his eyes to see a bird nearly as tall as Nat's two-headed cat thing. The large bird-thing was covered in red and orange feathers with a tail as long as Jer's dragon. Cay couldn't tell if each feather was flame or had a bit of flame coming from under it. But no heat came from the bird.

"My name is Asheal," she said.

"A phoenix, another rare guardian," Layla said.

Cay wasted no time. He ran to Asheal. "May I ride on your back?"

"Of course, I am here for you."

"I'll meet you at Black Rock," Cay told his brother and sister. "I hafta do something first."

"Cay, you can't—" Jer tried to stop them.

"Let's go, Asheal." They lifted into the air on the phoenix's powerful wings, and the ground quickly disappeared.

"Go with him, Jere-micum," Mura stammered. "Keep him safe."

"Come on, Soo." Jer ran up Layla's foreleg and settled at the base of her neck. Layla picked up the dog when she wouldn't come any closer and set her near Jer.

As Layla stretched out her wings, Jer turned to Nat. "Watch Mura and I'll see you at Black Rock soon."

Chapter 48

Layla shot into the sky and flashed through the clouds. Soo buried her face against Jer as he fought to keep one arm around the large dog and the other tightly gripped to a spine spike. They continued to climb, and the world below that he could see between the clouds, blurred and started to spin.

They came alongside Cay and his phoenix. "Where do you think you are going?" Jer shouted, but the wind stole the little air that fueled his words.

Layla said something to Asheal in a language Jer couldn't understand. But it could have been that he was just too tired. Maybe if he leaned his head against Soo for a moment. Soo had become heavy in his lap.

Layla roared, but Jer could barely lift his head. The air rushed by. They descended fast. His breathing came easier, and the fog that had filled his head cleared. Soo snuggled against him. Cay sat up from lying along Asheal's back.

"Forgive me," the phoenix said.

Jer shook the last of the fog from his head. "What happened?"

"Asheal has only recently become a guardian. Most of the time we fly high above the world and even return to the Almighty's throne frequently. As the Almighty's host, we do not need air in the same way that humans do. Up as high as we were just flying there is little air, not enough for what you three need to survive." Layla took the lead as she swooped in front of Asheal.

"I had been given proper instruction, but in my excitement for my first mission with a real human, I forgot. Again, I am sorry." Asheal spoke quietly.

"We seem to be all right." Jer patted Soo, who kept her face hidden but relaxed in front of him. "Cay, where are we going?"

"I left her behind."

"Who?"

"Lor. She looked out for me, made sure I was safe and that none of the bigger kids or Kint hurt me as often. I didn't want to leave her behind all alone. Mura said we'd go back for her as soon as we could."

Cay and Asheal surged forward. They swooped lower over a farm with a house, barn, other structures, and lots of green fields.

Layla circled over the same property. "I can't land without destroying some of the crops or being seen."

Jer scanned the ground for a clearing. "Is seeing a guardian bad?"

Layla made a third circle over the farm. "We try to stay out of sight as much as possible, but as there are legends of our kind all over the world, you can see that we aren't always successful in that."

Cay pointed and said something that Jer couldn't hear from this distance. Jer's gaze followed where his brother indicated, and he saw a girl working in the fields. They flew too high for her to notice them yet. Asheal descended toward a clump of trees not far from the girl.

"What about the stream? Could you land there? It seems to be free of trees, and I need to wash Soo before she terrifies Cay's friend."

"Exactly what I was thinking. We will make a good team, Jeremicum." Layla turned toward the ribbon of water on the far edge of the farm.

Jer glanced at his clothes as he slid down her front leg. He splashed into the knee-deep water. Because Soo had lain against him during their flight, his shirt and the front of his pants were now smeared with blood. "Great." He undid some of the buttons and pulled his shirt off. Goosebumps rose all over his skin. Jer pushed the shirt under the water and rubbed it. A few of the stains came out, though not many.

Layla moved above him, blocking the sun's warmth. Her front foot reached back to him a few moments later. A piece of root was stuck on her claw, the same type of root they'd washed with before meals.

"Thanks." Jer took it, broke it up some more, and mashed it into the stains on his clothes. He rinsed off the shirt and splashed his legs, shivering again. He repeated the process a couple of times before placing the shirt on a rock on the bank and coaxing Soo to come down. It didn't take as long to clean her fur as it did his clothes, but when Jer climbed up onto the side of the stream, his shirt was almost dry.

A blast of hot air nearly knocked him off his feet. Layla raised her head and smiled again. He and Soo were dry.

The tall plants behind him rustled. Jer whirled around. A badger, two rabbits, and bunch of birds lined the edge of the field. "I didn't call you. What are you doing here?" The animals just sat and stared at him.

"Your ability is already growing stronger. You have yet to know what you are capable of, Jeremicum."

Jer turned back to the creatures. "Can you lead me to Cay and Lor without being seen by the farmer?" Each animal turned and headed into the field. Jer grabbed his shirt, yanked it over his head, and followed.

Chapter 49

Asheal landed near some trees behind the pile of rocks Cay once helped remove from the fields. He jumped down. "I'm going to go get Lor. Can you carry us both?"

"Possibly, but Layla would be able to without any problem."

Cay nodded and turned, took a step, and spun around again. "How long have you been my guardian?"

"Since your first breath." Asheal's voice sounded like a song. It danced in his ears and somehow calmed him.

"Then why'd I get beaten so much? Why didn't you save me? I needed help."

The large phoenix rested on the ground like a hen on a nest. Her long neck lowered so she could look Cay in the eyes. "Of course, I knew, Calebus, as did the Almighty. You have never been alone. Yes, you did suffer a little, but what you didn't see is all the times you weren't hurt. All the times the Almighty sent me to protect you. The times I knocked over milk jugs in Kint's wagon as he neared town, slowing him down so he couldn't return and beat any of you before you were tucked away sleeping. Or times I entered his home and kept him from leaving. The times I made him so sick he stayed in bed so you could heal. So many times, my sweet Calebus, too many to count."

Asheal brushed her head up his arm, then raised it to look at him again. "The Almighty has His own reasons for requesting that you remain here for the time you did. It may have been to teach you to care for others as fiercely as you do. Such a deep concern for your friend's welfare that you would risk your own safety to rescue her could never have been developed had you not suffered the hardships you did here on this farm. The Almighty wastes no moment as He grows His children."

Cay didn't get angry often. But the more he thought about this, and the more Asheal explained, the more he tightened his closed fists. In fact, all his muscles were tight, and heat filled his chest. "And it was the same for Nat and Jer? The Almighty wanted us to suffer to teach us things?"

Asheal's head rose high, and she stared down at him. "Never accuse the good and holy Creator of everything of doing evil, Calebus. All He does is right and good. But this world is infected with a sickness, the wickedness of the evil one. If he had his way, you would have died years ago and never been able to do the glorious works that are to come. The Almighty has a plan for you, Calebus, and Nataline, Jeremicum, Mura, and so many others. They are plans for good and not for disaster, to give you a future and a hope. And not just for you, but He plans to fill this entire kingdom with that same hope and to have their futures restored because of you and your family, Calebus. You must only trust the Almighty and follow His will."

Cay stared at the bird covered in flames that didn't burn him. Some powerful being created him yet allowed evil to wreck his life. A powerful guardian had been sent to watch over and protect him from everything, yet he still got hurt, didn't have enough to eat most days, and remained separated from his family and their love. This all-powerful Creator, let him endure pain so that he could learn to help and care for others? If the Almighty was indeed *all* mighty, couldn't He just wipe out Thedo Brax and all the evil?

Asheal lowered her head again. "May I ask you a question?"

Cay sighed and stuffed his fists in his pockets. "I guess." Mura said the same thing to him many times, and it always meant he would learn he was wrong. He hated that, but he hated feeling this anger too. He wanted to understand.

"Does Lor care about you?"

"Yes."

"Why?"

"Because we look out for each other. I've always had her back, and she has always had mine."

"Did you make her do that?"

"No." That was a dumb question. "Nobody can make another do things."

"Kint made you work long hard days."

Cay sighed again. "But not so we would like him. He only wants the work done. Kint doesn't care if we like him."

"But what if he demanded that you love him like a father even though he treated you that way? What if, when you refused, he hurt you even more until you loved him?"

"I couldn't ever love someone like that. You can't make someone love you."

"The Almighty could. He could have made everyone believe in Him and love Him. Wouldn't the world be better then?"

Cay's head hurt. It seemed like that would have been better—no evil in the world. No one hurting anyone else, no men stealing thrones, no one taken from their families—but Cay knew somehow it wouldn't be better. "But that wouldn't be fair. Or maybe it wouldn't be kind. I don't know … but it doesn't sound like the right thing to do."

"If you had forced Lor to care about you, would you try to save her now?"

Cay stopped to think about that one. If he'd made Lor protect him and watch out for him, and she hadn't done it because she wanted to, would it be important to him to help her now? Lor mattered because, out of all the kids on the farm, she had *chosen* to watch out for him. That made a difference. "No," Cay finally said.

"The Almighty felt the same. He didn't want all of mankind forced to follow Him. He wants everyone to choose to love and obey Him. So, the Creator of all things gave mankind that freedom. But many don't choose Him. They follow their own wicked hearts, and others get hurt. Like you. Like your brother and sister. Like Lor. The Almighty doesn't want your pain. He's not pleased because of it. It breaks His heart. He wants everyone to willingly choose to follow Him."

Cay needed time to think about it more, but right now he needed to get Lor before any of them were spotted. Surely a phoenix and a dragon would be noticed soon.

He turned and crept along the edge of the millet field, his head pounding with all the information Asheal had told him. The plants were almost done blooming, but already his eyes watered, his skin itched, and his nose tickled.

Lor had been near the middle of the field when he landed. Her head popped up on the far side as she moved between the next rows to remove weeds and check for bugs. She worked toward him in the thin space between the plants, choosing to crawl rather than bend over and hurt her back and legs.

Cay sat close to the edge without entering the field that made him feel terrible. He watched her draw closer. He gave a low whistle when she passed the midway point. He tried again when she neared.

Finally, she looked up. She stared at him for a moment but didn't move. Then she shook her head and rubbed her eyes.

"It's me," he whispered.

She got up and, staying low enough not to be seen over the tall stalks, raced to him. "Where have you been? You left me here all alone. Do you know what happened when Kint found out you were gone?" Her words were cross. She usually only sounded like that when she talked to the troublemakers like Wart.

"I'm so sorry. I wanted to come get you, but Wart beat me up in the corn by the stream. I couldn't come back *and* get away. I didn't want to leave without you. Really, I didn't. But I'm back now. I came back to take you away too."

"I can't leave. He'll catch me—and you too. He has guards now. If I step off the property, they'll see me, and Kint has promised to kill anyone who tries."

"I can get you out, I promise. Trust me."

"You can't. You're stuck here now too."

"I have a way."

She sat back on her heels and stared. A rustle came through the thick millet, and Lor covered her mouth with to silence her scream.

A badger waddled toward them. Then a bunny hopped nearby. The noise grew, and Soo pushed through, came to Cay, and licked his face. Cay hadn't made friends with animals, not even dogs, before Soo. Lor had been bitten once by a dog Kint kept to guard the property, so she backed away from Soo. Cay was getting used to this huge creature, but it still made him jump to have her big tongue slide up his face.

Cay pushed her nose away and wiped off the slobber as Jer appeared.

"Lor says there're guards. I didn't see any. Did you?"

"We ended up at the stream. Nothing there."

"Who are you?" Lor hissed. "How come the guards didn't catch you?"

Jer turned to her. "We have some … *interesting* transportation." He reached out his hand toward her. "I'm Jer. You must be Lor."

She backed away from him too.

"Nice to meet you." Jer put his hand at his side and turned back to Cay. "We need to get going. We have to meet up with Nat and Mura."

"Asheal said it would be better if Lor went with you and Layla."

Jer looked at the girl for a moment. "If you trust her, I will too.

Where are we taking her?"

"I think I know someone who can help." Cay got to his feet and brushed off his pants.

Several chattering birds flew by them. Jer watched them closely. "We have to go. Someone's coming."

Lor still sat on the edge of the field, arms crossed. "Who are you?"

Cay stepped in front of her and braced his hands on his knees. "Lor, this is my brother. Now, we have to go. I'll try to explain later." He reached his hand for her, but she didn't take it.

"Brother?"

Cay took a hold of her shoulders. "You looked after me. Let me look after you now. I *can* get you out of here. But Jer can't carry you. Come on, please, Lor?"

A loud male voice came from the front of the millet field. "You nasty varmint. What are you doing in my field? Get."

Lor and Cay looked at each other. "We have to go now." Cay's words barely made a sound.

She nodded once.

"Go with Jer. I can't go through the millet. Remember it makes me itch and sneeze. Kint'll hear us. Asheal and we'll meet at the stream."

Jer, Soo, and Lor raced through the millet. They stayed out of sight as Cay darted across the path and behind a bush on the other side.

Kint yelled at whichever animal Jer had sent to distract him— possibly the badger, since it had disappeared. Cay crawled toward where his guardian waited.

"Girl? Where are you? You had better be working this field or so help me …" Kint's voice was so close, Cay froze. He didn't want to make any noise that would get him caught.

"GIRL!"

Cay couldn't breathe.

Asheal roared.

Chapter 50

Lor followed Jer back the way he came. Of course, he only knew where to go because the two rabbits led the way through the tall thick growth that looked like overgrown grass. Cay had called it millet—whatever that was.

"You're going to get us both killed," Lor hissed. "Can't you hear Kint yelling for me? If I don't show up soon, all the guards are going to be in this field hunting us down." She stopped and turned back toward the farmer. "Tell Cay thanks and all—"

Jer grabbed her arm. Soo blocked her path. She tried to jerk free. Jer held her tight, but not enough to hurt her. "My little brother cares enough about you to leave our sister and me behind to come rescue you. We've got men chasing us, and he insisted on coming here to get you rather than going someplace safe. Are you really going to turn your back on everything he's done?"

"I don't want to die." Tears filled her eyes.

Asheal let out an odd combination of a roar and bird's caw. The farmer stopped yelling. Jer thought a shadow passed over, but he couldn't see the phoenix. A shimmer slid through the sky just above the millet field. Lor didn't seem to notice any of it.

"Come on, while that man's distracted." Jer pulled her.

Lor followed, reluctantly. "Distracted? By what?"

"Those who are helping us." They crossed a path and entered another field. The tall stalks had fat leaves and ovals with feather-like ends growing from the tops. "The stream is on the other side."

"I've lived on this farm almost all my life. I know the stream is on the other side of the corn."

Jer stopped before they reached the stream. "My friend is going to take us away from here. Don't be frightened. She's here to help."

"What does that mean?"

Jer stepped through the plants. He couldn't see Layla, though he felt her presence. The light shimmered, and he could vaguely make out her shape. "Layla?"

"I'm here, Jeremicum."

"Who are you talking to?" Lor pulled her hand free and stood still.

"Asheal thought you could carry us better."

"Yes, I am aware. The girl will be frightened," the dragon warned, "so be prepared."

Jer stepped behind Lor, who was a little shorter than him.

Layla slowly faded into view. "She is going to scream," Layla said.

Jer covered Lor's mouth and held her tight. "I told you not to be afraid. She won't hurt us."

Layla's head rose. She leapt from the water, snatching Jer and Lor in one foot and Soo in the other. They shot up so fast Jer closed his eyes against the wind that brought streams of tears. Lor went limp against him.

"Are you two all right?" Layla looked down at them.

"I think she fainted, but otherwise we're fine."

Cay and Asheal came alongside them. "Is she—?"

"We're fine. Now where are we taking her? She can't come with us. It will be too dangerous."

"Asheal do you know Gan-Nonin?"

The phoenix looked to the dragon, and they turned right over the fields. A few minutes later, they landed on the edge of another farm. This one had skinny plants held up with sticks and string. Some had pink flowers while others bloomed purple. This field would be much harder to hide in. The other fields nearer the house weren't even knee high.

Jer lowered Lor to the ground. She moaned and stirred. "Cay, I don't know about this."

"I know the boy who lives here. He helped me get away from Kint and get to you. Watch her, and I'll be right back." Cay ran to the house.

Asheal and Layla faded into shimmers of light again. That was probably for the best, since Lor's eyes were opening.

She squirmed away from him. "What? What just happened? I saw a … What was that thing?" Her head swiveled from side to side. "Where are we?"

Jer stood and offered her a hand. "Away from that place. Hopefully were someplace safe now."

She didn't take his offered help, but instead climbed to her feet on her own. They walked toward a corral near the house where a gray-haired man pointed Cay toward the barn. They caught up with him just as he entered.

"Gan-Nonin?"

"That's me? What can I do you for—Oh, hey kid, how are you? Got to where you were going all right?" His brows scrunched up, but he never slowed down his words. "Whatcha doin' back here? I thought you were runnin' away from some place nearby. Thought it wasn't safe to come back and all." He glanced up. "Hey, you brought friends with you." He waved. "Ma can fix us some lunch if you're hungry—not much, mind you, but it will stop the ache in the belly. Why don't we—"

"Excuse me," Jer interrupted him. "I don't mean to be rude, but we need your help."

"Of course, of course. Whatever I can do. Happy to help."

It would be immensely helpful if he would close his mouth. Jer didn't say that—as much as he wanted to. "Cay?"

Cay pointed to the girl. "Gan-Nonin, this is my really good friend Lor."

"Nice to meet you. Always nice to meet a friend of a friend. Makes us all closer, don't you think? Any friend of the kid's is a friend of mine. I always say—"

A lot! Jer shoved Cay in the shoulder.

"Lor needs someplace safe to stay. She is a hard worker who can help—if she is treated kindly."

Gan-Nonin stepped forward and put his hand on Lor's back as he turned her around. They stepped out of the barn. Jer and Cay followed. "You know, Da just hurt his back. I've been trying to do all his work and mine too. I could really use some help. You came at just the right time and all. Harvest will be coming in soon—another month maybe. But there is still so much to do now." Gan-Nonin led Lor to the house forgetting about the brothers behind them. "Ma has an old dress that might fit you better than whatcha got now. We'll get you somethin' to eat and then maybe you can give me a hand later." He pushed open the door. "Ma, guess what? We've got some help around the farm …" He kept talking as Lor glanced back over her shoulder at Cay.

"He's a good guy. You'll be safe here," Cay assured her before the door closed in their faces.

"Come on. We have to meet up with Nat and see how Mura is doing."

They returned to their guardians and were back in the air within moments. Cay called to Jer, "We need to go back to the house and grab Mura's weapons. I forgot them."

Jer shook his head. "More of Brax's men were on the way. It won't be safe."

"Asheal and I will fly over and make sure no one is around. You and Layla can guard us from above. It will only take me a second."

"Only if it is clear of soldiers." Jer didn't like the idea, but Cay was right. Mura may not be able to fight at this moment, but that wouldn't always be the case. She'd need her weapons at some point.

Chapter 51

After Nat watched Jer's red dragon streak after Cay and his flaming phoenix, she paced for several moments. Mura was unconscious again, still laid on the pegaus' back where Layla had put her. "Is it safe to move her? Should I ride with her?"

Peryum, Mura's pegasus, pawed the ground again. "I won't let her fall. I give you my word."

Nat walked toward JabRil. The only animals she'd ever been around before meeting her brother and his big dog were rats. She didn't care for them. They nibbled on her toes when she slept and made holes in her blanket. Here, she stood in front of a two-headed, flying cat with a scorpion's tail about to climb on his back and soar through the air. She didn't like heights and had always tried to get one of the other girls to climb the ladder to clean the webs out of the corners at the ceiling.

JabRil nuzzled against her with his heads.

"I won't—"

"Let any—"

"Thing—"

"Happen—"

"To you—"

"Either."

"You can—"

"Trust me."

Nat took a deep breath and nodded. She moved to JabRil's side. He lowered his front allowing her to climb on behind his wings. "Where do

I hang on?"

"You can—"

"Lay—"

"Down—"

"Like Mura—"

"Between—"

"My—"

"Wings—"

"But you—"

"Will be—"

"Safe—"

"If you—"

"Choose to—"

"Sit up."

Nat decided she liked the idea of lying down with her face buried in his soft fur better. The striped spots had longer fur. She'd never felt anything so soft. The tan lion areas were dense, thick, and fuzzy. They tickled her palm as her hand ran over him, but she gripped his fur anyway.

His wings stretched out, and the muscles in his back rippled under her. She held her breath as JabRil ran a few steps, his wings beating hard. Then only his wings moved as air brushed against her skin. Nat dared turn her head and saw Peryum flying beside them with Mura securely on his back. Tufts of white passed between them. Nat squeezed her eyes closed. She was in the clouds. That was too high. Entirely too high.

"Peace—"

"My sweet—"

"Girl—"

"I will—"

"Not—"

"Drop you."

Nat tried to ease her grip from JabRil's fur. She remembered books she'd read. A science book about a man who tried to build wings he could wear in order to fly. Another mentioned brothers building a wagon that would fly and carry people. They were so excited about their work and how much it would change the world. Nat wasn't excited. Her heart pounded in her ears; the sound drowned out the rushing wind. This was not a safe way to travel. It just couldn't be. If the Almighty had intended for people to fly, He would have given them wings.

Nat forced herself to take a slow breath. But the Almighty had given these creatures wings. JabRil's warmth seeped into her and drove away her tremors. She marked the rhythmic rise and fall of his shoulders with each beat. The strength in her chimera made her stronger as if it leaked into her body with each stroke.

Nat dared to open her eyes again. Peryum flew a little lower than JabRil. Beyond Mura, Nat could see a line twist and wind like a snake as it cut through the green hills and darker mountains. It only stopped at a walled city with its web of lined streets. Then the snaking path appeared again on the other side of the city. Nat watched each city pass by until she saw one full of dark buildings blanketed by tendrils of smoke.

She sat up. The wind whipped her braids behind her like ribbons in a breeze. "Is that Fairlight?"

"It—"

"Is."

She strained to see the girls' home but couldn't make it out in the haze and numerous buildings. JabRil stretched his wings out straight, leaned to the left, and turned away from the city. A shudder passed through her before she lay down again, grabbing hold of her chimera and letting his strength fill her once more. Her eyes drifted closed. She'd been up all night training. Then the battle. Now flying. A deep tiredness settled on her, and the steady movement of the wings lulled her to sleep.

Nat startled awake as JabRil settled on the ground. She shivered as she sat up. They were surrounded by jagged gray peaks. Splotches of white sat in the shadows here and there. Was that snow? She'd read about it many times and always wondered.

She slid off JabRil's back and rubbed her arms. Puffs of fog floated from her lips with each breath. Why'd Mura want them to come here?

A creak came from behind her. She turned to see a door almost hidden among the large boulders. Wisps of smoke curled into the sky from a slender pipe coming out of the top of the rock. A tall man stepped out. His dark hair and short beard had a few threads of gray. His shirt couldn't hide his wide shoulders and the many muscles across his chest and down his arms. Tall black boots came up to his knees, and he carried a sword in his hand.

Nat looked around for anything to hurl at him. Rocks of all sizes surrounded her. How many could she throw? Some were too big for her to pick up—even with her power. And Mura said not to use their abilities around strangers. The rocks were too big to use the strength of her hands alone. Did she leap back on JabRil and order him away?

Peryum stepped passed the chimera and walked toward the man. When the pegasus turned sideways, his sword dropped to the ground.

"Your Majesty." He leapt forward.

"Majesty?"

The man seemed to notice her for the first time. "Aye, this is the rightful queen of Purlan."

"But Mura said my mother was the king's daughter." Nat's head spun. Air danced around her body without filling her lungs. "Is she my —?"

The man left Mura still on Peryum's back and came toward Nat. His bushy brows, met each other as he squinted and looked at her. "Queen Mura has no children, but her sister had three. A girl and—"

"And two boys. They'll be along shortly. So, she's not my mother?"

He bent deep at the waist over his hand. "The queen is your aunt, Highness." He rose and stared at her again. "So, she has found you at last. Good. That is very good."

Was he talking to himself or her?

After a moment more, he turned and returned to Mura's side.

The queen.

Her *aunt*. Why hadn't Mura said something?

"What happened?" He sounded like Mistress Swanson when something got broken and she was asking who had done it.

"Brax's men found us. She fought them but was wounded. I tried to stop the bleeding—"

He carried Mura and disappeared inside the hidden structure.

Nat didn't follow but flopped back against JabRil relieved by his warmth. "Queen?" She shook her head. "Aunt." She took hold of Ril's neck while running her hand in Jab's mane. "Highness."

"A daughter of—"

"Rhe king's—"

"Daughter—"

"Would be …"

Nat shook her head. "Yes, but I never thought of it like I was …"

"A Highness—"

"Of the—"

"Kingdom."

"Exactly." Nat missed her brothers. More than she'd ever missed anyone. "I need Jer and Cay."

Peryum settled and blocked some of the mountain breeze. "They are coming." His snout brushed against her. "Everything will be fine soon."

"Promise?"

"All things work for the good of those who love the Almighty and are called according to His purpose for them," Peryum said. "His promise is what counts."

Chapter 52

Jer held onto Soo a little tighter as Layla flew up the sheer mountain sides. They landed on the top of one of the middle peaks; Asheal and Cay touched down right behind them. Jer slid down Layla's leg, and Soo eagerly followed. JabRil and Peryum lay a little distance ahead of them. As they neared the two, Jer realized that Nat was snuggled between them.

"Where's Mura?"

Nat didn't look at him. "Queen Mura?" She pointed to a bunch of tall rocks at the end of the flat section they were on.

"Queen?"

"Who's the queen?" Cay stopped close to Soo, hugging himself tight.

"Mura," Nat said.

"If she's the queen …" Jer scratched his head.

"Aunt."

Cay's teeth chattered. "Ant? What's an ant? Like the little insect?"

Jer stepped in front of Nat and stared directly at her. He crossed his arms and tapped his foot. "Okay, Sis, I know you're not one to say much, but we need a little more information here. What do you mean, Mura's the queen and our aunt? How do you know that? And where is she right now?"

Nat stood and put her fists on her hips, but, outside of the protection of the two guardians, she shivered. She rubbed her arms too. "The man in there." Again, she pointed to the rocks. Jer now noticed part of a door he hadn't seen before. "The man came out when we arrived. He called her Queen Mura. He said that she is the one who should be ruling instead of Brax and that our mother is her sister. Then he carried her inside."

"Is she all right? Who is the guy?" Cay inched next to JabRil as the chatter of his teeth grew louder.

"I don't know. He didn't introduce himself. He just called her 'Queen' and took her away."

"And you let him?" Jer's voice rose.

Nat shoved both hands against his chest. "What was I supposed to do? He's at least twice my height and built like a statue. I have no weapons other than my stone's power, and Mura said not to use that around strangers. He knew her. Knew who she *really* was."

"So, what if she is the queen, and our aunt?" Jer couldn't understand her anger.

"She lied." Nat stomped her foot. "Why didn't she tell us?"

"Highness?" A male voice called from the rock structure. "Are you still—" The warrior stopped short when he saw Jer and Cay. "Oh," he bowed, "good, you are all here now. Come. Come inside. It's too cold out here." He waved them all to the door.

Chapter 53

Nat huffed as Jer slipped in front of her and Cay and stopped at the doorway. He made a big show of protecting them again with his hand resting on his knife. "Who are you? What have you done with Mura?"

Nat rolled her eyes. What did Jer think he could do against the big man?

Cay struggled to hold Mura's swords in each hand, but they were too heavy. The tips slipped into the dirt.

The large man's lips wiggled like he was trying not to smile—but he wasn't doing a very good job of it. "I'm Marcus. I grew up with the queen and your mother. I served as their personal guard for a time. Queen Mura is in the bedchamber." He pointed to his right, but Nat couldn't see much around Jer's back. "I have finished treating her wound, and she is resting. Please, Highnesses, I mean you no harm. Come in out of the cold. I can prepare something for you to eat."

Jer glanced over his shoulder to Nat, one brow raised high.

Now he wanted her opinion? "I don't know. He seems okay," she whispered.

Soo walked up to the man and sniffed him. Her tail wagged, and she continued toward the fire burning in the hearth. Jer nodded and entered the odd structure. Cay dragged Mura's swords behind him.

Inside, it looked to be part cave with mostly walls of the same stone as the mountain. But also, in other places, wood had been added to fill in gaps or create doors.

Cay pushed around them, dropped Mura's weapons with a clatter, and joined Soo by the fire. It burned bright in the pocket cut into the stone wall. He thrust his hand out. "Oh, that feels so good."

Marcus smiled as he ambled to a long shelf waist high against the wall. "I didn't mean to leave you outside. I thought you followed me, Highness. Your fear is understandable after what you have been through." He pulled bowls and vegetables off shelves and out of wood cupboards. Next, he pulled a long knife from his belt. As he talked to them, still with his back turned, he started to cut up the many colored foods in front of him. "It is an answer to prayer that she is free of Brax and has found you three."

"If she is the queen, what did Brax do to her?" Cay had turned his back to the fire but still stood close to the warmth.

Marcus choked so hard it echoed in the room. "He deceived her, betrayed her, and murdered her betrothed. Then he held her in prison until she agreed to wed him."

"Huh?" Cay stared.

Nat turned to her little brother. "He tricked her, turned against her when she thought he was a friend, and killed the man she was supposed to marry so that she would marry him instead."

Cay's gaze narrowed. "I didn't like him before, but I hate him now."

"We all have good reason to hate and fear that man." Marcus glanced over his shoulder at them. "But now that you have reunited, there is hope again that things will once more be put right."

Jer looked at Nat and then at Cay. "What can we do?"

Marcus stopped and turned. "Do you still carry the Savior Stones?"

The three siblings looked at one another again.

"Yes, I know about the stones. I guarded those who brought them to the home where you were hiding the night you ended up with them. I was one of the soldiers sent out to find suitable places for you to live until the time came that you would be brought back together and trained to face Brax."

"You picked that horrible farm for me?" Cay nearly yelled.

"I was injured before I completed my task. Another was given the responsibility to place you. Soon after I healed, I came here to aid any I could in escaping Brax's death squads. A neighboring kingdom lies not far beyond these mountains. I have helped many get there."

As Marcus returned to the food preparations, Nat wandered down a dark hall on his right. She pushed open a door that wasn't quite closed on the other side of the wall from where Marcus stood. Mura slept in a big bed covered in thick blankets.

Mura's face never had much color—much like her own—since being locked in a dungeon and in a building in a smoke-filled town didn't allow for much time for the sun to tan them.

Nat crept to the far side of the bed and pulled Mura's right hand from under the covers. Nat ran her finger over the burned fabric from the man with the fire stone. Pieces of it disintegrated away, revealing red skin underneath. Nat had suffered worse burns cleaning out the stove.

Mura didn't stir.

"What are you doing?" Jer whispered.

She waved him over as she gripped Mura's wrist with her right hand. Nat pointed to her wrist. Jer grasped it. Cay came through the door, and Nat put a finger to her lips before waving him in. He took Jer's wrist, and Nat closed Mura's fingers over Cay's wrist completing the circle. Their stones glowed through their skin; teal, red, blue, and Mura's white. Hers almost looked like a swirly S as it showed through her pale skin.

Mura drew in a breath and tightened her grip. Her back arched and her chest expanded. Like when they'd linked hands during their practice, Nat's skin buzzed and her heart beat like she was running up the stairs.

Mura's blue eyes fluttered open. After a moment, they focused and blinked. She pulled her hand from the children's.

"Come, Highnesses, time to eat. Let the queen rest."

Mura glared at Marcus, but he waved them out with a kind smile.

Chapter 54

The children left the room, though Mura still felt their silent questions beat against her thoughts. Marcus pushed the door closed behind them and came to her side. "Why did you tell them?"

"Why *didn't you* tell them." His question was more from confusion than anger.

"They have a horribly broken world to deal with. They don't need my failures on top of all that."

"You didn't fail anyone, Majesty."

"Stop calling me that!"

"I will not." Marcus rarely raised his voice or refused her. He had always been more like her closest friend than a guard for the heir to the throne. His gaze pinned her to the bed. "As the next in line appointed by our God-ordained king, you *are* our rightful leader. That you are kind and graciously accept all who come to you for aid is not a fault. It is a testament only to Brax's wickedness. Thedo Brax is the servant of the Father of Lies. That is nothing against you, but everything against him. You were betrayed—nothing more."

Tears choked her words. "But I carry the stone that allows me to see into another's heart. I—above all—should have seen his wickedness and stopped him before he hurt so many. Their blood stains my hands as much as his." She held her quaking hands out to him, showing her palms. Clearly there was blood on them. She saw it every day.

"There is nothing but pure white skin from being trapped too long in the dark. Your hands are as white and pure as your soul. You must stop carrying this blame. It is not yours, and it does not become a queen."

"Perhaps if I had someone to help me carry this burden, I could better face it."

He lifted the covers just enough to see her side through the gash in her gown. "Whatever happened when the young highnesses linked arms with you, it has sped your healing. The scar looks about a week old already."

He had changed the subject. Even without her ability to read his thoughts, she knew that. "So, you still refuse me?"

"You need none other than God, my Queen. Rest now." He turned and left the room. Mura covered her face with her hands as she let the tears come. It had been a long time since she'd allowed herself to feel this pain. She sobbed and curled on her side.

The bed moved and weight pressed against her. Calebus lay beside her. He reached toward her and rested his small hand on her check. "I don't blame you. Brax is a bad man, and together we will get your throne back."

The amount of trust and love filling his touch and flooding her body almost caused her pain.

"There is no other as kind as you, my sweet Calebus."

He smiled. "I learned that from you."

Chapter 55

After Mura fell asleep, Cay slipped out of her room. Jer and Nat were curled under blankets by the fire that had grown bigger than before. Marcus handed him a blanket too. "Rest now. We have a lot to do in the morning."

Cay had been awake for a whole day. His stomach was full, and his family and Lor were safe for the moment. Though he knew he should ask what they had to do, he wrapped the fuzzy cloth around him and wiggled next to his brother. Sleep sounded so good.

The next morning, Cay awoke to bright light coming through the windows. Marcus chopped vegetables on the stone shelf again with a steady *thunk, thunk*. Jer wiggled and yawned. Nat groaned when he bumped into her.

"Sorry to wake you. No real way to prepare a meal without making noise." Marcus smiled at them. "Jeremicum, sir, could you be so kind as to hang that pot of water over the flames, and Calebus, sir, could you add a couple pieces of wood when he is finished?"

"Sir?" Cay giggled under his breath. "If Kint could hear that."

Once they'd both completed the requests, the three children helped each other fold the blankets and put them in a neat pile near the stack of wood for the fire.

Breakfast was cheese and a pan of vegetables fried up with eggs and something Marcus called bacon. It tasted almost as good as tarts.

Marcus picked up their wooden plates when they were done. His smile was huge. "Come outside I have something to show you, Highnesses."

None of the guardians were outside that Cay could see, but it felt like Asheal was still near, so either she was in a cave or she'd made herself invisible again.

"Today, you begin your training." He tossed a sword to Jer. It was still in a leather case and his brother caught it easily. Jer pulled it from its sheath. The sun sparkled off the metal.

"Is this mine?"

"I would be honored for you to have it, Highness."

Marcus handed Cay a matching sword and walked to Nat. He offered her a bow and a long basket of arrows. She crossed her arms.

"Mura fights with two swords."

"That she does, Highness, but she also carries the stone that allows her to know her opponent's next move almost at the same moment they do. Sir Jeremicum told me that you control things with your thoughts." Marcus readied an arrow in the bow and pulled back. He aimed out over the side of the steep mountain they were on. "What better weapon than one that sends a projectile out into the air for you to control. Direct it around your companions and into your enemies without ever aiming." He shot the arrow and, rather than flying straight, it wobbled in the air, continued up for a moment, then lost all its speed and dropped out of sight far below them.

Nat reached for the bow. "It is going to take some practice to catch a moving arrow."

"A great deal of practice will be required of all of you." Marcus moved to stand between Jer and Cay. "Now let me teach you about the sword."

The sun was high overhead and, though the wind up in the mountains was quite cold, the heat from the sun beat down. One minute,

Cay shivered, and the next he sweated; adding to those discomforts, his right arm felt ready to drop off. Marcus had put the real weapons aside and given him and Jer heavy wooden sticks to work with. Jer held his in his left hand as he swung it and whacked Cay's almost out of his right hand.

"What are you doing?" Mura leaned against the open door.

"Training the highnesses," Marcus said, barely glancing at her.

"Then you have decided to aid us?"

He turned and looked at her. His arms dangled limp at his sides. Marcus hadn't been swinging a weapon and even his arms were tired. He tipped his head.

Cay took a closer look at his aunt.

She wore clothes very much like Jer's and Cay's.

"Are you wearing my shirt and trousers?" Marcus asked.

No wonder they looked so big on her.

"As there were no gowns in your home, and I cannot go about with a gaping hole in the side of my dress, yes. Now, stop changing the subject and answer my question. Have you changed your mind?"

He sighed. "I will *always* assist you, Majesty. But you will only be able to remain a little longer. Brax's men will find you here. I'm sure they suspect me of helping others escape."

Mura took slow steps toward them. "So, you won't join us?"

Marcus sighed. "You know I cannot."

"*Will* not." She stood directly in front of him but had to look up because of how tall Marcus was.

"Majesty." He paused at the way she glared at him. "I am not royal born."

"And I have no throne, no betrothed."

"The throne is there for the taking. It is rightfully yours, and when you regain it—as you must—you will see that I cannot."

Cay looked to Jer and Nat. They watched the grownups talk too. Did they understand what was going on better than he did? "Maybe we should go inside." But nobody moved. Cay turned his back on Mura and Marcus to face Jer and tried not to listen. But Jer wouldn't practice with him, and he couldn't stop hearing the adults.

"You think me some lofty thing so far above you that you are unworthy of me. The truth is, I am so far beneath you, that you could squash me with your boot and never even notice. I ask you one last time. Come with me."

"I cannot," Marcus said with a bow of his head.

Mura put her first finger and her thumb in her mouth and let out a loud whistle that made Cay's eyes squint closed. "Peryum."

"You can't leave, Majesty. Your healing is not complete."

"As you said, Brax's men will come." She walked to where the silver pegasus landed and stroked his neck. "Come, children. Call your guardians. We must leave." She sounded so sad Cay wanted to go to her and give her a hug, but she climbed up on Peryum. As she tried to straighten, her bottom lip pinched between her teeth, and her eyes smashed closed.

"You're still in pain. Majesty, please, wait a little longer." Marcus stood at her side.

"You know nothing of my pain, sir."

"I know it better than you think, Majesty."

"Do you know what's going on?" Cay whispered to Jer.

"Not really."

"She likes him." Nat came to stand by them.

"Well, I like him too, but—"

"No, silly." Nat shook her head and leaned closer to his ear. "She wants him to be her boyfriend."

"Like kissing and stuff? Yuck." Cay scrunched up his face. "Are you sure?"

"I've read about it in tons of books."

"Maybe I don't want to learn how to read." Cay shuddered.

"There are other things in books besides kissing." Nat turned to Jer. "Are you going with her?"

"I am." Cay moved further away. "Asheal, come please." The Phoenix rose from a peak nearby and landed next to him.

Jer looked between Mura and Marcus. "Are Brax's men really coming here?"

Mura closed her eyes again. "A troop of soldiers is two days from the base of the mountain. You have three days, four at the most if you wish to remain. Then you will need to find a safe place elsewhere."

"I think we should go, Jer." Nat swung her bow and arrows over her back, walked to the edge of the area where they had been training, and called JabRil. The chimera landed beside her, and she climbed on.

Marcus walked to Jer with Mura's two weapons and the two swords he'd given Jer and Cay earlier. "Go with them, Highness. Watch over her until she is strong enough to protect you again."

"If Brax's men are coming, wouldn't you be safer with us?"

"God has always taken care of me, sir. He will again."

After taking the swords in one hand, Jer extended his other hand. Marcus grasped his forearm. "Thank you, sir, for all your help."

Marcus bowed even while holding Jer's arm. "It was one of my greatest honors, Highness. I will pray for you without ceasing."

Layla landed without being called. Jer and Soo took their place on her back. Marcus waved as they lifted off into the clear sky.

Chapter 56

They flew south over high peaks and sprawling cities. Mura didn't think there was anything left of her heart to break. Yet, Marcus had found the only remaining piece and shattered it. She had no one.

Layla brought Jeremicum even with her. "Auntie, where are we headed?" His huge smile was infectious.

The Bottomless Sea stretched out on the other side of him until the distant edge touched the sky. "There is only one place I believe Brax doesn't know about. You might be safe there for a while."

"We will be safe only if you stay with us," Calebus yelled over the wind on her left.

"I agree. From now on, we stay together." Jeremicum and Layla slipped behind her to fall in line. Nataline followed him, and then Calebus slowed enough to follow.

Behold, I am with you and will keep you wherever you go, and will bring you back to this land. For I will not leave you until I have done what I have promised you. The words of the Almighty to one of His prophets of old floated to her on the breeze. It lifted her tears to be blown away on the wind.

They flew over a huge body of water unlike anything Jer had ever seen. A town passed under them. It looked like little more than a fat blob from this height. Then they sailed up cliffs higher than the Black Rock

Outpost and down the other side into a wide green valley with a lake in the middle of the many jagged peaks.

Jer startled for a moment as it looked like Peryum, traveling ahead of them, was going to fly back straight into the mountain side. But he landed in a long cave opening that looked like a smiling mouth. Layla landed beside him with plenty of room to stretch her wings. JabRil and Asheal soon found places alongside.

The floor Nat slid down to was covered in a thick layer of dust that the guardians had stirred up with their landing. Nat sneezed a couple of times, as did Jer. Cay leaned down and touched the ground. Like a wind had come from the back of the cave, much of the dirt and small rocks slid over the edge out of sight.

"Thank you, Calebus," Mura said.

"Where are we?" Nat looked around the cave with its many openings along the back wall and then out to the valley and the lake.

"This is known as High Stone Lair. It is very hard to get to as there are only two hidden paths—if you don't come from above. The sides are too hard to climb, and this ridge serves as a boundary between Purlan and the kingdom to the south. Liam the Pure used it as he gathered his forces years ago. Anyone allowed access was blindfolded and led in by one of the handful of people who knew the way. I don't think Brax knows of it." Mura wiped the sweat from her forehead with the back of her hand. Nat didn't think it was that warm. "We will have fish and fresh water from the streams that feeds the lake. There are many rooms in here for us to use …" She swayed on her feet. Only Jer's quick action again that kept her from falling.

"Marcus said you were not healed enough yet." Jer led her to a tall flat rock and helped her sit.

She winced in pain, but after a few slow breaths she spoke again—muttered, really. "The mighty Marcus doesn't know everything." She sighed. "Peryum, is the hidden treasury still intact?"

"Yes. It has been well guarded."

"Good. Show it to Jeremicum, please." She turned to Jer. "I want you to take a few coins, not enough to bring attention to yourself, mind you."

"Attention is never going to be a good thing, I fear," Jer said.

"You are quite right. Attention will not be a good thing until all is made right again. Go into Hallow Tide and buy us something to make beds with and any other simple supplies you think best."

Jer nodded. "I still have most of what Olrog paid me too."

"If you get a broom and a pail, I can clean," Nat offered.

Cay stepped close to Jer and Mura. "I can go with him."

"Not yet, Calebus. Jeremicum knows the ways of a city. He knows how to bargain for the best prices and what to watch out for. He will be safe alone, and Layla will watch over him. Later, when Jeremicum has become comfortable with the ways of Hallow Tide, he can take one of you with him."

"What do you want me to do?" Cay took another step toward Mura. Cay needed to be near her. Something was wrong, and it was more than her injury. He wanted her to be that strong woman she always was when she'd visited him. But he didn't know how to help her.

"Have Asheal take you down by the lake. Collect branches for a fire to keep us warm tonight and others to use as torches." Mura turned back to Jer. "Maybe something we can use as rags and a little oil would be good."

Jer nodded again.

Mura looked back at Cay. Her face was wet with sweat while Cay shivered. "You and Nataline can explore the many chambers and pick out the best ones for us to use."

Cay made many trips with Asheal to bring back wood. There would be plenty for a fire for the next several nights. They piled it all in the corner out of the way.

Jer pulled Nat aside. "You seem to know the most about how to treat wounds. You watch over her while Cay and I are gone. I'll try not to be long." Jer looked back at Mura, now slumped against the wall. "She doesn't look good. See if you can find a place for her to lie down."

"If there is a place that sells medicines, sometimes called an apothecary, I could use a little vinegar, yarrow, and willow bark. We will need cups and something to put our food on too."

"I hope I can remember all this."

"If I had something to write on, I could make you a list."

"I can read a little, but not as well as you, I wager." Jer moved toward Layla. "You'll help me remember, won't you?"

"Of course." The dragon almost purred.

Soo came over to join him. "Not this time, girl." He brushed her thick fur. "Stay here and watch them. I'll be back soon."

The Journey is
Only Beginning

In only a matter of days, they were settled into High Stone Lair. Nat and her brothers worked every day training to master their weapons and control the abilities given through their Savior Stones. Mura's wound healed, though her soul and spirit still remained crushed.

"What is going to happen next?" Calebus asked one night as they settled around the fire to eat.

Mura pointed to the children in turn. "Each of you will continue to train until you are strong enough to face Brax's men. Soon we will go and see who we might help as we seek out the others with the stones and look for two people we can trust to carry the rescued stones we have."

"We need to find others. People who will fight with us, too, like King Liam did." Jer raised his hand high as though he held a sword, ready to charge into battle.

Nat leaned in to make sure she had everyone's attention. "I think the first place to start is to learn what happened to our parents."

"That sounds like an excellent place to begin our next journey," Mura agreed.

Glossary

bailey – The courtyard or outer court of a castle

caravan – A group of travelers, such as merchants, journeying together for safety when passing through dangerous territory

chamber pot – A portable container, especially for urine, used in bedrooms

constable – An officer of the peace, having police functions, usually in a small town, or rural district

dorm – Short for dormitory, a room containing a number of beds and serving as communal sleeping quarters

farrier – A person who shoes horses

headmistress – A woman in charge of a private school

host – Warrior angels

inn – A small hotel

institution – An organization devoted to the promotion of a particular program, especially one of education

knapsack – A leather bag for clothes, food, and other supplies, carried on the back by soldiers, or hikers

lye – A strong solution used to make soap, drain cleaners, and oven cleaners

manacles – A wide shackles for the hand; handcuff

muck – To remove animal dung

naïve – Having or showing a lack of experience or judgment

nanny – A person, usually with special training, employed to care for children in a household

nickers – Short pants

petticoat – An underskirt, especially one that is full and often trimmed and ruffled and of a decorative fabric

quarries – Excavations or pits, usually open to the air, from which building stone and slate are obtained by cutting or blasting

revel – To take great pleasure or delight

stable – A building for the lodging and feeding of horses and cattle

scrutinize – To examine in detail with careful or critical attention

shackles – A ring or other fastenings, as of iron, for securing the wrists, or ankle

silo – A structure, typically cylindrical, for storing grain

skeins – A length of yarn wound on a reel

spectacles – Eyeglasses

skulk – To move in a stealthy manner; slink:

tankard – A large drinking cup, usually with a handle

tavern – A public house for travelers and others; inn.

toiling – Hard and continuous work; exhausting labor or effort.

wharf – A structure built on the shore of a harbor so that vessels may be moored alongside to load or unload

About the Author

Michelle Janene (Murray) is a church secretary and writes Christian fantasy and historical fiction. She lives in Northern California with two crazy dogs and the characters of her imagination.

If you enjoyed *Lost Stones: A Savior Stone Chronicle* please review it on your favorite site.

Join Michelle's email list and get a free novelette at
MichelleJanene.com
You can also connect with Michelle:
Facebook: Michelle Janene-Author or Strong Tower Press
Twitter: @MichelleJaneneM
Instagram: michellejanene_author
Pinterest: www.pinterest.com/michellejanene
Goodreads: Michelle Janene
StrongTowerPress.com

Other Books

Check out these books also by Michelle

Mission: Mistaken Identity

The Changed Heart Series:
God's Rebel
Rebel's Son
Hidden Rebel

Seer of Windmere

Barbarian Hero

Guardians of Truth

Culling a Miracle

Lost Stones

The Last Good King

The King's Vengeance

Thice a Bride

Dragon Fire